Stream-of-consciousness is more than a method in Michael Boylan's *Naked Reverse*. It's a distinctive character trait of the central character and narrator, Andrew, a philosophy professor who lives inside his head—until, of course, he doesn't. We meet our hero when he is in the process of divorcing and emotionally disentangling himself from Barbara, a woman who led him around by the nose. He seems to have married her because of a syllogism whose conclusion he couldn't escape even though he would have liked to. This, I suppose, is a particular vulnerability of philosophers. (It is no accident that "Barbara" is scholastic shorthand for the first and most effective of Aristotelian syllogisms.) With Barbara still on his mind, Anthea pops into Andrew's life. ("Anthea," by the way, is a nickname for Aphrodite, the Greek goddess of love, beauty and desire—and Anthea lives up to her name.) The problem with Anthea is that she is being pursued by violent brutes, posing a challenge for which a philosopher is not well prepared. This and other dangerous situations call for decisive actions from Andrew. Will he be up to the task? And what is to be Anthea's fate? By the end of the book, Andrew has been transformed into a man whom Barbara couldn't have dominated. But is he up to the challenge of Anthea? Find out what happens when a philosopher meets the real world: ten rounds, no holds barred.

Jeffrey Reiman, William Fraser McDowell
Professor of Philosophy, American University

NAKED REVERSE

A novel

MICHAEL BOYLAN

PWI Books
Bethesda, MD

Cover Design by Greg Simanson
Edited by Joanna Jensen
Proofread by Lydia Johnson
Majanka Verstraete, Book Manager

This is a work of fiction. Names, characters, places, brands, media, and incidents are either the product of the author's imagination or are used fictitiously. Any resemblance to similarly named places or to persons living or deceased is unintentional.

ISBN 13: 978-0692-729106 (PWI)
ISBN 10: 069-2729100
Library of Congress Control Number: 2016900050

THE ARCHĒ NOVELS

CHAPTER ONE

JUNE 1982

IT IS NOT A VERY LONG WALK from the nine-hundred block on East 57th Street to the "El" train station at 63rd Street and Cottage Grove, but it was one that I had never made before. Many times I had driven in the car along this street, but always quickly and without regard. I never paid any attention to the area except to make a mental note that this was a "high crime" area. After all, it was south of the Midway—a large strip of land which constitutes a kind of boundary between the protected University area and that tangle of dirty streets to the south and west. The Midway itself is divided into three sections. The first section forms large basins that are over an acre across and serve as intra-mural playfields for the students at Chicago University. In the winter, I think, they actually flood one of these basins to make the city's largest ice skating rink. This was nothing to me for I have always eschewed athletics both from the point of view of participant and spectator.

But anyway, these things did cross my mind as I carefully descended into the first basin down a steep slope and over the green pasture. It was an expedition that I had never made before. This may sound a little strange for one who walked much of the time about Hyde Park, but I had never ventured onto—or rather into—these green stadia. I had nothing to do over there. Here was the University and over there the squalid reminders of urban blight. It was almost as if I were making some kind of historic trek down. Down deep into the recesses of Hell's fifth circle. But no, that is a little too dramatic. I have a tendency to overstate things a bit at times. Fortunately, I usually recover and put things right again by the second draft.

I should like to make one thing clear from the outset: I did not feel any guilt about having never made the trip across the gulf that constituted the Midway. I merely mention the fact so that you can understand why it was that I felt so unusual and extra conscious of my environment as I shuffled along with my black Samsonite briefcase (the kind with the expandable bottom for ease in 'stuffing'). You see, most of the time when I am walking somewhere I can't tell you what it was that I saw or when. I generally am thinking about some problem or other which I am working on and fully intend to solve before the next invited paper I am asked to give. So you see, it was a unique set of circumstances which occasioned my walking as I did without a single thought about Philosophy of Science or anything to do with that ugly, grey-stoned prison which was now behind me.

As I ascended from the last basin and over the small third strip, I had the feeling that I was in a foreign country. Well perhaps that's a little strong again, but at any rate, it was an area which I did not know, and it was damned humid. I turned right and walked up 60th and then left again at the gas station on the corner of Cottage Grove. At this corner I could see Washington Park and that absurd statue of Father Time and the monument to the ages.

I say that the statue was absurd. This judgment does not reflect the genre of the artist, but rather my approbation of his accomplishment. I turned my body in disgust and saw on both sides of the street low income urban renewal housing. As I went down the street, little black children darted in and out from under stairwells and from behind garbage containers (you know, those large industrial bins which can hold a week's garbage for twenty families). It was only early June, but already the flies were buzzing around these receptacles of rotting animal and vegetable matter. This was the playground for the poor underclass. Their wretched lot started to pull me back into the real world.

The garbage was ripe. In another month, perhaps, the flies would be replaced by yellow jackets. On the corner of the next street was a newspaper stand with a group of old men hanging around talking with each other and passing the time. They were shabbily dressed. None of them had purchased a newspaper, though there were crumpled racing forms in their back pockets.

As I approached the ancient wooden structure that stood elevated (where the nickname 'el' derives) above the road, I passed a clinic which advertised in block letters: GREEN CARDS WELCOME. Coming out the door was a youth, perhaps twenty or so (though I am not a good judge of age), who popped something into his mouth. He walked with a jaunty stride which effused bravado. I wondered to myself whether this young man was taking "uppers" or "downers" and whether the physician who ran this "clinic" was actually just a medical pill pusher who soaked the poor and the government alike.

There wasn't much time for such speculation for I heard the rumbling of a train and I hurried up the steps past a man unconscious on the stairs and I rushed into the small station. I reached into my pocket for the fare, but my fingers could not locate the correct change.

A man pushed past me.

The train was stopping. I located the change and thrust it under the glass but the lady who operated the turn style wouldn't let me pass. She was counting the money! She hadn't counted the money of the person who had gone before me. I pushed against the turnstile to try and hurry her. She hit the button, but because I had pushed the stile it had to come back to go forward. This delayed things more. Finally, I was through the stile and out on the platform just as the doors to the train were closing. The conductor wouldn't open them again for me. I sat down and waited for the next train. This must be the feeling that society's disenfranchised often feel. It rarely happens to me.

Again, this jarred me back to the world and away from my fog of discontent. What did I know of the lot of these unfortunate souls? All I had was a guess, for that is all one can possess from such flimsy evidence (only the slightest hypothesis supported by no verifiable record). It is just this and nothing more, but it is enough. Enough to nurture these slight germinations which grow and flourish with each passing incident in the receptive environment of the rotting decay of man's irrational insecurities that generated hatred. How insidious are such events even when accidental physical features are logically mistaken for those of essential predication.

I could prove nothing, of course, but that was not the point. That is never the point. Legislators and judges who ask for such deserve to be laughed at with emotional acridity. The proposition that "if there is no physical evidence (that which fits into this narrowly described category that is subject to prejudged interpretation of sense data, etc.), then there is no crime" is, of course, patently false. It should be corrected to read that if there is no evidence (under our procedures for observing such), then there are no crimes which may be criminally prosecuted. There may be multiple crimes which may occur (even with *de jure* sanction) which fall outside such subjectively random criteria.

But all this was only a diversion. I loved getting off on such little spurts. I suppose that is why I went into philosophy. I loved to follow up a point to its logical conclusion. There is something very self-contained about this activity. It can occupy an active mind and keep it contented. But sometimes other issues cut into the scene. Barbara, for example. But that is enough of her right now. She is history. She has *driven me* into freedom. It is to her that I will owe my salvation from the grand leviathan of self-contained arguments. I should be coming to praise her and not to bury her.

The train came. From the great distance of one half mile you can watch the train approaching from Jackson Park. It was from here that all "B" trains originated (or so it seemed from the little map which I studied from my seat on the train). The cars moved along the old tracks with the discordant sound of metal scraping against metal. Why don't they get a quieter system? This elevated train system has to fail federal guidelines—at least for noise pollution.

Why, if I rode this thing every day I'd go deaf (or at least have my capacity for hearing diminished). But who'd file suit? The poor blacks who live in these neighborhoods? What chance would they have against Lockport, Southport, and all the other powerful white enclaves? Better to put money into a Loop Mall on State Street and pay for the mayor's yearly trip to Europe than to do anything to fix up this crumbling rapid transit system.

Well, with a dialogue like this I was feeling pretty self-righteous. I could knock off a dozen or so tin horn politicians. No trouble. I felt like standing up right then and there and giving a speech. "Friends of the oppressed and downtrodden . . ." Afterwards everyone would come up and shake my hand. They would declare that they never heard anything so stirring and that I would be the man to bring them out of the filth and poverty in which they lived. I would unite the family once more and be at once the great synthetic agent of everyone.

"You want to buy some incense?"

This question broke the glorious train of my thought. I looked up and saw a fellow dressed in Arabic clothing with his hands stuffed with little green sticks. I tilted my head as the words he was incanting just began sinking in. "Incense?" I asked. But the fellow took my question as an order for the goods and pressed the green sticky items into my hand. The smell was revolting. I could not believe that anything could be so poorly made. The powder which was supposed to burn at one end of the wand was already converting my hand to its peculiar hue.

"Dollar."

The words didn't register.

"Dollar." The old hammer, anvil, and whatever began knocking together in my inner ear and presently I became aware that this blighter was soliciting funds from me. Now you might be amazed that someone who is an associate professor of philosophy at Chicago University and holds a Ph.D. from Cambridge University would be taking so long about an action which by all rights should have been apparent to him from a number of independent signs quite a spot earlier than it was. To this charge I reply, "Guilty, my Lud." But again, this is getting us away from the point. When things are getting a little on the overwhelming side, I tend to give the old tote the run of things, you might say. My tone alters from the serious writer of papers and essays to a kind of stooge. It is my small attempt to keep a kind of perspective on things.

So it was when this Arab (I call him this knowing full well that he was not an Arab, but just a man wishing to construct a heritage) pushed the incense into my hand. I did not do the obvious thing of hurling the flaky stuff back into his face while yelling some obscenity, but rather reached into my pocket and gave him four quarters.

I don't know why I gave him my money. I was not afraid for my personal safety (though this fellow could have taken me out quickly, no doubt) because at that moment I did not regard myself or my personal safety very highly. I had one vague idea in mind which I did *not* want to confront. There were no overarching schemes or designs; they sat behind me in long-term storage. What I had before me was unknown. Well, I should correct that part of it was already being determined. I had, for instance, just made my first investment. With this realization I quickly shoved the green gems into my pocket before they completely fell apart.

CHAPTER TWO

"I'M NOT SURE WE CAN cash a check this large, sir."

"What do you mean?" I asked, staring through the bars at a stodgy man.

"We have our policy, sir."

"What the hell do I care about your policy? Look, you have enough money there. I saw the last lady give you a twenty and you lifted up that little drawer and the bills were lying around in piles."

"But sir, a check is a little different. . ."

I was getting fed up with this incompetent yahoo. I mean, there he stood with his smelly white shirt with big yellow stains under the armpits, only rivalled by a phony toothless smile. I felt like kicking this little mindless cog back into the flywheel to give him a little excitement and enable him another perspective. I had half a mind to raise my voice to great heights and begin to swear at him in German (pretending to be one of Hitler's long lost youth corps commanders), but this empty-headed conglomeration of fatty globules would not fully appreciate the high aesthetic spectacle to which he was being treated, so I merely declared in my tv announcer's voice, "Not all checks are alike. This is an American Express traveler's check. It is good anywhere: across the U.S.A. and around the world. An American Express traveler's check is as good as money, *so ask for them by name*." I tilted my head to ascertain whether I had made my point. The man was looking straight ahead, so I added my closer. "Now cut the shit and give me my money."

The two-pronged approach must have touched the man to the very core of his person. He lit up when he heard me recite the sacred litany. This man was not as stupid as I had taken him for. No, he could recognize the words of advertising wisdom. No arguments based upon common sense could have moved him from his entrenched position, but this recitation from Madison Avenue struck an existential note and instantly he went to his superior to see whether it was all right to give me my thirty-eight dollars change.

He was back in a flash with a smile which (had it been any larger) would have threatened to expose his teeth. He cheerfully handed me my money and my ticket and gently reminded me that my bus would leave in ten minutes. I didn't take any chances. I glided over to the newsstand to pick up something to read. I had taken nothing with me, but I was determined not to purchase anything more complicated than Time Magazine. I had nothing to worry about. The newsstand was filled with items especially designed for reading levels of fourth to sixth grade. I made my selection and climbed onto my bus so that I could get a seat to myself. I didn't like to sit with other people, so I set my jacket on the seat next to me so that it would appear that there were two of us. Then I leaned back in my seat and pretended to be asleep. That way, if anyone got onto the bus and wanted to sit next to me (thinking perhaps that I had put my own coat next to me), they might be reticent to ask to sit down because they would see I was asleep.

Lots of people were boarding the bus, but no one was sitting next to me. I smiled. It was worth taking a light jacket in June just for the privacy that it potentially afforded. Besides, there could be some cool days in June what with the rain and all. However, the real reason I brought my spring weight coat was because I liked it so much that I couldn't bear to leave it behind.

It was rapidly approaching the departure time, and the bus was filling up more than I had expected. Why would so many people want to ride the bus? Why was I riding the bus? I glanced down at my watch.

We were five minutes late. The bus driver wasn't even on the bus yet, but was talking to another driver just outside the door. Our man looked like a seasoned fellow, rather short but surprisingly thin. He was nibbling his way through a glazed doughnut which had lasted him fifteen minutes. Eating at that rate must be what keeps him so thin, I thought, consciously aware of the few inches around the waist that I could stand to lose. We were now ten minutes late. Finally our jockey said his good-byes (having now finished his repast) and with one hand grasped the strap of a large thermos of coffee and slung it over his shoulder. Then with the other hand he smoothed back his slick greasy black hair and slid into his seat. He took his time about getting settled. He showed a certain pride in what he was doing—as if he were an airplane pilot checking a large console of dials and whatnots before taxiing off. However, modern busses are much simpler by comparison: steering wheel, gear shift, gas pedal, and brake. These modern cowboys don't even have a clutch to contend with. The whole pantomime seemed singularly ironic to me, though I must admit that the vibration from the motors made one believe that this was a powerful machine that was fully at his command.

We were just pulling out when a young woman raced toward our bus. She wanted to get on. I suppose this must happen now and again. I expected the driver to instantly stop for her, but in a second or two it became clear that he had other ideas. This cowboy probably didn't want to lose any time. After all, he wouldn't be the cause of our wasting any precious seconds.

The people on the bus didn't like it. There is a spirit among bus riders for the oppressed and luckless. I suppose it is because only the poor and downtrodden ride busses anymore and they have real sympathies for unfortunates who miss the bus (why, the same thing could be their unlucky lot—or might be the next time they purchase a soiled *billet*). So it was that a large public outcry arose among the ridership entreating, or rather demanding, that the bus driver stop the bus and let the little lady on. Now I had the driver pegged as a rather independent sort of guy who wanted to show everyone that he didn't give a damn what they thought of him, that he was the

captain of this ship and dared anyone to mutiny. Well mutiny was
what they were doing.

It was up to him to quell it with firm command and a toughness
of spirit. This was not to be, however, for the bus driver was also a
red blooded American male who, when he saw that the suppliant
passenger was a rather well constructed female, decided that perhaps it might be in his own benefit to let her on. I can ascertain no
other motive for his stopping the bus.

I was surprised at his change of heart, for it had seemed clear to
me that he had had every intention of thumping the gas and zoom-
ing out of the stagecoach station. Needless to say there were some
hoots and jeers at our navigator when he changed his mind. This
is also standard procedure. We thoroughly stand up for an under-
dog and dislike someone in authority putting down the helpless.
Now, let us assume that the bus driver was in a kind of position of
authority—after all, he could roll the tank over and blow us up if he
wanted to. But when that person in authority changes his mind and
says, "Hey, you are right. I'll change pronto," then we castigate him
for his weakness and spineless disposition. It is a losing situation.

Anyway, she got on the bus. Naturally, I moved my spring-
weight coat over in case she should choose to sit with me. There
weren't very many open seats available for her and she was greeted
by many of the men with inviting leers (most of which, if I had been
in her place, would have turned my stomach). Not that in her situation I wouldn't want a little male company, but some of the slobs
who were on that bus came across in a very indelicate way, which if
she had any sensitivity at all (and I was certainly convinced that she
did), she would be offended to her very core. So instead of sending
my eyes to do the work of Fortune, I turned my head and studied
her progress in the reflection against the window to my left. She was
approaching my seat and looked at it once before sitting next to an
old lady across from me.

I had lost, but somehow I didn't mind. If I had to lose such an
opportunity, better to an old lady than to some sailor or whatever.
Still, I could not help feeling a longing for this woman. She was

younger than I was, but older than an undergraduate student. Perhaps the typical age of a graduate student (though this is not much help, for the span of ages in this group is quite considerable). Besides this rather imprecise stab at her age, I couldn't tell much else about her. This is not surprising, since I am not much for physiognomy anyway.

I did not want to stare at her, but somehow I was drawn to her face. It always seems to be the case that we are especially attracted to that which we cannot possess. I don't mind admitting that I cherished some rather lascivious thoughts, but soon I was able to distract myself in the private affairs of the world via the mindless news magazine that I had purchased at the bus station.

We were driving north. I had a ticket that would take me to La Crosse. I don't know why I chose that particular town. Perhaps it was the beer festival. Not that I was particularly fond of beer or public festivals. In fact, if my memory serves me correctly, I was around six months early or late (depending upon your perspective) for such festival frolicking. I have no idea what made me pick that town. I had almost picked it randomly. I had had a notion that it might be nice to go to La Crosse and so—no, that isn't quite correct. I had walked up to the ticket window and the man had asked, "Where to?"

"St. Louis," I said as that was the first thing that popped into my mind.

"Next window please," said the almost mechanical voice.

"Can't you sell me a ticket to St. Louis?"

"Listen, Buddy, see the sign? This window is for Wisconsin and Minnesota only."

I laughed. "You mean you have a separate window just for Wisconsin and Minnesota? No wonder you are losing money. That is the most ridiculous thing I've ever heard." I could have continued about how this had been the only window without a line (though there were two people now behind me) and that it was obvious that because the other windows had such long lines and that this window didn't, that something should be done to rectify

the situation. However, I didn't say any of that because this idiot
behind the counter had nothing to do with such executive decisions. Instead I replied, "Give me a ticket to La Crosse." I was not
about to wait in one of those other long lines for a silly bus pass.
There would have been no point in such an action, considering I
had already been standing in a slow moving line. This victim has
just been through too many such exercises in patience. I wanted to
get somewhere, though I was not all that particular where it was I
wanted to go. It was simply my intention to whip out a traveler's
check, get a little cash and my ticket, and sit back to enjoy the
view. And so I did, though I got the urge now and then to look
discretely over at the beautiful creature who had so successfully
delayed our departure.

I would occasionally let my eyes wander over in her direction—
on the pretense that I was looking at something or other on the road.
I would get an opportunity of looking at her momentarily until her
eyes might chance to turn my way, and then I shifted to my bogus
point of interest. All this served to distract and amuse me. It was
funny, but I really didn't feel any discomfort about Barbara—now
that I had finally taken off. Of course, I had thought of it many times
since my journey across the Midway. I had thought of leaving her
before, but my sense of fair play would never let me desert a responsibility. So when I got an opportunity to leave when it wasn't *my
fault*—I jumped at it. Well, 'jumped' is not exactly the right word,
but I did move without ambiguity (directly and with finality) out
the door.

I glanced at my news magazine. How boring. I looked outside
and instantly fell asleep. I was dreaming about watching a great
spectacle: A pageant of foreign delights. I was a guest.'Guest' is
exactly the right word. I was not really a part of the proceedings. I
could walk around and view the sights, but whenever I wanted to
buy anything, no one paid any attention. It was as if I was not there. I
was not a real participant. I was not an actual part of the fair. I was a
guest. And so I wandered about, wanting to taste various delicacies
while, at the same time, knowing that none would be allowed me.

There was a real mixture of emotions on my part between excitement at the novel environment and sadness at my status.

"Sir?" I felt something. What was it? Finally a booth that recognized me! Now was my chance. "Sir?" I felt it again. It was not the fair. I did not want to leave. Why did I have to leave just when—and then I awoke and what before my wondering eyes should appear, but the beautiful form of the goddess Isis.

What was she doing? I revived in earnest, content to leave the magical fair. What I wanted was here.

"Sir, wake up. We're in Milwaukee."

What did I care? I was not going to Milwaukee. I was going to La Crosse.

"Milwaukee?" I stammered.

"Yes, I thought that you might want to get out. You see, there has been a delay, so even if you are going further everyone is getting out. We will be here at least a half hour."

"A half hour?"

"Yes, there is a mechanical problem. If it is going to be longer than that they will switch busses. I thought that you would like to know. I did not like waking you from your sleep. You seemed to be lying there so peacefully, but they did call us off the bus."

I looked around and the last people were departing for the terminal even as she was saying this. "Well, thank you," I said. "That was very kind of you to wake me, Miss . . . ah—"

"Brevist."

"Brevist. Yes, Miss Brevist." I wanted to repeat the name to see if she were going to correct me by putting 'Mistress' in front of her surname. It was just an instant that I paused, but hearing no correction I continued, "Thank you very much. Can I buy you a cup of coffee to say thank you?"

She paused a moment as if she were trying to size me up. At least that was what I thought she was doing. I must say that her pause was quite a bit longer than mine had been. I felt sure that I had been too forward. I should not have blurted out such an invitation so quickly. She probably thought that I was trying to "pick her up".

But before I could continue with my train of thought, she replied in a different voice than she had demonstrated before, "Okay, just a quick cup. We really do not have very much time."

I nodded. I was trying to be a bit low key. You see, I did not really know what I was doing. I had been staring at this beautiful goddess surreptitiously when I traveled to my fair in dreamland — only to be awakened by this same goddess of womanhood. Did she awaken me with a kiss as in the fairy tale? Alas, not.

To be more realistic, she probably wasn't a maid and she didn't kiss me, but poked me on the shoulder. All the same, the situation was a very confusing one for me. I did not know exactly what I wanted out of it. I did not even know what I hoped might happen in my fondest dreams. Not really. I was very confused. Was I trying to pick this girl up? No, I firmly decided. That wasn't what I wanted. I fled Chicago looking for something that I had lost. Though if you pressed me on the subject, I'm not sure I knew what that was.

Well, here was a start: talking to people. Meeting strangers and finding out how those outside academic circles drink their coffee. Yes, this was my real project. I wanted to take a survey: put my finger on the pulse of the real America.

I picked up my case and my jacket and followed my goddess into the terminal. Though I have not been to many bus terminals, but nonetheless I feel I can say with confidence that the bus terminal in Milwaukee is not one of the high points in bus terminals. It is a hygienic wonder of the world (in an *ersatz* sense). It is not the ideal scene for enjoying a cup of coffee. I wasted one quarter on the stupid machine when the cup jammed then tilted over. I failed in my attempt to save the day and ended up spilling some coffee on my pant leg. I was more successful on the second try.

When I had procured the coffee, I came over to my charge and handed her one of the cups of coffee.

"No, I wanted the black," she said.

I had handed her the wrong cup. I drink mine with cream and double sugar. But my mishap on round one had me in a flurry. I then gave her the cup of black coffee and took back my own.

"I'm sorry, I must still be asleep. First that machine jams and spills some coffee on me and then I hand you the wrong cup."

"Where did it spill?"

"On my pant leg, there." I tried to gesture, but my hand was holding the cup of coffee and I didn't want another mistake.

"I'll get you some water." Before I could tell her to forget it she was up to the drinking fountain (such as it was) and back with a wet handkerchief. She rubbed the stain with firm short strokes. It was almost as if she were jabbing my leg. But I did not mind. I rather liked feeling her thin hand against my leg.

"It's that damn cream and sugar you put into your coffee that makes this thing so stubborn. You really should drink your coffee black. It is much better for you. Cream and sugar are only empty calories, and cream, you know, clogs your arteries."

I felt like dumping out my coffee altogether. But then this sensation gave way to another and I felt resentful at her telling me what was or was not good for my body. Who was did she think she was? Lecturing me, a professor of biology once removed, what was or was not good for his body! I should be outraged. I should dump my coffee down the back of her dress!

This was a little exaggerated. My field was strictly philosophy of science with a concentration in biology. And I was only an associate professor and not a full professor. I made mental notes of this, but still I was in a combative mood stemming from her words of advice. Since she would probably not understand any complicated defense of my drinking coffee (as one part of my brain began to consider it, I did not think a biological tact would be easy to maintain), I decided to try a different approach: "I like cream and sugar. It is one of my little indulgences I allow myself." I thought that this speech conveyed all that I wanted. It was apropos to the tone I wished to maintain and avoided directly all talk about material obstructions in the old aorta.

"Well, those 'treats' you give yourself are not really treats at all," she began, having successfully taken out the stain in my pant leg, "if they end up putting you in a coffin."

"I dare say," was my retort, not really knowing how to respond to her. Did I want to be nice? (This thought was perhaps connected to the nagging question that I had in the back of my mind about whether I was trying to pick her up. I had answered this question in the negative, but the verdict was not all together final and there were some strong lingering doubts.) If I did, then it seemed that I should avoid all talk of any unpleasantness.

Better to change the subject. Barbara always had a way with that retort. She was a master of the *non-sequitur*. In polite circles, i.e., anyone who got their degree from an Eastern U.S. university or from somewhere in Europe, this was a telling repartee which would quell any further promulgation of the untidy bit of nastiness. I was about to *faire le même* when she put in, "I should think so. It is surprising what people put into their bodies. Why, you would be surprised by some of the things that happen in our bodies."

"Yes," I said with a lilting voice. I was not quite sure how to take her, she was so aggressive in her cause. "But surely one can fuss a bit too much about such things. One cannot be constantly worrying about the absolute health value of this and that. Why, there would be no time for anything else, don't you think?" I felt that I had given a perfectly measured response to her repartee.

"Oh it really does not take so much time. Once one understands the basics, the rest comes almost automatically." She was speaking down to *me*! "Sure it takes a little reading, but there are magazines you can get, like 'Health' for example."

"I see." This little vixen was pretty sure of herself. She felt as if she had me. Her voice spoke with conviction. Perhaps she was the apostle of Galenus sounding the second coming with Hippocratic facility. However, none of this really bothered me. I was so entranced with her visage.

I am not sure that *individually* her features were very striking, but *ensemble* they made my head spin. Her nose was perhaps a little long and it turned down slightly. Her chin was sharp and her eyebrows were a little thick. She had light brown hair which she wore rather short. Individually, I could criticize any one of her features. Why was it that I was taken by her so? Her build was slight; she could not be over 5 foot 3 inches or so, but there was something which delighted me. I was amused by the modulation of her voice and the intensity with which she brought forth her case. I was a willing spectator/victim to her barrage of arguments.

"Look, I don't want to come on too strong about this, it is just one of my interests. I guess we all fight for something. I fight about sugar and cream." She finished her coffee and got up. "Well, it was nice talking with you, but I think it is about time to re-board the bus."

These words made me heavy with sadness. It had only seemed an instant that we had been together. Why was she suddenly taking flight? Being as it was early evening already, I had been about to suggest a quick journey to a place close by for a bite to eat. Her abrupt exit had taken me by surprise. She seemed to me to be a person who went about in short intense bursts which related to each other only vaguely or by some principle of which I was not aware. The whole episode left me feeling quite confused and disconcerted. I finished my coffee (feeling slightly ambivalent about all the sugar and cream) and then I got up to return to the bus when who should return but the little goddess snow bird.

"Bad news," she said.

"The President has been shot?"

"No, the bus engine has to be overhauled."

"Oh?"

"Yes. And they cannot get another bus here for the transfer for six to seven hours."

I looked at my watch. It was seven ten. "That would be one or two in the morning," I put in sternly. One must be stern about bus company errors. "They should put us up for the night."

"Are you kidding? You have been flying too much. Busses won't even buy you a sandwich for the wait."

"But our tickets are good for the—" I looked up at the board for the first morning bus on our route. "Do you see that?" I pointed to the schedule board. The first morning bus was at seven twenty. "We could rest up here and take the morning bus."

She looked at me rather skeptically. It was as if she were debating what she should do. Did she want to put herself under the 'protection' of such a seedy character as myself? What might I try to do to her when we got to the hotel? Was I the type to press myself upon a poor, defenseless young thing? You bettcha. I tried to hold back my anticipation, but I'm afraid that as an actor I am only a feeble imitator (what is the mirror image of a mirror image?).

"Well, it is getting rather late. And this bus depot is not the most pleasant place in the world." She paused as she pursed her lips and gave the problem deep consideration. "Oh, why not? Can you fetch my bag for me? I'll call the Marc Piazza for a couple of rooms."

I quickly hopped to it with a spring to my step which I had not had since I passed the oral defense of my dissertation at Cambridge eight or nine years ago. This might be a glorious evening. I did not know the hotel she mentioned, but I hoped it would be a nice place. It was quite a coincidence that she knew so quickly where she would call. But perhaps she knows the city well.

I lifted the suitcases (bag became plural: one medium and small one), and suddenly realized that there was a bus arriving from Chicago in ninety minutes. It would be the last bus of the night from the windy city until the early morning one. Why hadn't she mentioned it then? Perhaps no one had told her and she was unaware of the schedule. That must be it. I was the recipient of a little stroke of luck. I might now take my time and capture this little creature. The thought made me feel very comfortable. I, who had never been an exceptionally lucky individual, was going to be the lucky winner of Miss Brevist. I smiled as I approached her (I must admit that the load was rather cumbersome). Little did she know that another bus was leaving at eight-thirty!

She waved to me. Apparently she had gotten a taxi. Then I noticed something in her hand. It was in the hand which was waving. There in her hand, grasped securely, was a bus schedule. She had a bus schedule. She must have known about the eight thirty bus all along.

My mind became confused. She knew about the bus schedule and yet she told me that the next bus would not be coming until two in the morning. She must have known that I would suggest staying at a hotel. Yes, that was it! I came to this marvel of deductive reasoning just as we were getting into the taxi. That was it—she was picking me up!

CHAPTER THREE

I SHOULD TELL YOU RIGHT OFF the bat that I am not a person who usually stays in the posh hotels. Oh sure, I've stayed in some nice ones before, but they were always at philosophy conventions. Then, the University was picking up the tab. I'd get a nice room and have a few big meals and everything would be free. But when I was picking up the tab I generally went to the Holiday Inn or Hotel 6 (when the rooms actually went for $6). When it was my dime I leaned toward reasonable, functional establishments. Don't get me wrong, I really prefer an old fashionable hotel any day of the week to one of these mass produced pre-fab jobs with their plastic sterility. University professors—even at Chicago University—are certainly not lords of the manor (though some pretend they are and much of the etiquette of the academic life pretends to being gentry). But with Barbara and her expensive tastes, what little we had was spent on shoes, purses, and other clothing accessories that were always beyond our means. I had not bought a thing for myself in five years.

When expenses are not evenly divided, then one has two choices: one person must make up for the other's excesses via frugality or else go bankrupt. I'm not entirely sure, but going bankrupt might constitute moral turpitude (the only way to fire a tenured faculty member).

Why, even though I had a little money given to me by my father when he died (which along with his insurance paid my bills at

NYU and Cambridge), her spendthrift ways soon put an end to that. I know that I am lucky that I chose to go off to England for graduate studies when I did. If I had waited a year (as Barbara's father had suggested so that I could marry Barbara just after her graduation), I'd have never gone. Her greedy claws would have seen to that.

If I seem a little bitter, I apologize. But in all honesty I am somewhat upset. I mean here I was a distracted student of philosophy and biology at one of the best universities in the world wondering whether I should marry this girl to whom I had been promised, or whether I should chalk it up to experience and continue on with my studies. The choice was not an easy one, but I felt that I had made a commitment. I made a commitment which I did not intend to break. Indeed, it took something extraordinary to force me into my present flight. However, all that is behind me now. At present, I was putting the finishing touches on my wardrobe (that is putting on the tie I had brought).I was traveling light. Besides my light weight jacket, I had a pair of regular pants and a pair of jeans, two shirts, two pairs of underthings and a toothbrush. That was it. What I didn't have I figured I'd buy along the way. It was June and I could get away with going to a restaurant without a sports coat.

We decided (that is, *Anthea* decided) that it was time to tell me her first name and then *she* made the choice to eat at Le Bistro. I seconded her choice. Le Bistro was a restaurant located right in the Mark Plaza. It was an exceptional meal (and I'm not complimenting the food). There were courses upon courses of various kinds of fresh and cooked vegetables and adequately prepared French-American dishes. (French-American means ersatz French sauces and spices combined with American-sized meat portions).

"You know, it is nice to see a restaurant serve so many tasty vegetables," I said somewhere in the middle of my gourmandizing.

"Yes. I am really a vegetarian you know. It's just that I sometimes eat meat."

"Are you a vegetarian by principle or just because it tastes good?"

"I don't know. A little of both I suppose."

"If you'd excuse me, I have always thought personally that the only way one could be a vegetarian was through palate and not through moral persuasion."

"I tend to agree with you, for myself, but I've know people who are really hyped about saving the whales and all that." Anthea lifted her right arm as she spoke as if invoking her clan on Mount Olympus.

I was about to mention that there were very few people eating whale meat these days. I'm sure that it was just a figure of speech, and I didn't want to turn this dinner into a philosophical discourse between Hylas and Philonous, but my ears perked up whenever I heard someone espousing what I considered to be a bogus philosophy. After all, I was a philosopher. I felt a responsibility to say something even if it meant that I would alienate myself from this delicate flower.

"But how is that?" I replied against my better judgment.

"What?"

"I'm curious to hear about a consistent moral position which supports vegetarianism."

"I am no lawyer. I cannot make their case for them before this court, your honor." I laughed, naturally. She had defused my attempt at the present, but I did want to get into it. I set down my machines of combat and relaxed to the quiet and low light at the place.

Our attention was drawn to the table next to us before we could say anything else. It was a couple in their early forties. She wore a slinky gray "A" skirt that looked as if it had come from K-Mart. He had denim pants and a short sleeve yellow knit shirt, probably from Lands' End. They were in different universes and she held the road map. He had wanted to order a hamburger, but she insisted on haute culture and got him snails. This fit her aesthetic for the occasion this was supposed to represent. The problem was that neither of them knew how to eat them. He picked up his clamp and tried to remove the snail with the clamp! The result was that it slipped off his plate and fell down to the floor. This brought a barrage of quiet curses as he blamed his wife for inducing him to order escargots.

Quickly the waiter glided over to assist, when the fellow decided that he would pick up the shell with his fingers and get the snails out that way. All he succeeded in doing was in pushing the snail further into the shell. This occasioned great frustration which the waiter vainly attempted to quell.

"If monsieur would use the clamp to hold the shell and the seafood fork to extract the escargot, it might prove more enjoyable." Now it didn't matter if the waiter knew any other French words besides 'monsieur'. His speech was delivered with the maximum amount of restraint, considering the circumstances. The man at the table then put a shell into the clamp and was about to apply the seafood fork, when the shell (which, in fact, had not actually been put fully into the clamp) began to slip from its place. The effect was for the shell to be ejected onto the adjoining table and into a bowl of soup which was carefully being consumed by a fastidious, middle-aged gentleman, who upon receiving this unwanted missile (which had stained his tie in its messy aftermath), sat bolt upright, said, "Oh!" and then, in a dignified, self-assured manner, walked out of the restaurant. This display really got to the boob, who threw down his napkin (an act which sent the other snails onto the carpet) and stormed out himself, saying as he went, "Come on Ethel, this ain't our kind of place."

Ethel, trying to remain calm and retain her aesthetic through all this and being acutely aware that most of the restaurant's patrons were at that moment watching her every move, tried to swallow a spoonful of cold potato soup. She was successful in getting the soup to her lips and into her mouth, but the swallowing required a concerted effort and thus resulted in her breaking into tears and following her husband out the door. The waiter quickly moved to the table and took the lady's purse which she had left. Soon she would be aware of its absence and the easier such restoration might be affected, the better.

"The snails seem to be a bit slippery tonight," retorted Anthea, returning to her meal.

"Quite."

"One never has such problems with vegetables," she said, taking another bite of her entree.

"Artichokes have caused a few raised eyebrows in their time."

"Technique, my friend. It's all in the wrist."

"Just so," I said with a smile so slight that it was hardly perceptible in the dimmed light. "Oh, by the way, how do you like your Coq Grenoble?"

"It is not a vegetable."

"Quite."

Anthea twisted a bit in her chair. She was quick with the repartee and I could just see her changing gears to deliver her reply. "A very delicate taste. Do you like yours?"

"Oh rather."

We finished our entrée and sallied forth to the dessert. I was astonished that someone of Anthea's slender size could eat so much and still remain as petite as she was.

I had only two sets of everything. I didn't think I liked her suggestion. I was no athlete. I was repulsed by the smell of victory and the tragedy of defeat. But even as she made the suggestion I knew that I would be there the next morning. It was very bad for me to say, "No". That was the way it always was with Barbara. She would decide virtually everything. It's not that I did not like to put in my ideas, for I flooded her with my thoughts on the subject (and to be perfectly fair to her, she sometimes adopted them), but it was *her* and not *me* who made the final decision about things.

I hated this about myself. I hated being pushed around. Ronnie would always tell me to stand up to Barbara (Ronnie never wanted me to get married—he said it would ruin my career). And I tried to follow his advice. But then there would have been a great fuss and I hated that as well. I always felt a modicum of guilt tinged with a sense of the absurd. It was absurd to become so upset over small, trivial episodes. What would it hurt to "show myself bigger than the situation" by giving in? Well, if giving in means showing oneself to be bigger than the situation, then I must be one of the largest personages in America.

I have only met two people who have not tried to take advantage of me in that way: Ronnie and Gambol. Ronnie was a good friend at Cambridge and Gambol was my dog when I was a boy. I had loved

Gambol with a pure devotion. There was nothing that I would not do for that dog. He was a white and tan colored mutt that looked like a sheep dog. He was big, dumb, and ugly, but I felt closer to him than to any person. I used to go .on long walks with Gambol into Washington Park. The animal always followed my lead and never took his own initiative unless I gave him leave. But then, that's part of another tale. Just now I was sitting in my hotel room and thinking about Anthea. The resentment was wearing off. All that I could focus on was her wonderful face and that slim, young body. I remember when Barbara was young. Her outgoing personality drew me to her. She seemed to like me — at least she encouraged me. We had only been dating a year before we had sex. She was my first, and to this day, my *only* partner. I took her with relish. Sex was better than I had imagined it.

At the beginning I sometimes felt that Barbara didn't boss me around so much when we made love. I imagined that I controlled Barbara through sex. Well 'controlled' might be a bit strong. What I should say is that for the first thirty or forty times, Barbara allowed me to choose the time and manner of our sexual relations. I suppose that wasn't much, but as I was an ingénue, it made me feel powerful and masterful. But even that, too, went away. And I retreated more and more into my research. It never occurred to me to have an affair. I would never have done that. I believed too much in the commitment from a promise (actual or tacit). I guess that's the reason. At any rate, I never had an affair.

Anthea was to me a woman of mystery. Where did she come from? Why had she raced to get onto the bus? Where was she going? All these questions would probably never get answered. We would be on our separate ways and part again as quickly as we had met. What was the sense of it all? The whole encounter seemed so — pointless. I tried to glean some information about Anthea when we paid our room bills after dinner (on the principle that we might be a little pressed for time in the morning). I had walked slowly back to her room with her and we lingered outside her door. She asked me inside. I wanted to go in with her and follow the usual script. But I felt that to do so required me to make a positive decision, and 'positive decisions' were not my forte. I'm more the impulsive type. So I smiled instead and said I was a little tired and that I'd take a rain check. She contorted her face with a most unusual expression. I don't know what it meant. She was probably breaking up inside at what an idiot I was to pass up a chance with her. After all, was not this whole thing cooked up by her? Was not the raison d'être of this capricious sortie to get into the sack and have a few intense physical feelings? That may have been the biological plan for *homo sapiens*, in general, but at the moment I could not feel right about pursuing that outcome. And if it didn't feel right, why do it? But then, one could counter, why not? What was I losing? My wife and I were separated. I no longer felt any commitment towards her. We would be getting a divorce as soon as the papers could be drawn up and signed. So what was the impediment? Here you have a good look-ing younger woman who is aching to hop into bed with you, and there you are balking. Is it not really because you do not have the nerve to say *yes* to her? Is not the real reason for your sitting at this minute alone in your own room a piece of evidence which shows your lack of intestinal fortitude? No, that was not it. I had courage to some degree. It's just situational. I remembered when Ronnie and I had gone to a pub and it was after a football match and the place was filled with footballers who were their usual rowdy selves. We wondered whether we should move over to the saloon. "It's getting a might smelly in here," said Ronnie.

"Very thick."

Ronnie wore wire rimmed glasses which fogged up rather easily. Besides, the smoke was getting under my contact lenses and nothing feels worse than foreign material between the lens and the eye: a suction is created and the foreign particles are scraped across the cornea. Such is a standard account of a corneal abrasion (a rather uncomfortable infirmity indeed—and the reason I gave up contacts shortly after I married Barbara).

"Shall we tip a few on the other side?" I suggested after an interval in which the bad atmosphere of the public bar took on an added mean-ing as a little pushing and shoving started between a few of the lads.

"Quite."

So we tried to make our way along the bar to the door which separates the two halves of the tavern. We had just gotten to the end of the bar when a rather obstreperous chap interposed his body.

"And where do you think you're bloody well going?" The bloke appeared to be a footballer who had consumed a large quantity of liquid refreshments during the course of the day. Such people, Aristotle claimed, are not responsible for their actions (due to ignorance of the particular — what was going on around them during their drunken sojourn). One thing we did not want to do was to get tangled up with a man who was not responsible for his actions.

"Just getting a breath of air, mate," said Ronnie crisply.

"Isn't the air in here good enough for ye?"

Instead of answering this dilemma question, Ronnie simply replied, "Excuse us, please."

"Oh you want to be excused, do ye?" It was clear that this townie did not like the University "gown" folk. He was just itching to put us out. I could see it coming. I do not know if Ronnie did, but before I suspected a blow I pushed myself to the side so that I was not behind Ronnie.

"Here's a breath of fresh air for ye," began the drunken ape as he delivered a sharp blow to Ronnie's midsection. I reacted immediately. Without hesitation, I swung a left hook to the lout's jaw. At the same moment I felt a stabbing pain in my left hand. The force of my blow sent me sprawling on top of the burly bully as all confusion was breaking out in the establishment. Both Ronnie and I were on the floor, lying on top of the footballer as the constables arrived (the barkeep must have seen something coming and called them early because they were there in only a couple of minutes). Anyway, most of the patrons were hauled away. That is, anyone who looked like a footballer was taken away to dry off. Since we were clearly students we were left to take care of ourselves. Ronnie and I laughed at how the big lug had been knocked out by a little chap like me and that the jerk had also managed to have himself arrested on top of it all.

Ronnie did not feel very fit, but he had no internal damage. I had sustained a small fracture in one of the bones of my hand.

"It is lucky you were there to give me a hand," he said in the cool autumn air. He walked along, slump shouldered with his hands deep into his tweed sport coat pocket for warmth.

"I gave you a hand all right. It's my left hand. I think I may have broken something. How about your stomach?"

"Don't know, really—we'll have to pop over to the district surgery tomorrow for x-rays."

We walked a bit further, not talking. The wind had picked up some over the fens and we were both very cold by the time we reached our rooms. "I think it's about time for a top coat," I said as I began to shiver.

"An extra sweater will do it. Bad luck about the hand, but if you're going to be my body guard you will have to toughen up those bones."

Me, a bodyguard! Even now the thought makes me laugh. It was the only time in my life that I have ever hit anyone. My hand became quite a joke among several of us graduate students. I was given all sorts of advice on how to avoid such side effects of my brawling antics in the future. They ranged from odd diets full of protein to soaking my hand in Epsom salts dissolved in warm water. I was curious about how toughs manage to hit people without smashing up their bodies. Apparently the trick is to plan your blow so that it ends its momentum at impact. One wants to hit a chin and stop and not to hit "through" the chin. The information was useless really, because I never intended to hit anyone again. But still, the knowledge gave me a kind of peace of mind.

The incident was a very spontaneous one. That is the way that I imagine all *acts of courage* are: they just happen. You either do them or you don't. This is why I did not worry about such things since I knew that if I were ever put into such a situation in the future I would either do my bit, or I would not. There really is not much time for fooling around in events of this kind. Because situations of courage were those of split second timing, I knew that my failure with Anthea tonight was not of the same genre. It was not as if I said to myself that I was going to ask her to my room, or whether I would try to seduce her once she was in my room (or her room or any room or even in the hall), because I had made no such resolution to myself. In fact I had no plan at all. I was just trying to enjoy what was being presented to me without going out of my depth. In fact, as I sat back in the token wooden chair in my room, I thought that I was rather happy with my caution. After all, the experience had been rather pleasant. I had enjoyed the conversation and I might even enjoy the little run in the morning (though I didn't see how I could run very well in my crepe-soled heavy shoes). But I did not have to go very far. It wasn't as if I were running a marathon. We would just go down a couple of blocks and look at the lake and come back. If she wanted to run farther] she could. The very thought of it made me want to get some sleep.

I put in my call to be awoken, brushed my teeth and hopped into bed. As I lay there I began to wonder about La Crosse. I had no idea what kind of town it was except that it was rather small and had a few breweries. Perhaps I would install myself in a cheap hotel and fritter my life away drinking the local suds. I was rather fond of pretzels. In fact, once while on holiday from Cambridge I went to Munich and lived in a hostel run by nuns. For sustenance I lived for days on wurst and beer. It was a perfect combination. You would put a little wurst on the piece of hard bread and smother it with Bavarian mustard. Then you wash the whole thing down with a liter of beer. Since a liter is around a quart and since I only had one meal a day (outside of the frühstück one had in the morning, which at the hostels run by the nuns consisted of two large rolls and a very large cup of coffee), it had a considerable effect upon me. Those were very happy days. I was doing what I wanted: sightseeing, attending a lecture at a local university, and finding a quiet bench in a park that was in the shade and reading for hours at a time. I had a moderate amount of money to support modest vices, such as traveling.

I readily went to sleep at promptly 23:00 (since the nuns locked the doors at 22:00). The mattress was lumpy, but it did not impede my drifting through my memories of my solitary sojourns. If this was heaven, then kill me tomorrow.

Staccato. Thump, thump. I emerged from my pleasant reverie. Then I became aware of a knocking on my door. I didn't pay any attention. The knocking continued. I opened my eyes and tried to recall where I was and where Barbara was. Then I remembered. I pulled on my pants and went to the door. It was Anthea. She had a worried expression on her face.

"Can I come in?" she asked, pushing inside and shutting the door before I could answer. She was carrying a little bag that seemed stuffed with something. She shut the door after her and went over to the bed and collapsed on it. I went over to help her, but in an instant she was erect again. She was dressed in a powder blue running outfit. *Very chic,* I said to myself. The clothes exuded an air of calm self-assurance which stood in stark contrast to the pained and agitated attitude which characterized her body.

"You've got to help me," she said in a low, almost inaudible voice. She was sitting up on the bed, holding the bag tightly as if it were a baby.

I wondered instantly if she were in trouble with the law. Was she asking me to harbor a fugitive? Would I be a party to breaking the law? This would have bothered me tremendously, for as much as I liked this beautiful waif from the Greyhound terminal, I would not break the law for her. I would not go out of my way to help the law arrest her, but I wouldn't help her escape. I wouldn't unless she were the clearly innocent victim of societal injustice. Then the scenario would be different. The law would be the bad guy and she would be the fugitive—David Jansen fleeing from the one-armed man. "What's the matter?" I asked.

"I can't tell you. You've got to trust me."

"What kind of trouble are you in? Who's after you? What have you done?" My questions were coming across rapid fire. I had so many. This is what I'm trained to do: assess the paradigm and search for anomalies. Instantly a calm little interlude in my sordid existence had changed natures. It was different than I had imagined it had been. Did that mean that it was really something different all along?

Anthea sat there holding the bag. It was just a brown paper bag like the kind this hotel uses to line its waste baskets. Then I looked again at my waste basket and shot off another question, "Is that a waste basket bag?" Now, this question might seem a little out of line concerning the apparent gravity of the situation. But my mind was full of many questions. Who was this girl, anyway? What sort of person was she? Was she a criminal? She had seemed so nice. She had been so charming the night before. She wasn't coarse or common the way one imagines most criminals to be.

"I don't have time to explain now. I need your help. Two men are after me."

"Why? What have you done? Are they policemen?"

I had to get that question out. I wanted to help, but I could not let my emotional reactions be the guide of my conduct. My philosophy had taught me that. I had to know so that I could gauge my behavior accordingly. Her expression changed. It was as if I had accused her of being a prostitute or a drug dealer. I didn't think I was *charging* her with anything. I was only asking a simple question. I mean, I knew practically nothing about this blossom of a woman. She was good company. She was attractive. She has just enough *attitude.* In short, she was pleasant to be around. But what had this to do with her soul? I had a right to know about that.

Anthea's demeanor quickly changed. She became filled with a calm cold control which bordered on anger. "Who do you think I am?" She got up and started for the door. "I was stupid to come here. I should have known you wouldn't help." I stopped her by interceding between herself and the door while I grabbed her shoulders to stop her. She tried to free herself from my grasp. She was a powerful woman and I was a weak puny man, but something gave me an unusual strength which I didn't think I possessed.

I pushed her against the wall. The exertion made me breathe very hard. "Look, you weren't wrong to come here. I want to help. Will you stop being so bull headed? I only asked you a few questions. What would *you* do if the situations were reversed?"

"I'd help you without reserve."

"But without a certain amount of information?" We stared each other down for an interval.

"Listen, I am not acting, don't you see? If you want me to help you I have to know a few things."

"There isn't time, don't you see? It may already be too late. If those guys get me they may kill me."

"Tell me what I can do. I'll help," I said instantly.

She looked at me suspiciously and then apparently decided that she would have to trust me. "We've got to get out of here," she said.

"Fine. I'll get my things." I slipped into the bathroom and finished dressing.

"No. You don't understand. They may be covering the elevator. They may be covering the stairs. They may be coming to your room at this very moment."

"*My* room. . ." I said coming out of the bathroom relatively ready for whatever was to face us. My voice portrayed my anxiety over this new development. "I thought you said that there were only two of them."

"I saw two of them. They were waiting outside the elevator on my floor. I went down the stairs to your floor after getting a few essentials together."

"And what you're saying is that there may be more of them. Some may be guarding the stairs, some at the entrance to the building— they may be all over! In that case we're sunk."

"Not necessarily. We know that they are looking for me." I didn't interrupt her here and ask her how she knew this, but instead I let her continue.

"They probably know about you if they pumped the staff, as I believe they have. By the way, did you get that wake-up call?"

"No," I said. "But that does not mean anything. I've been in plenty of places that have forgotten to give me a wake-up call."

"I'm not so sure," she said.

"Look, it would have been to their advantage for them to know where I was if they were after me. By sending a wake-up call they'd pinpoint me."

"We've got to chance it." I didn't understand her words. She was standing near the window now. She was not clutching her bag in the same manner as before. In fact, she was holding it rather carelessly. "We've got to trick them. I'm sure that they did not expect me out so early and so probably I made it here unseen. They may know where I am. At any rate we need an escape vehicle." She reached furtively into the bag and pulled out a C note.

"Take this and get us a car."

"A car?" I asked in a voice which portrayed that I still didn't understand the scheme which she had concocted in her brain. Besides, I did not know the city. I could probably make it back along Wisconsin Avenue to the bus station, but beyond that I was not sure. I could probably get a car through the hotel, but that would be nix since it could be traced to us by the goons too quickly. But then there were the yellow pages.

"Do you know a place or should we look one up?" I asked.

Anthea had beaten me to my solution as she was already heading for the desk and the phone directory. She appeared to know the city somewhat and quickly located a place for us.

"Now you get the car. Let's see, it ought to take you thirty minutes to get over there and get the car and five minutes to get back. Let's set our watches together."

I felt as if I were in the army. We were engaging in a combat mission. I had missed all the wars (thank goodness) and so took a neophyte's pleasure in the planning of our escapade. As she talked, her short, carefully cut hair bobbed slightly in beat with her nodding head. There was an intensity to her eyes that I had not seen. She was ravishing.

I am rather embarrassed to admit that I felt at that moment like taking her in my arms and kissing her intensely. But this was hardly the time for that. I got my instructions and left.

I went first up toward her room to see if I could get inside and bring back her small bag with the shoulder strap. I don't know why she hadn't brought it with her when she packed her brown bag. The whole thing seemed so peculiar. I got to her room and unlocked the door. In the center of the room were two bags. I went to pick one up when I heard something behind me. I looked back and standing in the doorway was a man holding a gun.

CHAPTER FOUR

"WHERE DO YOU THINK you're going?" asked the man with the gun.

"What do you think *you're* doing?" I replied, not processing fully that by the simple fact that he held the gun it meant that he was the more powerful of the two of us and that he could cancel my further trip plans. I knew all of this in the abstract, of course, but when one is actually confronted by a gun one tends to see the situation in an untrue light: either you think that you're dead or you believe that the other would never use that device for any reason. I thought the latter and so did not appreciate the true gravity of my position.

"Listen fella, I don't like smartasses."

I tried to fathom why he took me for a smartass.

The man stepped inside the room and shut the door behind him. I realized that this move was not one which was to my advantage. With the door open it was less likely that he might do something to alter my state of being, but with the door closed he might resort to a number of tactics designed to make me divulge the whereabouts of Anthea.

Before he had the chance to apply the screws, the door burst open. The man with the gun nervously spun around and I was certain he was going to shoot the intruder. I based my conjecture on my reading plenty of detective stories. Connected with literary background,

I also gathered that my time to make my move was now. I was supposed to jump on my captor who held the gun and wrestle him to
the ground, recover the gun, get the girl and the undying admiration
of everyone in the town. It would have made a nice ending, except
that the ape who held the gun was unlikely to even budge if I hurled
myself on him.

I was no match for him and it would be stupid for me to try. So I
just watched this gorilla spin around and thrust his gun out at arm's
length. The man coming in managed, "Mike."

"Oh shit," said the primate with the gun. He was obviously a
boss of some variety who knew the intruder (most likely one of his
men). "Oh shit," he said again as he dropped his arms to his side and
turned his head back to me in disgust. "You know that I almost blew
your head off? How many times have I told you that you should
announce your presence? Knock, you dummy."

It seemed rather odd for Mike here to be calling his henchman a
dummy in his Polish-Serbo-Irish-Chicago Accent of the First Ward,
the highest paying territory in the city's very unorganized system
of bosses. It might seem strange to someone who does not live in
Chicago for an insulated university professor to have some idea
of your typical Chicago thug, but it is not really so odd at all. In
Chicago certain things are accepted. Crooked dealings are one of the
things that everyone accepts.

The evening news casts interviewed prominent crooks and talked
with them. The restaurants and bars are full of them. Unlike other
cities where the crime element operates outside the law, in Chicago
they constitute the government and the civic business organizations.
You might say that crime is a respectable business in Chicago. Just as
one might have contact with municipal leaders of any city in which
one lives (nothing strange in that, even for a university professor),
so also does one have contact with mobsters or people in the pay of
mobsters. In Chicago, the only difference is that these civic fathers
are also miniature fathers ("dons") in their own right. There isn't
any mob violence any more. All the disputes are ameliorated in
the city council where all the various criminal factions send their

representatives. It is democracy at its finest. Guns (for the most part) have been replaced with patronage and a padded voting register full of voters as difficult to find as ghosts.

Interspersed with the established groups are a number of "small time punks". These individuals or small groups are allowed to pick up the scraps and the gristle that is too unprofitable for the larger groups to handle. Since they have a low overhead (and don't have a city payroll to support), they can afford to take on the less lucrative "business" ventures. It all made perfect economic sense, for deep down these big-time and small-time thugs were American entrepreneurs in the true sense, except that they cringed at paying taxes or submitting to regulation.

I had these guys pegged by their personal style as small-timers probably run by a traffic court judge or some other municipal post under the radar. There were five or six of them bumbling around with their third grade minds, breaking society's fine collectables and then kicking the larger pieces out of the way in their wasteful quest.

They never bothered cleaning anything up nor did they bother with meticulous care in their destructive missions. This all seemed relatively clear to me, being a citizen of Chicago for seven years. What wasn't clear to me was what Anthea had to do with them and what exactly they were going to do with me.

"I'm sorry, Mike, but Joey said that youse had her. Sose I got Billy up from his station. He'll be ups in a minute." The words dribbled off this monkey's lips as if he were the proud winner of a spelling bee, finishing the final word to insure his victory. The result which ensued was contrary to the expectations of this proud contestant.

"You idiot! Does this look like the girl? Does it?" The expression on the other's face changed from pride to one of saddened disbelief. He hung his head as a scowl formed on his visage. "I don't know what I'm going to do with you thick headed bimbos. I come up on this guy opening Miss Brevist's room and your black buddy runs to you and says we've caught the girl." This speech was the center of his attention. If we weren't on the third floor, I'd have run to the balcony and jumped away.

"If you guys can't tell the girls from the boys, we'll have to send you over to The Lighthouse for the Blind to make pencils."

This last phrase seemed to be recited as if it were an oft repeated threat. But even if it had been, the crestfallen man winced as if he had been hit across the wrist with a switch. He stood silent, tall and erect. Then Mike turned to me.

"Now tell me where she is," he said with determination, holding his gun as if he might pistol whip me. "We can still get her if you tell us where she is."

"Why do you want her?" I asked.

"Listen, I'm asking the questions," he said, taken aback.

Just then Billy and Joey came back. They flew in the door and looked around. "Where is she?" asked Joey, the short, thin black man.

"What does it look like?" said the penitent one.

"What do you mean, Sam?" said the Billy, a short fat man who appeared to me to have severe ego problems.

"Just whats I says, youse gumboats." This was apparently a sharp repartee by Sam.

"Holy fuck, you mean I've come all this way for nothing," said the fat Billy. "Joey put us on to this and you trying to tell me he didn't know shit about what he was talkie' about?"

"That's exactly what I mean," returned Sam. "This sharp-eyed gumboat, who won't get glasses even though he's made several visualary mistakes!" Sam seemed very content with his winning sentence fragment. And even stranger still, the others felt he had delivered a stunning oratory. Even as this stirring event was taking place, Mike was losing no time. It was time to reconvene his interrogation session with me. In this mode, he was focused upon his mission. He would not be deterred in any way by what was going on between the others.

"Listen, we don't have a hell of a lot of time. It'll be much easier if you just tell me where the girl is."

"Why? What has she done to you?"

Apparently Billy, who was left out of the Sam-Joey debate, wanted to be a part of this one and took a step towards me and said pugnaciously, "You heard the man. Spill it." After which he delivered a sharp blow to my stomach which sent me to the floor and into a state of semi-consciousness.

I heard confusion and yelling around me and then there was quiet. It must have been an hour or so before I could straighten up. I had never considered myself middle-aged, being only in my late thirties, but my body at that moment felt as if it were twenty years older than I was. I never felt so bad in my life. I stumbled up to the bathroom where I ran some water over my face. It worked, but I still felt awful.

I was an associate professor of philosophy of science specializing in biology and yet I could not understand why I should feel so terrible in my head when I had been hit in my midsection. Part of it I suppose was shock, but the rest of it was unknown. Perhaps I hit my head when I went down. But then I could generate a thousand suppositions and revisions and then reverse them in an instant. This did not do anyone any good. I had to concentrate on what was at hand and what I was to do now. I looked about the room. The suitcases were gone. I felt around in my pocket. My room key was gone. But they had left my driver's license and I checked the small change pocket of my jeans where I had put my one hundred dollars. It was still there.

They must have gotten my room key and were now probably carrying her away, unless—unless she had gotten away. Then a black thought passed through my consciousness. It was an hypothesis that might offer causal explanation: what if she had set me up for this all along? This thought didn't strike a concordant tone. There were no purifying showers—only the dark menace of that thunderhead.

The fact was this: Anthea sent me back to her room. What hypothesis might explain the fact? Well, she might have sent me back to her room as bait so that the others might flock to the room and leave an opening for her to escape. There was not enough evidence to confirm this hypothesis with certainty, but it seemed plausible to me. In fact, as I thought about, it occurred to me that my hypothesis would give her maximum opportunity for escape. Assuming that she was self-interested and didn't care a peep about me, such a motivation might well prove to be the most rational available to her. Otherwise she would have been in the room waiting for me where the goons would have caught her. I went back to my room. It was locked. I went downstairs and got another key. The room was empty. My case was gone. Anthea was gone. My traveler's checks were gone. But this was no problem; they were redeemable! Always trust television advertising. I went to the American Express office and found that I would have to wait another half-hour for the place to open. So I strolled over to the car rental place she had told me about. I inquired and my hundred dollars got me the information about where she went as well as a little Toyota with which to follow.

I went back to the American Express office and waited another hour for my checks to be replaced. So there I was, sitting in my very own Toyota with my wallet full of traveler's checks and Anthea's destination, Tomah, Wisconsin, firmly in my mind. I realized that I probably wouldn't reach her, but I had nothing else that was occupying my time so I decided to set out on my little adventure. I wondered whether the goons were following her, too. I did not see how they could be, since they seemed to be so stupid, but one never knows. After all, they did find her in Milwaukee so they might not be as dumb as they appeared, or they might have someone who did the investigating for them. I did not know and I did not care. I did not care about a lot of things. My stomach was in knots from a variety of emotions. I did not like the idea that I may have been tricked. How else could I interpret it? If she had followed the plan that we had set out, she would have been caught. She was not caught, therefore; she must have not followed the plan. "Not following the plan" meant that she must have cut out immediately after leaving me. That must be it. There, is no other plausible explanation. I could think of no other explanation. I wanted to let my mind wander along the long stretches of the six lane highway that comprised Interstate 94.

I did not know why I was following her. I did not care for a person who could leave me for the wolves. I had always been someone who put high stock in loyalty and fidelity. Now, in just two days I had been shocked out of that bedrock security upon which I had built my life. Driving to Tomah was a pointless action, yet I suppose I wanted to know—wanted to know for sure if she had devised a plan for her escape which included me as the fall guy. The lust after knowledge proved to be the fatal flaw of Oedipus. Would it prove to be my undoing as well?

Did I really want to be here on the road watching an endless train of green highway signs flashing their ever important messages? There were two sorts of signs that were posted adjacent to the shoulder of the road: first, mileage/speed limit/caution for cattle crossing the road; and second: advertisements. The most catching to me were the Burma Shave signs. They were spaced out a mile or so apart: Our fortune / Is your / Shaven face / It's our best / Advertising space / Burma-Shave. They gave some continuity to the drive.

What was I doing? Why was I going after a person I didn't care about? Was it because I could not decide where else I wanted to go? Was I just following the path of least resistance? I thought back to Barbara and my graduation from New York University in 1966.

"You aren't really going to England, are you?" Barbara was agitated.

"You know I am." I did not like her maneuvering me. She always did it, and I tried to fight it, but she always won out in the end.

"But I will be graduating in only another year. Couldn't you wait for me?"

"Look, I have been accepted at Cambridge University next year. I am not asking you to give up your college to join me. Why do you insist that I give up my schooling to be with you?" I consciously looked away from-her. I knew that if I was to have any luck with her I had to avoid eye contact.

"Does this mean we're finished?"

Her question was delivered in a tender, hurt tone. I felt bad. I looked into her cute face (I say 'cute' because she was not, in truth, beautiful, but actually rather plain) and I felt sorry for her. The corners of her eyes were stretched downward. Her lips, which had been pursed, were now long and quivering. What was I doing to her? Was I a bad person? She asked me if we were finished. How the hell did I know? A year was a long time. Perhaps we *were* finished. But that was only one part of me talking.

"Why do you ask that?'

"You're so eager to get away from me," she said, turning her head away from me and getting up from the stone upon which we had been sitting. It was late afternoon and the sun was playing tricks with its refracted light. I looked at Barbara with the background of the sky. She looked tragic. I felt drawn to her. I wanted to make her feel good. I wanted to tell her that I was not the kind of person who deserts another. I wanted to say all this but instead I said, "You don't understand me at all."

"That's an easy thing to say."

"Oh?"

"Certainly. I have been very close to you in many ways. I did not think that I was throwing myself away on someone who considered it a momentary fling!" She had me and she knew it. I was a chump for guilt. Feeling shame or guilt is a sign of a good soul. She knew I was not only about animal lust (though to be perfectly honest, I could not say for certain whether this was the case or not). I was not the kind of man who would use a person and then discard her. Her body was now directly in front of the sun so that she blocked out the central rays. Only the peripheral aura surrounded her. I felt terrible. I could not express myself. She seemed at that moment to be so right and I appeared to myself to be so entirely wrong. But what was the nature of this "wrong"? Was it merely a mistake made by a naturally good person or the true expression of a twisted and ugly personality? Sometimes I wondered whether *I* was really the bad person. After all, the name "Barbara" in Aristotelian logic stood for the only valid form of the syllogism: A-A-A-first figure. No matter what you substitute for the terms, it is always valid.

So many times when Barbara talked about the "future"—*our* future, I should have been happy. I should have felt cascades of relief over having such an important life decision behind me, but instead I felt scared. I felt as if I wanted to run to the East River and swim away. Was this the attitude of a mature, responsible fellow?

Here was Barbara, who with all her faults was willing to attempt at making a go of it. She was not timid over making commitments which would bind us together in perpetuity. Why was it so much easier for her? Were women different that way? Nonsense, we must all be the same. But was *Barbara* any different in that way? Why was she so sure about *me*? It didn't seem possible that someone was willing to risk it all like that. She had no assurances about me. How well did she really know me? I had been her constant companion for two years (four academic terms). That was a rather artificial environment. How could she be sure about other possible environments?

"I don't consider you to be a momentary fling. You know that." I was sincere.

"Oh really, is that so? What *do* you consider me to be? I'd like to know."

She was approaching me again. As she walked her shadow preceded her, looming large in

her path. I watched from where I was sitting on the ground in front of the rock as she completely engulfed me in her shadow. I felt a chill as I felt compelled to look her in the eye. A paralysis gripped me; I could not respond. But then, she did not expect me to. Her next words told me that. They were in exact harmonic ascension from her last speech as if she were merely indulging in an emphatic dramatic pause. "Your college tramp to play around with? You made certain promises to me, mister. I believed you."

I tried to remember the so-called promises that I was alleged to have made. I couldn't remember them. It is true that I had told her that I loved her. And it is also true that I said that I needed her. And perhaps I might have said something like, "Wouldn't it be grand to be so happy always! But did those statements constitute a promise of marriage? This was clearly Barbara's logical implication.

And 'BArbArA' was the only universally valid figure in Aristotelian logic. She was claiming that I promised to marry her and now was backing out when I had no other use for her.

But perhaps there are more ways to promise marriage than by simply saying the words. Maybe I promised her in other, non-verbal ways. It could be true that I acted as if I wanted to marry her or at least acted in a way that I knew she was interpreting as being in a way that testified a desire for marriage. And because I knew she was taking things in that way and since I did not correct her, I was giving my tacit approval to her interpretation. If this was true, then I was guilty as charged. And if I was guilty I would accept the punishment. I would not back out of an obligation.

"I don't deny that I probably—" I began trying to let her know that there was something to what she was saying and that I would *probably* acquiesce if only she would let me down quietly.

"Probably!" she jumped on the word. "There is no *probably* about it."

"All right," I said looking up at her from the ground. Her black hair had a sparkle of light around it as if the ends of her hair were live wires emitting sparks.

"You are right. Everything you say is right." She was silent. That wasn't enough. "I have an obligation to you. I will keep it. You don't have to worry." There, I thought, that should do it. Now we can go back to being normal.

"An *obligation*. You call me an obligation!" That did it. She was now breaking into tears. I got up and held her to me. In order to comfort her I knew what I would have to say.

"Now, now dear, you know that I don't think of you as an obligation in the sense of an onerous burden."

"But that's what you said. You said 'obligation.'"

"I know that was what I said, but I misspoke myself. You are a responsibility. A glad responsibility; one that I am happy to bear." The words came out and I waxed on for a while until she seemed pacified. Don't get me wrong, I wasn't being insincere. I really loved Barbara. I could feel genuine affection for her. After all, she was really the first and only woman of my life. It was just that I had some lingering doubts about the marriage thing. I was only twenty two and somehow it seemed a little early to be calling it quits. But there I was. I was not the kind of person who turns his back on a promise (even one which had never been explicitly made).

The whole situation seems comical to me today while sitting in the car driving to

Tomah. I think that it might have been best in the long run if I had entered into a real discussion with her—where her and my feelings might be set out and examined. The trouble is that with most of us philosophers, we do not do well in the emotion game. If I had told Barbara that I could not be sure of my feelings just yet, she would have been hurt, of course, but that hurt in the short run would have been better than what we had experienced in the long run. I did not know why I had been incapable of making that important decision and acting upon it. I just was not decisive. I remember my father telling me that a real man was one who could make decisions and then stick by them. I suppose by that yardstick I failed miserably.

But what a foolish set of criteria for measuring one's worth. It tended to promote the Gary Cooper strongman image of the single man standing out alone. What an outmoded and ridiculous set of values this was! I laughed to myself, but even as I was doing this I came back to the unpleasant reality that I had flinched in a crucial life decision and that my action had increased the pain between myself and another. It was my *weakness* that had caused the trouble. I hadn't made the right decision nor did I stick by my real instincts. I turned on the radio to put some happy thoughts into my head when one of those green signs flashed even better news to me: Tomah 14 miles. Then there was a more troublesome Burma Shave series of signs: If you / Don't know / Whose signs / These are / You can't have / Driven very far. I hit the gas a little harder and zoomed ahead to my destination.

Once in Tomah I searched for the local Wisconsin Rent-a-Car office where my Toyota (but more importantly, Anthea's car) was due. I asked for directions at a gas station and soon pulled up to a small lot with perhaps six cars in it. This was on a very different scale than the office in Milwaukee, which seemed to have a hundred or more cars ready to rent.

I stopped the engine and walked inside the little wooden hut. It had unpainted exterior walls and a flat metal roof with one small pipe protruding which was probably the chimney. As I walked inside I was hit by the smell—kind of like being in an old moldy trunk. The walls were forest green with one sign hanging, slightly tilted, that said, "In God we Trust—everybody else *cash.*" The space of the hut was used efficiently. Three paces inside and you were at a plywood counter. The layers of the wood were starting to separate.

The wall to the right of the counter was lined with hundreds of magazines and comics and a few newspapers which were stacked in a pile and ready to go. The hut looked as if it doubled as a newsstand.

"Want a paper or a magazine?" asked the middle aged man sitting in an unusually tall swivel chair which enabled him to reach half of the magazines and comics without getting up. He had a tick in his right eye and a hair lip which he compensated for by pushing his lips out in front of his face as he rhythmically made a smacking sound. On his head he wore a faded red yachting cap with an anchor ensign on the bill.

"Not really. You see, what I want is some information—" I started impatiently. The contrast of my fast talking to his slow locution was quite apparent.

"Mighty fine magazines we have here."

"You don't understand. I've got to get some information in a hurry."

"Or maybe you prefer a comic book. Lots of people like Spiderman or the Fantastic Four."

Then I saw his game and ordered three magazines.

"Which ones you want?"

"I don't care, you pick them."

"Well, I would, you know, if I knew what you liked. But you being a stranger I couldn't very well do that, could I?"

"Give me your three most expensive magazines."

"Well, okay." He paused and then swiveled back. "Are you sure you want to buy *Glamour*? Not too many men read that you know."

"It's a gift," I said just wanting to get this transaction over with so I could find out about Anthea. This man was wasting precious time.

He brought the magazines over to me and I paid him. The periodicals were in sad condition, but I was not really interested in reading about *Today's Hunting*, *Raising Hogs*, or *Glamour* (the last of these was also months out of date).

"Thanks kindly, come again," he said smacking his lips.

"Hey, just a minute. I want to know something about a car that was brought in to you this morning. It was a young woman, do you remember?"

"Don't get too many customers, you know. This car business is really only a sideline. We keep four cars in the lot and the rest are picked up every six months."

"If you don't get many customers, you should remember this one. Did she come in?"

"Don't suppose I'd make any money 'cept for the garages. You know, they pay me something to use the cars as loaners. Folks have their car break down, they need transportation. They come here."

"I hate to interrupt you, but did a young lady come in here or didn't she?"

"Yep. 'Bout an hour and a half ago."

"Well? Anything else?"

"She brought her car in. It's that little Pinto over there."

"She just left it?"

"You her relative or something?" This country rube didn't want to give me any more information unless I had a "need to know." I had to tell him something.

"I'm her brother," I said. "She's been missing for a couple of days so I'm out after her."

"Don't look like her brother," said the vendor, "Look more like a husband or a lover."

I didn't respond. I was not going to let some rube from Tomah be so insolent. He was getting too nosey. Besides, he probably did not have any more useful information. I began to walk away.

"Last I saw of her she went next door."

I heard these words even as I was walking away. I acknowledged them with a motion of the head and kept walking at the same pace.

Well, I should mention that this car rental place was on a corner. The only thing the vendor could have meant by "next door" was a supermarket which was fifty yards away or a used car lot that was one hundred fifty yards away. I decided to try the car lot first.

Like the magazine store/car rental place, this used car lot also had a gas station on the premises. Presumably there was not enough business in any one area for there to be such stark specialization as having a single business at a single location. The car lot side of this conglomerate had three strings of plastic pennants in assorted colors flapping in the wind. These strings looked to be several years old since they were not in the best repair. A number of them were missing from the strand and a few had been ripped or worn so that only the torn part was flapping in the breeze. The lot had a variety of cars ranging twenty five to thirty years in age. Each car had its price indicated on the windshield in soap-inscribed numerals. There were probably twenty cars or so arranged orderly in four rows.

I decided that the only way I'd find someone to talk to was to go over to the gas station side. I moved off the gravel lot which held the used cars to a blacktopped surface which was home to the gas station. Inside a trailer that had no wheels and sat squat on the ground, I found the proprietor, a man who stood my height, but who carried a considerable paunch. He was in the process of reading a "girlie" magazine and chewing a considerable wad of tobacco that seemed near to the spitting moment. I half wondered if I should wait for that momentous event or whether I should intercede in the drama.

"Excuse me," I put in.

"Aaagh." He spit early into a bronze spittoon on the floor but missed. "What do you want?" The man was upset at having his routine interrupted.

"Yes, I'm looking for a young lady who might have come here a few hours ago."

"What she look like?"

I was naturally pleased that I had finally found a man who was not concerned with lining his pockets to give any information and who was not after accumulating all our respective histories before giving an answer.

"Well, she is about five foot four or so with light brown hair which she cuts rather short." I gestured with my hand to show him how her hair flipped up around the side of her head.

"Sure I remember her. She bought a car from me, a seventy four Pontiac Le Mans. A very nice car and a steal for two hundred dollars."

"You sold her *that* for two hundred dollars?" The price seemed a bit high to me for an old gas guzzler like that.

"A good deal too, you should see my cars. Run like kittens. I fix them all up myself when they come in here. Only use the best rebuilt parts. Why I bet that car has another fifty thousand miles in it."

I doubted this very much, but I was, of course, in no mood to argue the case. I wanted to know which way Anthea went. Perhaps I could follow her and catch her at night fall in the closest town along the route. But the station attendant/used car salesman could not be of any help to me. His was a rather straightforward, honest existence: he merely took his cash when it was handed to him and studied the poses of the various presidents who graced our legal tender. He had no interest in my elusive beauty who had driven away into parts unknown. There were three routes she could have taken: north to Black River Falls, west to La Crosse or southeast to New Lisbon along the route we had just taken. Without any information, I could not know. It seemed useless to me to just randomly pick one direction since I could not be sure that it would lead me to my destination.

I walked back to the newsstand and turned in my car. I decided that I would use my bus ticket to La Crosse and get out of this stupid town as soon as I could. After purchasing another magazine, I was given the directions to the bus station (which was located in the lobby of the Grand Hotel).

I started towards the hotel at a steady pace, but I soon slackened it and then stopped all together. I was standing next to a park in which there were four or five little children playing on the slide. I went over and sat on a swing. I felt the full brunt of what had happened to me earlier in the day: Anthea had left me. She had been using me. She probably knew that she couldn't continue on her bus ticket, because obviously the ticket had been traced and followed. So she planned to make an unplanned stop. This too had been anticipated. She had used me to make her escape.

I was not exactly sure how I felt. There was a feeling of being made into an object for the utilization of another. That did not sit well. Then there was the frustration that I felt after chasing her and not being successful. But most of all I felt appalled at the lying and disloyalty that she had shown to me. She had made me think that she was friendly to me. A friend does not sell another to save her own skin. Loyalty demands sacrifice for others. Anthea had clearly been out for herself. I grabbed the metal links that held my swing. I wanted to crush those metal links. I barely noticed the children leaving the playground.

I was consumed by my own situation, but without my normal power to analyze and evaluate. The fact was that I felt for the first time as if I were all alone. This made me uncomfortable. I felt a panic rise within me which made me very nervous. I felt an instant urge to go somewhere and do something familiar. I looked over at my white knuckled hands holding the metal links that suspended me. Then I leaned back and thrust out my legs. There was the slightest movement. Inertia had been broken.

Then forward an inch or so kicking my legs in the opposite direction. Then back again. I wasn't thinking. I was just doing what was available to me. It riveted my attention. There was nothing else in the world except me and my slowly developing momentum. I suddenly became aware of the sky as I leaned far back. It was clear without any clouds. Then back again to the red dirt beneath the swing that had been carved into two channels with a mound between — the long work of others who had conquered the sky through kicking the dirt. I saw and was going, but there was no thought of conquest. Caesar be damned, I was a slave to the forces of physics and I felt satisfied.

I had to fight the feeling of being alone. That's what dad had told me. He said that mommy had gotten into a car accident and that she was never coming home because she was dead. I did not really understand this. When he told it to me I merely nodded my head. I did not really believe him. But then she did not come home that night nor the next nor the next. Very soon it became apparent to me that she was never coming home.

*   *   *

I remember that we went to a funeral home in Queens. Since we lived in the lower west side of Manhattan, we didn't often travel to Queens. It was like going to a foreign country. My father had chosen that my mother's service at the mortuary be in a closed casket. That way we wouldn't have to remember her as dead and waxed up artificially. We could just remember her the way she had been to us, buried in a closed coffin so that I never again saw her face. I suppose it really hit me a couple of weeks later that never again was I to share the things that she gave me, for she was no more. This thought was unacceptable to me. I would not recognize it. I dreamed that mommy was really just on a trip and would return again to be that kind of support that she had always been.

"Why are your pants TORN?" My mother didn't accept nonsense. She stood in her classic pose with her hands holding her hips with elbows out creating judgmental triangles.

"I was playing."

"That does not answer my question." My mother would point her index finger my way.

"Well, we were over in Battery Park—you know where they have those large rocks?"

"Go on."

"We made a game of jumping off the rocks, but I couldn't do the landing so I fell on my face and ripped my pants."

"Andrew, you are a dunderkopft! You need to look after yourself. Forget all these crazy ideas. Be a safe little boy for your mama."

After her speech she would turn and go on whatever task she was at—such as making dinner.

It was good advice. She was killed by drunken driver, but then again she was passing in the other lane on a curve where she could not see oncoming traffic.

I often think I owe my love of philosophy to my mother.

The thought of something dying is very difficult for a twelve year old. Here I was, just growing up. I had reach the significant age of twelve. I had dreamed of reaching twelve. That seemed like such a grown-up age to me. I thought that it meant that I was now in a new stage of life. I was some sort of proto-adult. I distinctly remember my birthday dinner (I never had parties because I didn't have enough friends for one) and how proud I had been. My parents were proud too. It was probably one of the happiest moments of my life.

Now I felt ashamed of it all. My mommy was dead and I no longer felt like such big stuff. I started doing the *New York Times* crosswords. I was acutely pained, constantly. When my thoughts ventured to my mother I began to cry and secretly went to play with my dolls. Dolls were such wonderful things. They always did what you told them to and they never died. I played with them for a couple of months until my favorite doll broke and then I stopped. I was too ashamed of what I was doing to ask my dad to fix it for me.

I think that it was at this time that I began reading. I would play a bit with Gambol and then the two of us would cuddle up in a big chair. We called it the darning chair because mommy used to make repairs to clothing in that chair. I had never been much of a reader at all. I never liked school that much and I only read the things that had been assigned to me in class. But I got to like reading. With the smell of Gambol and the warmth of his body the pace of life seemed to change for me. Reading is easy so long as you don't try to rush it. I would rest my book on Gambol's back and actually anticipated a slowing down of everything. I could read for hours and hours. I loved almost all books: biographies, mysteries, "the classics" —anything I could get my hands on.

My dad hired a housekeeper who stayed around during the day and fixed dinner. I didn't like her (Mrs. Kicksmueller was her name). When she was around I would go to my room to read with the door shut. I would lie on my bed (lower bunk) with Gambol at the end. I shoved my feet into his side. We were sovereign within my secret domain (even more enclosed on the lower bunk and the snap-on reading lamp).

Now, to be perfectly honest, my room was rather plain. I had a bunk bed in case I ever wanted to invite any of my friends from Manhattan or Staten Island over to stay for a weekend. (I never had one friend over. Moreover there were only two kids that I would have considered inviting over, but since mother had died, I felt that this was no longer possible.) I also had a matching maple dresser and desk which had a small attached book case (though I got most of my books from the library, preferring to get rid of my books once I had finished them). I did own several volumes of Dickens and Victor Hugo which I allowed to grace my book shelves. I would not allow anything put up on the walls. I wanted them bare. On the windows were venetian blinds and on the floor was thick wool pile carpet. It wasn't the most beautiful room in the world, but I was well satisfied with it.

I slept on the top bunk, high above my room. One could feel a sense of power from that height. I lorded over the room and felt a sense of security when I went to sleep (I never used the top bunk guard rail designed to keep you from falling out of bed and breaking your neck).

I suppose it took me a long time to accept that my mother was dead. No event in my
life had been so shocking to me, not even my father's death six years later. It is not a subject about which I am fond of thinking. But somehow as I was swinging there high into the sky, so that the entire swing set began to vibrate even though the posts were securely fastened into ground by cement, I sensed that same intense sadness that I had felt as a boy. Was it the *same* feeling which had never been allowed completion, or some other analogous distress that was affecting my old feelings, much as waves in a ripple tank interfere

with each other, causing patterns of amplification and distortion. There was, of course, no way to realistically determine this from my distorted subjective standpoint. There was only helplessness.

Just then a thought struck me. What if Barbara had set out after me? She might have felt so bad about what she had done that she was following me to bring me back. Perhaps she was here right now ready to take me home. The thought was a strange one. I knew in some part of me that such a speculation was highly improbable. (One might even say impossible!) But somehow there was a thread of plausibility in it that intrigued me. What if she had felt ashamed in the arms of Giles Coughlin? Perhaps she concluded that she really wanted me all along? When I left the apartment, she might have been struck with great remorse and gone out after me.

I knew that this was only an illusion in my mind, but the-thought was comforting. I could make it seem almost plausible by working my imagination in a particular way. At any moment I might see her walking down the street. It would be Barbara, all five foot four inches of her with her black straight hair. The thought suddenly became very uncomfortable when I imagined her actually walking down the street. I didn't want to see Barbara. It wasn't because she was a rather plain woman whose face could become very nasty when she yelled at me, but because I finally felt that I could put something behind me. I felt that Barbara was history. As soon as I reached La Crosse, I would be calling a friend of mine at the law school to file papers for divorce. I did not want anything more to do with her and yet the thought of her coming after me had a certain appeal to it.

I nursed that thought along as I came back to earth from my swing. It was time to go to the bus station. I wanted to get to La Crosse. So, I departed my vacant park. Playtime was over. It was time to execute my escape plan. I had half-forgotten the directions, but the locals on the sidewalks were friendlier than the mercantile class. When I got to the hotel it was four thirty in the afternoon. I saw a bus pulling away. That couldn't be my bus, I thought. But when I got to the reception desk at the hotel, which also doubled as a ticket counter for the bus, I noticed that the bus schedule was posted and the last bus scheduled to leave for La Crosse and Rochester was the four fifteen.

"Was that the four-fifteen that just left?" I asked a short skinny boy of about seventeen who was working the desk. I felt kindly toward the boy because he wore thick wire rimmed glasses.

"The bus that just left was the?" The boy was a bit flustered by me, the out-of-towner. "Yes sir, the four-thirty," he said, hastily looking at a schedule that was under a large piece of plate glass which served as the counter top at the reception area. "I mean the four fifteen which generally leaves at four-thirty." He looked a little confused.

"I mean it gets in a little late. It comes all the way from Milwaukee!"

He spoke the name 'Milwaukee' as if he were talking about the largest, most important venue in the country; 'Milwaukee' that great metropolitan center of culture and cosmopolitan elegance. "It's the last one that leaves today, except for the five-thirty for Millston and Black River Falls. That one only is ten minutes late; it originates in Madison." I hadn't asked for all this information from the floppy haired young man, but the information was not unwanted. I was stuck here in town unless I wanted to go to Millston, Black River Falls or Minneapolis (the destination of that bus which the boy had failed to mention. After all, who would want to go to Minneapolis when they could go to Millston?). Or I could rent a car from that old fool in the newsstand. No, I had enough magazines for the day. My only other alternative was to get a room and catch the morning bus.

"Would you like a ticket for the five-thirty, sir?"

"No, I was just curious about the schedule. I'll tell you what I would like, though, is a room for the night. Do you have one free?" I asked this question with a straight face even though I could see the hanging collection of keys for the hotel. Only four of the twenty keys were gone. This was certainly not the Waldorf Astoria.

The boy turned around and hesitated for a moment. He wasn't, I hoped, trying to give the impression that the hotel was really quite full. He picked up a key and slapped it down on the counter.

"Here is one of our best rooms," he said, "Would you sign the register please?"

I signed and put my address. The clerk did a double take when he saw my name on the register. I decided that they were not used to such unusual names as Viam here in Tomah, so I picked up my key and started away when the stammering room clerk called me back.

"Mr. Viam."

"Yes?" I said, only turning my head. I felt like lying down.

"Oh, I'm afraid I have given you the wrong key. I didn't know. Honestly, she didn't say you would be coming, so naturally I assumed she'd be alone."

My curiosity was piqued. I turned and walked back to the clerk.

"Here," he said, handing me another key. "This is our second key to room twelve, the best room in the house. I suspect Mrs. Viam, your wife, will be waiting for you."

Chapter Five

YOU MIGHT SAY THAT was startled by this news. *Dumbstruck* would also be a good term to describe my state, for I could not talk when the young man handed me the key to Room Twelve. My wildest nightmares had come true. What could I do? I could not leave. There were no other busses. I could have rented a car, but that option did not present itself at that moment. As I had feared.

Barbara had found me out. Somehow, she had tracked me to Tomah, Wisconsin. What was I to do? She was always one step ahead of me when it came to the practical ways of life. There was no turning back. I needed a place to stay. They wouldn't put up a man in a separate room from his wife. I started up the stairs in the Grand Hotel, listening to the soles of my shoes sing as they mounted and exited carpet that had forty years of grime within. This paean to filth and decay drove me inevitably forward even as I unlocked the door and saw coming out of the bathroom dressed in my brown slacks and gold shirt none other than Anthea Brevist.

"Mrs. Viam, I presume?" I said in an ironic tone. She was as surprised to see me, it appeared, as I was to see her, and yet she tried immediately to cover this up.

"Oh, Andrew, how nice of you to drop by." She walked over to the chair and got out a hair brush and went through her hair with short rapid strokes. "How did you *ever* find me?'

"Never mind that just now. I have a few questions for *you*," I said closing the door and walking over to the bed where I sat down. There was so much I wanted to say that I did not know where to begin. I just sat there trying to think of a rational ordering of my concerns so that I could get in mind a series of questions which would lead me in the direction I wanted to go. There was so much I wanted to ask. I had so many mixed emotions seeing Anthea there in front of me that I did not know what I wanted to say, however, she (perhaps feeling a bit guilty?) began the conversation. "I was so sad that Joey, Mike and the gang got hold of you back in Milwaukee." She brushed back her short blonde hair with her right hand.

"You set me up.

"You don't understand. They were going to take me back to *him*."

"But I could have been killed."

"Oh, they wouldn't have killed you. They could not hurt someone unless it were an accident. They're not the brightest you know. People call them the *Keystone Cops.* "

As she spoke she fiddled with buttoning an unbuttoned-button on her, I mean *my*, shirt—that is, the shirt she was wearing which was really my shirt. The sun was coming in the window, bathing the chair in which she was seated and the floor around her in a trapezoid of soft summer afternoon light. This almost served to isolate her as if she were in a spotlight or framed in a picture. I had to admit to myself that even in men's clothing she did look rather striking. She was one of the most beautiful women I had ever been so close to.

"They didn't look too friendly," I said.

"They're not *friendly,* but they're not killers either. Killing is not Clay's style."

"Clay?"

"Oh, didn't I tell you? Clay is the man who I'm running away from."

So our situations were more similar than I had imagined. We were both fleeing obligations. I was becoming more confused by all this as her explanation progressed.

"Husband?"

"No."

"Lover?"

"You see, Clay is a business man. He made his money making plastic washers in a business he built himself." Anthea liked to express her words with her left hand in the air and her right hand in her hair.

"And those apes back in Milwaukee were plastic washer workers?" I saw that this was going to be an involved explanation, so I lay back in the bed and propped my back up with pillows. I hadn't realized how tired I was until I did this. It was relaxing to watch her sitting in the chair gesticulating and trying to be as *matter of fact* as she could about the whole episode.

"No they are his 'boys'."

"So he is a small time punk?"

"Don't let him hear you call him that. He's been working a little messenger service out of the north side near to where the Ravenswood 'el' tracks pass over Diversey." I nodded even though I had no exact knowledge about the location. I had never used the 'el' much.

"Well, I don't know how much you know about messenger services," she said as she rolled her hair around her right index finger.

"They are supposed to take bets from people and then send them over to the race track via messengers. The reality is that they are bookies. Am I correct?"

She caught her right index finger into a snag in her hair. "Well, "she began again after extracting her finger, "In a business like that— he calls it a 'club' you know, I think to put him under the jurisdiction of a low cost, city official—"

"One who could be bribed easily," I put in. Such conclusions were not hard to come by to one who has lived in Chicago any length of time.

"Exactly, well in his business he needs to have a little protection. You know, someone who will keep things in order. It is a little risky to be in the messenger business." She folded her hands in her lap.

"Especially when you are really in the bookie business."

"Especially!" Her tone of voice was between registers. I don't think she liked the matter of fact way I could surmise Clay's real operations. I think that she supposed that just because I was a man unexperienced with women that I was naïve to the ways of the world, as well. I wished I could have told her that as long ago as Aristotle, man's knowledge has been known to be compartmentalized. One can know things in one area and not another (contrary to what Plato thought). But I am sure that this reference would have been meaningless to her so I did not bring it up.

She paused and then continued. "So Mike and company are Clay's little force of body guards, establishment bouncers—you know." She lifted her shoulders and raised her palms up to heaven.

"Goons."

"They are his staff."

"So you've been the woman of a punk." The truth of the matter demanded expression. She avoided my gaze. This was not the sort of treatment she had been used to. She desired the "treat me as a bubble-headed idiot" routine, which included, "Let's indulge in euphemisms to cover up what we're really doing." It is one thing to sacrifice someone and leave him to his fate as she had done to me and admit openly that that is what you did and quite another (and in my mind a more mendacious route) to pretend that what you did was not egoistic and completely self-serving. This was what she was doing. She was looking out for no one except herself.

Anthea got up to close the blind. As she walked, I observed how my clothes clung to the parts of her body which were different from my own. There was something stimulating to see a beautiful woman dressed in your clothes. She sat down again, but did not seem to be comfortable. Finally she looked up and said, "Look, I'm really sorry about Milwaukee. I wanted my clothes and that was the only way—"

"If you had wanted your clothes, you would have gotten them when you went back for that brown bag."

I wasn't going to let her off so easily. Her mouth changed shapes when I called her on her lies. I loved to look at her face. There was something about her—not identifiable with any particular feature or characteristic—which drew me to her.

"I wasn't thinking that fast. I knew I needed some money and all my sundry items, but I was not sure how I could escape, or if I could escape." She paused. "When I was in trouble, I went straight to you."

I wanted to take her in my arms and forget about all this crap, but for some reason I carried on this dialogue. "You came to me for help, eh?" I tried to put a sarcastic, incredulous tone to my voice.

"Yes. You were so kind the night before, and besides, who else could I go to?" She got up and walked to the window again. Then she said, "I put my stuff in your briefcase when you did not come back right away and put on your clothes. I thought that I would be less conspicuous than I would be in a running outfit." She had her back to me. My pants clung to her shapely derriere. "I went to the car rental place and got a car for the westernmost section of Wisconsin."

"You could have gone to La Crosse. That's further west. I'm sure they have an office there." I do not know why I said that. But as I delivered this ridiculous repartee I got up from the bed and walked over to her. "I looked on the map. It was the first city I saw," she said. I believe that was the truth. For who in their right mind would choose to go to Tomah?

"How do you know you're not being followed?"

"I don't. That's why I checked into the hotel under *our* name. You see, I found your address in your briefcase."

"I see," I said moving closer to her. She turned her head to me. There was a look of concern on her face. I put my hand on her cheek to stroke away the tension. "You know, when I checked into this hotel they told me my wife had already checked in. So they gave me the key to this room — my room — our room. I guess it's our room for tonight." She smiled.

Then I kissed her. I pulled her little body close to me so that I could feel every undulation

beneath the clothes which she was wearing.

She tilted her head and said quietly, "I don't mind. It's our room tonight." These words intensified our embrace. I was concentrating on the tips of my fingers which were stroking her entire body.

Then I took off her shirt and exposed what I had been lightly touching moments before through the medium of a wrinkled cotton shirt. The blind was closed, but still some light suffused and bathed her body in a warm glow. I watched as she stepped back and slid her other garments to the floor. The soft light accented the curves of her body caught in relief against the gentle shadows on her smooth skin. I was mesmerized. It was as if none of this were happening and then suddenly it did seem real. She had taken control and relieved me of my garments. And I became aware in a sliding moment of time about what was happening and what I was doing. She led me to the bed and we lay down in an embrace.

*   *   *

"Let's have some dinner, maybe you'll feel better after dinner," she said sincerely.

"I don't know what happened," I said, but this was a lie. I knew. It was the reality of the situation. When that reality hit me I suddenly realized that I was not sure if I really wanted to be doing this. Now this is not exactly true either. I wanted to be with Anthea and I wanted to have sex with her, but at the same time there was a lingering anxiety: Barbara. I had thought of Barbara. "What an ass," I bet you're saying. "Here you've got a beautiful woman in your arms and you've got her where you want her and you go and think of your wife! What a loser!" And you'd be right. But it wasn't that way at all. I wanted Anthea right enough, but I felt suddenly that a situation was occurring in which I didn't exactly know what I was doing. You see, I like to make my choices and not be led into them. But that's a lot of rationalization. The truth of the matter is that when it became real and the spell of fantasy had been broken, I sensed Barbara. Now I don't know if I was feeling sorry for myself or what, but nothing progressed properly after that.

"Don't feel bad. It happens. We've got all night, you know."

I smiled. I'm sure if anyone would know about it she would. But that didn't concern me just then. I felt somewhat ashamed. Would it have been better to have stayed at a distance from her? Should I have slept on the floor and kept my distance from this siren? The entire idea was ridiculous. As we got dressed, I decided to talk to Anthea at dinner and find out something about her. Our first conversation had been centered around me, but in very general terms. I had not wished to divulge any specifics. Now I wanted to do things differently.

* * *

The place we went to was a chicken and ribs place. There are no fancy restaurants in town, but this place was supposed to have edible food. Anthea wore her running outfit and I wore the clothes she had had on during the day. Indeed, we were a sorry pair.

"You'll have to get some new clothes tomorrow," I said as we sat over some sorry looking salads.

"You too," she put in. "Your clothes can't last both of us — they're hardly lasting you."

Something about Anthea was fascinating to me. I thought she was a beautiful woman, though objectively speaking she was not as ravishing as she appeared to me. She told me about her boyfriend. His name was Clay Macdonald and he was about twelve years older than I was. He was married and had three kids. He set her up in an apartment in "New Town" toward the lake in a very fashionable district. They had met when she had been a checker at a supermarket. "I had gone from an airline stewardess to a waitress, to a ticket taker at professional wrestling matches to that job as a checker at the A&P."

She was very matter-of-fact, "I was tired of the long hours at such low pay." She had, according to her account, kept her job at the A&P for a while. She didn't want to become overly dependent upon Clay. But finally, she gave it up so that she could have some time to relax.

"My family was not poor. Daddy made a bundle of money, but he never liked to spend it. He lived as if we were poor except for our house in Evanston which was on the north side of town along the lake. When I was through with high school I rebelled and went to junior college to be away from home. I got tired of reading boring books on stuffy subjects and so I went to flight attendants' school. It was just as stupid, but there was a job at the end of it.

"I flew for about two and a half years until I developed a phobia about being among so many people in a plane cabin. So I had to quit."

I nodded my head. The thought of working around a full plane of people over and over again would put me in the nut house. Anthea talked so easily. She seemed to really be at ease with me. For a woman who had been so timid, or rather cagy about what she was going to tell, she had suddenly opened up in an extraordinary way. After she quit her supermarket job, she was Clay's woman for four or five months when she got tired of that, too. She appeared to me to be a woman who got tired of things rather quickly. I wondered how long it would take before she was tired of me.

"Anyway, I left him. I wrote a note and withdrew the money I had saved from my jobs and left. I didn't take any of *his* money; only a few clothes he had given me."

Anthea stimulated my own private self-reflection: just a week before I could not have imagined that I would be talking to such a woman as this, much less sleeping with her. I wanted to tell her about myself. I wanted to tell her about my so-called friend Giles Coughlin, Langlin Professor of Poetry at Chicago University. This was Mr. Giles Coughlin, who I never suspected of anything, until I found him in bed with my wife.

Now don't get me wrong. It was not as if I was heartbroken. I had grown apart from Barbara over the years. She was always such a boss. I rarely got my own space except for things she didn't care about, like my research. Our feeling for each other had transmuted into a kind of acceptance. It was almost as one accepts his job, a necessary evil. We performed our rituals and we had our various divisions of labor. We ate together, slept in the same bed, and had sex about once a month or two. It was a satisfactory if not a pleasant way of life. I could have been coming home to *anybody* really; it didn't matter. We rarely talked about anything except what we had to do and what we didn't like about the people we knew. Barbara did some copy editing for the University Press, which she did at home. We were each very busy and tried to keep it that way. If I wasn't exactly enamored with her it should still be perfectly clear that I would never leave her. No, I would stick by her. I thought of separating many times. I wondered whether I would be happier without her. I thought that

I would, but such a conclusion would not rule my decision because happiness is not everything in life. There was also devotion, loyalty, and perseverance. Barbara would fall apart (at least that's what I thought) without me. And I could not build my happiness over the body of another's pain. So we remained married.

Then when I found her with Giles in our bedroom two days ago, after I had turned in spring quarter's grades and was supposed to be working in the library, things were suddenly different. *She* was the offending party, not *I*. She had broken faith, not I. As far as responsibility demanded, I had gone the limit. She had given herself to someone else, and I was free to pursue my own directions. That's the way I saw it from my view looking in from the doorway to our bedroom with the two of them naked in the bed, rhythmically moving about. They had had the window unit air conditioner on so they hadn't heard me enter the apartment or walk down the hall. I opened the door and there they were.

A thousand thoughts suddenly rushed through my mind with the instant conclusion: she has broken faith, you may now leave if you like. I tilted my head and said, "Afternoon, Giles, Barbara."

They didn't respond. I walked to my closet and emptied the contents of my briefcase onto the floor and then stuffed an extra piece of everything into my case—including a lightweight jacket. Then I picked up my bank book (we had separate accounts) and began my exit route, heading for the Midway and the elevated train station on Cottage Grove.

Barbara and Giles never said a word. They paused, obviously. I'm sure that they expected me to go into some kind of rage at the sight. But I was completely calm in my behavior. Of course, a number of emotions were violently struggling inside of me, but the mode of my action was clear to me for the first time in my life and I felt good about what I was doing. For so long I had been led and maneuvered. I was not my own agent. Responsibility and shame had made me a prisoner. Now I was acting on my own. This may seem like a trivial accomplishment to many, but now responsibility and shame permitted me to do as I wanted. It was time to leave endless battles of

Troy and to embark on my Odyssey to—well, there the metaphor becomes a bit blurry since I had no one to go home to. All that I had was a clear exit strategy.

But I didn't tell all this to Anthea. I merely said, "I'm married, you know. I've left my wife."

She didn't seem surprised when I said that I was married, but when I said that I had left my wife her eyes displayed confusion. "Are you divorced?"

I didn't answer her but said, "Excuse me, that reminds me of something." I got up and called my friend Don at the law school. The public phone was in a small alcove next to the door. I possessed one of those new phone cards which gave me the opportunity of calling long distance on a push-button phone and have the cost listed on my home phone bill (now Barbara's home phone bill). All I had to do was to press "1" and hit in my number. It worked. Don picked up on the third ring.

"Hello, Don?"

"Is that you, Andrew?"

"That's right."

"For Christ's sake, Andrew, where are you?"

"In Wisconsin."

"Holy shit, we've been worried about you. Barbara called us and said you walked out Thursday and didn't know where you went. She's awfully worried. You should have called you know."

"I don't want to talk to Barbara. I want you to draw up divorce papers for me and Barbara."

"Divorce!" Don was bewildered.

"Yes, you heard me. I don't think she'll contest it."

"Don't you think you're going off the deep end?" Now there was Don the marriage counsellor.

"Nope. She's the one in the diving pool."

"Well, I've just talked to Barbara and I don't think she wants a divorce. Why don't you come home, and we'll all talk things out. You were always such a reasonable man. This isn't like you."

"Of course it isn't. And I'm glad of that. You tell her that I'll have my divorce. I've got grounds."

"What grounds?'

"Adultery."

"Oh." Don's voice changed. He was no longer the chipper marriage counsellor. Even across the phone wires I could sense his shock and dismay that I had revealed so confidential a matter to him. "Look Andrew," he began again with a new tone of agitation, "you should come back and work this thing out. Illinois is a no-fault divorce state you know."

"I don't care about settlements. She earns more than I do. Let her have the condominium and the car. That should satisfy her. We have our own bank accounts anyway." Don couldn't fault my logic. It would be one of the easiest cases in the world. No hassle or fussing.

"Look, Andrew, a thing like this takes time. Why don't you come back home so that we can get this settled."

"It's Friday night. I'll call you in a week or two. That should give you enough time." I hung up. That was one piece of business that I wanted out of the way. Then I returned to my Anthea. This little vegetarian was chewing away on a big order of barbecued ribs.

"That took a while," she said.

It was wonderful to watch her eat. She attacked her food with such delight. "I had to put in a phone call to my lawyer for my divorce."

"That was sudden."

"Not really. It's been in the works for thirteen years."

She didn't understand, naturally, but then to a certain extent, neither did I. We sat there eating

and making small talk. I was becoming overwhelmed with desire for her. We began touching legs and rubbing ankles under the table. I felt like I was a teenager (except I wasn't like that as a teenager). Some of the people at other tables turned and stared at us.

"The local population doesn't like this," I said.

"The local population is jealous," she returned.

When we got back to our room things worked out perfectly this time. I had one of the most physically satisfying nights in my life. I had energy stored up from years of marriage which had been bottled up without any but the most sporadic and perfunctory expression. We indulged in embrace after embrace, even waking ourselves in our sleep to revel in the sheer joy of two bodies in carnal knowledge. I didn't get a lot of sleep, but when I opened my eyes the next morning my drowsiness and aching body were not unpleasant, but tangible reminders of my night with Anthea.

CHAPTER SIX

WHEN I AWOKE, Anthea was already up and exercising.

"What are you doing?" I said, looking over at the clock. "It's only seven in the morning."

"I've got to keep my body beautiful for you," she said as she was engaged in rapid sit-ups. Her body was lean and muscular. It was wonderful just to view her exercising wearing only her bikini panties. I watched her as she went through several sets of various exercises which aim to tone up various parts of one. I almost felt like joining her in her labor. It is not as if I hate exercise, it is just that I have always hated competitive athletics. Walking is fine. I used to do it every day to keep fit, but I never went in for anything more systematic. My limit was always a brisk half-mile walk to work.

When she had finished and showered, I shaved and brushed my teeth.

I used soap for lather and for dentifrice—ah it was terrible for a dentifrice. Then we sat down on the bed and talked about what we were to do.

"Do you want to stay in Tomah a few more days? This is a rather nice room." I was happy where I was.

"I'm afraid that I might be traced by the car I just bought," she said.

"You really think that they are still interested?"

She made a face, "Some people would go to great lengths to get what you had last night."

"How about what *you* had," I replied. *This* Anthea reminded me of Barbara in two ways: she tended to be bossy and she seemed a little self-serving. If I was to be with her for a while, I wanted to make a few things clear. It was no good stepping from one problem into another. A clear resolve formed in my mind that I was going to be a little more assertive in my own behalf than I had previously been.

"Oh, you were great, but don't you agree that in love making that it is the woman who is the key element? It is she who brings the man pleasure." Anthea put her hands to the bed and stuck her head out like a goat. She wasn't trying to be ridiculous in her posture or in her argument, but she clearly was. Striking this combative pose, she thought she would intimidate me. All I could think about when I saw her in such a pose was that her breasts were hanging straight down and that she looked like a goat. The comic effect was a hindrance to my ability to speak (not, of course, the effect it was supposed to produce).

"But it is the *woman* who gets more pleasure," I returned.

"The woman?" This response startled her. It was obvious that she lived with a particular conception of a woman as one who brings all happiness and pleasure to male-kind (it is from thence that they derive their great Power over men). But I was intent to thwart her claim.

"Yes, have you ever heard of Tiresias?"

"No," was her reply. She seemed a bit peeved.

"He was a famous Theban in Greek mythology." At this she sat up. She sensed that I was about to make some claim based upon some area of which she was ignorant. To counter on my move, she walked over to the chair and began pulling on her clothes, as if to show me that she was only mildly interested in what I was going to say.

"You see, Zeus and Hera were having an argument over who had more pleasure in love making: the man or the woman."

When she heard the name 'Zeus' she lit up. "Wasn't Zeus the Greek god?"

"That's right. He was the number-one god and Hera was his wife."

"If they were gods, why did they have an argument?"

"I don't know—" I stammered. You see I'd forgotten about the *Euthyphro.*

"I mean, aren't gods supposed to have all-knowledge and stuff like that?"

"Yes."

"Well then they would have no need to argue with this Tirisis."

"Tiresias," I corrected.

"Whoever," she said. "A god has no need to argue because He knows everything." She had now finished dressing and was tossing all available clothes into my case minus a few things which she threw over to me to wear.

"That's certainly true, but—"

"So the whole story is a phony since it makes such fictitious assumptions."

I couldn't argue with her there. There was really nothing to say to that. I could have told her that the dispute was between Zeus and Hera and not between the two of them and Tiresias and how the dispute was finished. I could have gone through the entire story and point out how it illustrated the point that I was trying to make, but that would have been to no avail. She was ready to go and I followed her out the door.

I bought a map and asked her where she wanted to go. Anthea was unsure, but she declared a desire to go camping. We were in the car now. She was driving and we were on Highway 12 going toward Eau Claire.

"If you want to camp, that's all right. But I am not much of a camper."

Anthea turned her head slightly and tilted her eyebrow. She was sizing up my remark. She seemed to rather like the idea that I didn't know much about camping. (How could I when I had never been camping in my life?) I wanted to keep this last fact secret from her if it was at all possible without lying.

"'What is it that you don't like about camping?" She was testing me. I could tell. She wanted to see just how much I knew about camping. I could see that I was doomed. This woman just loved to lord over me. It seemed incredible to me that she could have been the mistress of a punk like Clay Macdonald, who I imagine had quite an ego problem and wouldn't have taken her air of superiority as I did. Perhaps she was compensating for all the bad breaks she thought she had gotten with him (or with many others).

"It's rather roughing it, isn't it?"

"You talk funny. Like a university professor." She laughed at the thought. I had not told her what I did. I thought she could have inferred it from my Hyde Park address. Most of the people who live on the nine hundred block on 55th-59th Streets either worked at the hospital or at the university. But then she may not have known Hyde Park that well.

"What's so funny?" I asked, knowing perfectly well what she would say.

"I was just thinking of you as a university professor. I have you pictured in a tweed coat with patches on the elbows. You would be so stuffy, just like you are with me, but this time it's in front of hundreds of young faces."

"I don't have a tweed sports coat. But suppose I am—ah, rather stuffy."

She turned her face at me in surprise. I wanted to tell her to look at the road, but I didn't. Instead, I said, "Your dream has come true. I am a university professor."

She turned and looked straight at me, "You aren't."

"Yes. Couldn't you tell by my address?"

"I thought you were a salesman or marketing man or something on that line." She smiled and shook her head, "You mean I just screwed a university professor?"

"That's right."

This thought seemed to intrigue her. It was as if she had approached a figure who was inaccessible to her, one which she had never expected to interact with in a tête-à-tête, much less a carnal adventure.

"Well professor, or Doctor, or —what should I call you?"

"Andrew."

"But that hardly seems appropriate."

"Cut it out." But she wasn't mocking me. She was genuinely in awe of my position. It was totally ridiculous.

"But you haven't told me why you wanted to go camping," I said, trying to change the subject. But I could tell that she was now different.

She was putting a certain distance between us. I didn't see why this should be. After all, nothing had really changed. But she continued in this way until she reached Eau Claire. Eau Claire is a fairly large small town. We decided (or rather, Anthea decided) that we would split up and buy some provisions separately which would make it harder to trace us just in case they were still on our trail and had tracked us this far. I claimed that she was being ridiculous and overly cautious, and she declared that I didn't value her enough to think that someone who was entranced with her would give up so easily.

Then it hit me. After she left to do her shopping I realized that she was probably going away for good. The stupid argument that she had just given me was only a ruse so that she could get away on her own. Her changed manner and her past behavior pointed to it: she had left me and I was on my own.

Everything that had happened in the past two days was over. The chase, serendipity at finding Anthea—everything seemed at that moment to be so ephemeral. Why was I doing this? I walked over to a tavern. It was only ten o'clock in the morning but I felt like a couple of belts. I ordered a whiskey. The establishment was dark, cramped, and smelly. The only outside light came through a window at the top of the door. There was no one else in the place. The whiskey tasted awful. I didn't want to be in there. All that would happen if I began drinking would be that I would become terribly depressed. I already had a good dose of that. It may seem hyperbolic, but I felt as if I had my whole life in front of me in a heap. It was an unorganized pile of junk. I needed some time to sort things out. Anthea had been right. Camping sounded like it would be just the thing. But I didn't know anything about camping. I knew that if I walked into a sporting goods store and asked them for camping gear I would get taken for everything I had. The whole thing seemed to be a mess. I decided that I needed some clothes and some food and something to put them in. At least I would have to buy a ruck sack. Probably I'd need something in which to cook my food, utensils, and a sleeping bag. That sounded like the minimum needed.

I left the bar and walked around looking for a sporting goods store. I did not find anything. Then I asked someone and they directed me to a place several blocks away. I had completely forgotten about Anthea. I knew that she was gone. I walked as directed and found the sporting goods store. Outside the store I saw something that made me feel excited. It was our car! She hadn't left.

Then I remembered that I had several things that I was supposed to get and hadn't. I had wasted quite a bit of time—perhaps an hour or more. I should have been done. But then, so should she have been done. I became suspicious. What if she had been found?No, that would have been impossible. What if she had been trying to lose me and was in the process of picking up someone else right now? That was possible. I decided to wait inside the car.

The door was locked. Anthea had lived too long in the city. City folk often get overly suspicious or cynical. I felt like an ass. If she wanted to go off with someone else, who was I to stop her? I had no right over her. Did I even want to stop her? I decided to walk away.

It was then that she exited the store. She saw me right away.

"Andrew, over here."

I was being called.

"Give me a hand with this equipment."

Did I want to return? I certainly did, but something held me back. I turned and just looked at her. Did I want to waste my time on someone who would only leave me in a pinch? Was this the kind of person I wanted to associate with? Then I squinted. The sun was glaring and my eyes were in pain. She was standing there with her arms full of things—which she had purchased for *us*. Look, I'm not marrying her. What do I care if she shifts for herself? We all have to do that in the end. It's no good when you only depend on another to do your shifting for you.

I walked back to the car. "I'll get the door if you let me buy you some more clothes."

She smiled. She was so beautiful when she smiled. I didn't know why it was, but I was hypnotized by that face and her large, trusting eyes. "That's a sucker, play" I thought, but even believing this I went back to her and loaded the car.

"Well, we've got almost two hundred dollars' worth of stuff in there," she said as she drove us to the town's department store. Her hair was pulled back over her ear today. She was sportswoman Anthea. The special look that it had had Thursday was gone today. We needed a few other things as well. Inside the store, I bought a cheap suitcase and some more clothes for myself. Anthea bought herself a pair of jeans and a sweatshirt which said *Lady of the Lake* across the chest. She also (at my prodding) bought a dress which we would store in the car (and a few other items essential for any trip). After dutifully procuring her food list, we set out along Route 53 toward Chippewa Falls. It was a nice drive. The day was beautiful and I slid down into the seat and lain back my head. Anthea was a steady driver; she didn't speed up or slow down. The two lane highway wasn't very busy so we didn't have to pass very many people. Anyway, we weren't in a hurry. It was now time to sit back and enjoy the sun, scenery, and Anthea sitting next to me happily driving the car.

We stopped in Chippewa Falls for a late lunch or early dinner. There is a local brewery there called Leinenkugel. Anthea tells me that it is typical for many of these Wisconsin towns to have small local breweries. The beer may be a bit uneven, but there is a special feeling one has visiting a small plant which has its own distinctive taste so different from the standardized taste of keg (CO, injected beers as are most of our major beers in this country). It reminded me of the art of the inn keeper explained to me in Cambridge by Ronnie. The beer there is actually aged in the publican's cellars. He uses his expertise to determine the conditions under which it should be kept and when it should be tapped. It is aged and served at cool (not cold) temperatures and in casks of special woods. Finally it is loaded into gravity controlled taps after which it must be served within a certain time or it goes bad.

I remember talking to many a proud publican about his system and the taste he strives after (for one shipment of bitter can certainly vary between establishments depending on the treatment given it). Some seek an even flavor while others try for that sharpness which renders its name.

At any rate I enjoyed touring the brewery and the late afternoon meal. The food was reasonably priced and the beer was free. Anthea was particularly talkative.

I was in very high spirits as we got back into the car and continued heading north. We passed through such thriving metropolises as Bloomier, Barron, and Spooner before changing to route 53 on our way to the campgrounds. The length of the drive was making me very tired and rather out of humor. I suddenly became very angry at Anthea for forcing me to go camping with her. I felt that she was just as demanding as a wife.

Then I thought about Barbara. I don't know what it was that soured me about Barbara. I'm not sure that we had that much to begin with outside of sex. I had only been on a few dates before and could not have been said to have had any real experience with the opposite sex. I had had no real loves before I met Barbara at New York University. I suppose it was at NYU that I first came out, so to speak. This was hard for me because I had always been so withdrawn. In high school I had been slow to physically develop. When I was a junior in high school, I was still only five foot five inches tall. I was very skinny and therefore pushed around a lot by the other boys in school. I hated athletics and never went to any of the sports events which comprised most of the school's social life. The only game I played was chess with my father.

Since my mother had died, I was very close to my father, though this is misleading because my father was a very private man. He would like to be alone for hours at a time and not talk or communicate in any way. Sometimes he would shut himself up in his study and stay in there for the entire day. I was left to my own devices. One thing I did was to collect insects and plant leaves. My father had bought me a dissecting scope and I had numerous books on taxonomy. I would go out to the city's parks in Manhattan and Brooklyn and search out rare specimens (rare being anything either that I didn't have or didn't have very many of). This part of the process that could take the longest. You see, lots of specimens look alike. Because of evolution there had to be diversity in every species so that selection could occur according to environmental pressures. Once you had a good number of specimens, it became more difficult to find added entries. One could go a long time (weeks) and not find anything new. I suppose it's kind of like fishing (though I had never been fishing in my life—the thought of a poor fish "drowning in the air" makes me ill).

When finally I had collected my requisite number, I would take them into. my room and examine at them under the microscope alongside my taxonomy manual. It was intriguing to classify a specimen. This is because no single individual is identical to the drawing in the book. This called for some calculated guessing. One part of the process was to examine the various parts of the organism separately. Sometimes this was a key to assigning it to a taxon.

I loved reading about various types of plants and insects and had a number of books on the subject which, along with science fiction, were my mainstays during those years. I never left New York City in my journeys. The MTA took me where I needed to go. I never left the city at all—even when classmates who had recreational housing in Connecticut or New Jersey suggested group outings. I knew my father would not have approved.

That's the way high school went. Then my father died just after graduation. I was already accepted to NYU. My father's estate plan was well conceived. The house was sold, affairs settled, and then there was a trust fund for me: a monthly income. Even my schooling had been settled from the life insurance. I would become master of the trust fund when I graduated from college or when I became 21.

The two events turned out to almost coincide.

During my first year in college I could not accept this freedom that had been thrust upon me. My preventative action was to take very heavy loads of courses so that I would not have time to do anything except work. After the first year (I also took classes in the summer) I had almost finished sophomore requirements.

It was then that I met Barbara. I wasn't sure whether I wanted to try and finish college in 2.5 years or whether I should do a second major. I didn't know what to do. I didn't like social events. I has stopped playing chess. I guess my only entertainment was going to obscure artist-run art galleries in the village when they had a new show. This was not to socialize but to come into contact with authenticity.

It was into this vacuum that Barbara first appeared. She was in a mathematics class with me. We had assigned seats and she had a seat just in front of mine. Barbara had a bad habit of forgetting her pen to take notes.

"Andrew, can I borrow a pen?" was her frequent request. I usually had two pens on me, but I always *made sure* I did when I went to math class. I used to buy nice pens—not the cheap 19 cent kind, but regular first quality writing implements. For my own notes I preferred a fountain pen, but for lending I always handed a Cross ballpoint. (Fountain pens become "grooved" to their owners so it would be bad for the pen to be lent to several people.)

Soon Barbara was asking me to help her with a problem or two after class. We went to a snack shop and sat down. "Would you like something to drink while we look at those problems?" I asked. She said she didn't mind so I bought a couple of milkshakes. (I don't know why I bought milkshakes since I didn't even like them. Perhaps it was because they were the most expensive things from the fountain and I did not want to appear cheap. "Cheapness" is the worst thing a student could be (or appear to be) when I was going to NYU. I brought the shakes over to the table and handed Barbara hers and then sat down. That was the problem. My chair stuck and pushed into the table, spilling the milkshake all over Barbara's problems and her skirt. I felt terrible. "I'm sorry. What an idiotic thing to do!" I was furious with myself. I suppose that everyone sitting in the snack bar could hear me and laughed with amusement. They were probably thinking, "What a jerk. Look at him. He just gets out with a girl and see how he handles it? That kid ought to be locked up securely." I just knew that this would be the end to everything. But Barbara simply smiled (after she had gotten over the initial shock). I handed her hundreds of napkins—I took apart one of the napkin dispensers and presented her the contents and she thoughtfully used twenty or so declining the rest. "Did I ruin all your homework?

"Well, it is written in pencil and I'm afraid the water has gotten to it."

"I feel so bad. I'm just so clumsy."

"Oh, it was not your fault," she began as she pulled at her black hair which was arranged in curls at that time. "The chair stuck. It could have happened to anyone."

There was some truth to that. But it was also true that it could have been avoided if I had reacted differently when the chair stuck. I could have stopped and alerted her to the problem and then collaborated on a solution. For example, I could have told her to stand up or to move to another table—a whole number of options.

But instead I made a fool of myself.

"The only sad part of it," she added, "is that it takes me so long to do this math. I just don't have the head for it."

"Oh, that's no problem. I'll come and help you. We can do it in the library tonight."

That was that. As I think back on it I wonder whether she tricked me into that somehow. She had asked me to help her with a problem. When I had asked her where she wanted to go, she had said the snack shop because it was so close to class. (It was really farther away than the library was from our math classroom. I even wonder, thinking back on it, whether there was some way that *she* made the chair stick. I don't know how she might have managed that as the time interval between my getting up and returning was only a few minutes. But if there was a way to have engineered the deed, Barbara would have found it.)Soon, working in the library became a regular thing. And from there it was casual appointments outside of class and studying together. Milkshakes were the gateway drug toward spending more and more time together.

One thing led to another so that before the year was out, we were mildly affectionate and I had kissed her. Now I should make it clear that at this time I was not really in the mood for a *long term* relationship. I was going into my junior year and I didn't want any commitments which might alter my career goals (which were at that time to live off the interest from the money my father had left me). If I could subside off $7,000 a year (and I didn't see why I couldn't), then I could avoid getting a job for my entire life.

As a junior in college, the prospect of having to go out and get a job seemed like the most horrible fate that could befall a man. Every job that I could think of was full of so much routine and boring tasks. There was so much repetition and submission to superiors and I had had enough of that at school. Why did I need any more? I wanted to live a life which would allow me freely to explore everything and have to do nothing in return.

Besides this, there was a feeling in the air around 1964 that there was more to life than serving the military-industrial complex (which was what every job was seen to be in that it represented the economy and that it fostered the forces which were spreading poverty and the *de jure* segregation in our country). Everything could be reduced to this evil genius and I, as an unthinking student of the times, bought my blue jeans (the new student uniform for conscientious young men of today) and railed in my private discourse against the materialism of society and dreamt along with LBJ of a great Society which would change all the wrongs of that evil establishment that Ike had warned us all about in his farewell address. It never occurred to me that even while I was denouncing materialism, I clung to my possessions and that income which might make me independently (if even on a small scale) wealthy (and with a 4-F draft deferment on top). I lashed out against the industrial establishment in which my father's money had been made and in which my money stood invested, drawing hefty dividends on which I was presently living.

I never saw the contradictions. I never saw the absurdity of little rich kids (as NYU is full of this species) running around trying to look poor with the uniform of blue jeans, Beatle haircuts, and shirts full of patches. The point was to look as if we were part of the downtrodden Proletariat because we were showing our solidarity with our brothers. But then we went back to our dorm or apartment rooms and put on our expensive stereos and ate our large meals with our top grade beer or wine (marijuana had not caught on yet with this set), and think nothing of the contradiction. We felt pure and self-righteous. I know that I did. What a jerk I was. If I was going to give mere lip service to something, I shouldn't have engaged in such deceitful fantasy that I was really one of the *people*. I did not really wish to become one of the *people* or I would have given away my money and joined up. Anyway, there I was amidst a fomenting time for students. It wasn't as bad as it was a few years later, but considering what had gone on before, it seemed quite *avant-garde*. Sex was also seen to be the up and coming thing to do. There was so much pressure about it that if a person was going out with another and *not* doing anything besides simply kissing on the lips, he or she was considered to be passé. No, maybe I should revise that, *he* would be considered passé. There was an odd feeling about women. They were supposed to engage in sex so that their men might not be passé, but it was important that it was entirely clandestine. They were supposed to engage in sex because they were overcome by the tremendous magnetism of the man. He would power her away from her pure unstained virginity to the base lasciviousness of their animal natures. The women were at the same time not supposed to want sex (thus making the *capture* all the more satisfying to the ego of the man) and also to be satisfied by the male partner (thus showing him that he could make even the coldest fish warm blooded (a change in species) at his very command). Since woman had to play this double role, it required a tremendous amount of secrecy. For if someone found out that the woman who was his steady had had sexual relations with one or several other lovers, then he might believe that she really enjoyed sex and thus his conquest would not be as awe inspiring. This was why every woman, even if she admitted other lovers, had to state with conviction that her man (that bozo who she was presently with) made her feel like she had *never felt before*. This new man had brought her the fullness of sensuality that she had not been able to achieve with another.

Now at nineteen, beginning my junior year in college, I did not have what you would call an overwhelming sex drive. I understand that this is supposed to be the time in a man's life when he is at his prime. It may be because I was a late developer, but this was not the case for me. Any sexual impulse that I felt could be easily contained and accommodated sporadically by myself. I was not eager and anxious to hop into bed with someone. However, because of the times, I did feel that this disposition on my part was the evidence of yet another defect in my character. I sometimes tried to tell myself that I was above it all, but I really felt that I was somehow inadequate as a sexual being. Why didn't I feel like going out on the prowl after young ladies? Why didn't I want to join the small clandestine orgies that took place on campus once or twice a year?

And then there was Barbara. I think that I might have been able to have avoided the usual games if it hadn't been for her. I was perceived by many to be her "steady". (I never asked her to be my steady nor did I even want this, except in the way that having a friend showed that you were attractive as a man.) We didn't go with the "straight" crowd or with the "beat crowd." We weren't really in any crowd. This wasn't because I was a staunch individualist, but because I was considered to be more or less worthless socially. I didn't have anything interesting to talk about with my peers about music (rock and roll), books (the latest best sellers), or the most important topic: gossip. I didn't know much about what was happening to whom—nor did I care much except that I would have liked to have had something to share with others. But I didn't know anything and the rule was that unless you knew something and shared it, that you didn't get anything in return. Since I didn't have anything, I didn't get anything.

Barbara wanted to be a part of the "straight" crowd. I didn't care. (The only difference between the "straight" crowd and the "beat" crowd was that the former dressed better and was even more secretive about what they did privately than the latter. The "beats" were less hypocritical about their sex and drug use, but then the straights were less hypocritical about their real ties to the establishment. I

always said that the big difference between the two groups was
that one pressed their blue jeans.) I suppose I really did care. I felt
more sympathy with the beats. I wanted to be one of the *people*. But
Barbara was just the opposite so we usually did things with her
friends rather than mine. This was not imperialism on her part. I
really didn't have anybody who would have wanted to do much
with me. This made me wonder at times why Barbara wanted anything to do with me. She was on the outside of the straight group
dying to get in and I was nowhere and not doing anything. Perhaps
she needed a boyfriend to get in; I don't know. At any rate we were
a rather nonphysical couple as I have said before. This didn't bother
me, because, as I have also said, I didn't want to get too entangled
with a woman so that I would have to marry her. One evening in
late November, Barbara asked me if I wanted to get an apartment
and move out of the dorms.

"Why would I want to do that?"

"You could have more freedom," she said with a smile. We were
walking next to each other on the way to the library. Suddenly she
took my hand. "You'd be eligible, you know, because next term
you will be a senior." At that time only senior men could get off
campus apartments. As I was so full of credits, I would be a senior
in mid-year.

"I like it at the dorm. I don't have to do any cooking." I did not
like the summers when I would live at my uncle's while he and his
wife took their long vacations. I had to cook and clean, and that
whole image made me sick.

"Well, I could cook for you sometimes."

"That is not allowed," I said. The rule for men off campus was
that they could not entertain any university women in their rooms.
At least in the dorm you could have a girl in your room as long as the
door was six inches open and you both had at least one foot on the
floor."Oh, that rule is never enforced. Who would know?" Barbara
surprised me. She had never before seemed to me to be one who
wanted to break-the rules. Anyway, what did she care whether I got
an apartment off campus or not?

"I don't think I would be interested," I said. "It would take too much trouble to move."

I felt a strange sensation. We were sitting in the lounge at her dorm (men weren't allowed in the women's rooms, but only in the lounge to the dorm. When we wanted to call for our date, we had to check in with a girl stationed downstairs who would have her paged). I got up and walked around a little. There was only one other person in the lounge, a girl in curlers sitting at the piano trying to play a Chopin nocturne and butchering it badly.

"Well, you do what you think best, of course." Barbara was looking out the window. I thought that we had finished with the subject, but then she turned her head back towards mine and said, "Of course, it is cheaper to live off-campus."

This seemed ridiculous to me. How could it be cheaper to live anywhere other than a dorm? Dorms seemed constructed on the principle of economy. The rooms were small and there was very little upkeep. What could be cheaper than eating the slop that they served in the dining hall? I walked a few steps towards to piano player. She had just struck a resounding discord. My mind seemed a little confused as if something were happening which I should know about, but didn't. I felt that there was a subtext to this conversation which I wasn't a party to. This gave me the feeling that I was at a disadvantage. I knew even then (though if you had asked me, I couldn't have articulated it) that Barbara was a woman whose very essence was scheming. What did she have in mind for me? If I could have asked the question *then*, I probably could have told you that she wanted me to take an apartment off-campus, but why?

"Cheaper?" I responded.

"Of course." She reached for my hand and guided me back to the sofa. "The only advantage to living on campus is that it qualifies you for financial aid. Room and board cost a good 15 per cent more on campus than off. For one thing, you don't buy all that unnecessary food that they charge you for at the food service. Look, you don't eat all that much at meals so you are bound to subsidizing those who do." Barbara was an economics major with a specialization in the stock market. Who was I to argue with someone like her? "And the rooms are relatively the same price even though you get a much higher quality. You see, the college does not have to meet the same standards as private housing. So the college can stick you in a decrepit lodging because it is the only supplier in the marketplace. They have no competition. Why do you think that so many seniors live off campus?"

The truth was that not very many did. But Barbara had a way with rhetoric that was convincing, even when she was factually wrong. I searched for some way to avoid her domineering will.

"But how do you know it would be any more pleasant?" This retort did not warrant a reply from her.

She merely lifted one eyebrow. I continued, "Perhaps I'll have to get financial aid."

"Don't pull my leg, Andrew." She was staring intensely at me now.

"Well, I might have to. You never know."

"Andrew, I know better than that." She did? How? I had never talked about my financial situation with her or anyone except the man who ran my trust. Barbara had told me of her own family situation. Her dad was middle class and struggling to put her through college. But after all, she was an economics major with an emphasis in the stock market. Maybe she had x-ray vision?

"I worked in the dean's office during my freshman year, Andrew, and we often had access to the confidential files of various students in the normal course of our work. I have firsthand knowledge that you would never have to go on financial aid."

She had done it: she caught me in a contradiction. I hadn't actually said that I needed financial aid, but the implication was there. Now I was putty in her hands. She added (to cinch the deal), "You know, you're always complaining about the noise in the dorms. Well, you won't have to put up with that if you change to an apartment."

And so the next day I signed up for an apartment effective net term. It didn't occur to me at the time, but perhaps it was that girl on the piano who was driving me nuts and impairing my better judgment. I did not like the fact that Barbara had known about my financial situation for so long and had not mentioned this to me. Why had she kept it a secret? Maybe the subject just didn't come up, or perhaps there was some other reason?

I wouldn't have known about this at the time, but student workers are never allowed to look into the confidential files of other students at NYU or anywhere else. She must have looked into my folder on the sly. But what motive could she have had? Had she looked into other folders? It is possible that she didn't look into the folder at all, but merely on the contributions' list. This is a list that the college keeps to solicit funds from parents over and above tuition. They usually have two categories: "loaded" and "really loaded". My name might have been on that first list since my father was dead and I had comfortable means. She might have then made the inference. What I didn't want to consider (even now) was the possibility that Barbara, little Barbara, sweet Barbra, who came from a family which was financially struggling, might have culled the list in order to find out which boys in the school came from wealthy families. Then she could try and meet those with whom she shared a class. Perhaps she tried to get a peek at their confidential files in order to confirm the fundraising sheet's categorizations. She might have intended to meet me only so that she could catch me and get her hands on my money. I said that I don't like to consider this possibility because it makes me cringe at my gullibility. Could I have been such a schmuck?

At any rate, I moved in to that apartment. It was a small studio apartment with cooking equipment and a refrigerator built in, but it served my needs. The bed was a Murphy which came down from the wall. The place was also furnished with a couch, two chairs, a table, and a lamp. It was a step up from the dorm, but it was not as nice as Barbara had pitched.

There was one window in the room which looked over the alley between buildings. In the alley there was a large light that was always on in the night. The funny thing about this light was that it was not held securely. Consequently, whenever there was any wind (which was most nights) the light would swing back and forth. The first week or so I was entranced by the light's movements. It gave a certain syncopation to the evening. I took to leaving my given light off so I could contemplate the patterns. Even when I pulled down the shade to the window, the light would still shine through the cracks and play its tricks. This was one thing that I both liked and disliked about the apartment. I could feel alone but at the same time be conscious of the outside world.

When I was a boy (after my mother had died) there were times when I went into the closet in my room and shut the door. The only light I saw was the ¾ inch gap at the bottom of the door. That became a tube of light. As my eyes would grow accustomed to the darkness, that tube of light became even more exotic to me: a Dan Flavin minimalist display. I suppose I could have taped newspapers or cardboard to the whole blind in order to block out all the light, but then my room in the daytime would seem like a prison. So I decided to think about my adolescent closet when my starry shade began to annoy me. The other point of nuisance was the noisy landlord's cat which was out each night and had a habit of climbing onto garbage cans. The problem was that sometimes the cans would tip over with a resounding crash followed by angry cat screeching. The apartment was supposed to be quieter than a dorm, but I think that the cat and the lighted room more than made up for stereos and parties.

It was only two weeks before Barbara came again to see the apartment. She had helped me move in, but she had not been back. I had only taken her to see my dorm room twice. I didn't like the pressure of being alone with her in a private space. On this occasion we first went out to a movie together and then had a coffee while we talked about our visions of the future. I told her about my plans to travel and live as I could.

"I want to get married or become a stock broker," she confided.

"Why don't you do both?" I suggested.

"It's not that easy. The financial world is not feminine-friendly. They say women aren't aggressive enough for the job."

I thought silently that such a criticism certainly didn't apply to her. We finished our coffee and Barbara suggested we travel to my studio apartment. I was happy that we stopped talking about the future. As we walked I picked up a small stone and pointed to a mailbox as my target. The stone fell short and wide of the mark.

"And what about you, Andrew? Do you plan to get married some day?"

"Perhaps," I said in a lilting voice. I picked up another stone and threw it. It missed and almost hit a car window. I decided to stop. "My aim is pretty bad this evening. Perhaps we should call it a night."

"Oh, come on, Andrew, it is only nine o'clock. You promised to take me to your place."

"Do you want an ice cream cone?'

"Okay, but only if we have it at your place."

"But I don't have any ice cream." I didn't like the idea of her coming into my private domain. That was one thing that I liked about an apartment: I could be all alone. Back in the dorm my roommate had been ideal for me because he was withdrawn like I was and didn't bother me. But it was for better not to have a roommate at all to get in the way.

"We'll find something. " Barbara was optimistic. We were now within a block. When we got inside she walked over to my cupboards and looked through them.

"Let's have some of that house warming gift I gave you over a little toast."

The prospect didn't seem all that bright to me. I had not touched the potted meat nor the wine. I had not had anything particular to celebrate.

But Barbara did not read my subtle cues. She made herself busy and in short order came up with the refreshment. We drank the wine and had the toast with the potted meat on top. To be perfectly truthful, it tasted better than I expected. Barbara had most of the toast and gave me most of the wine. I thought that we would only be drinking a glass, but before I knew it we had finished the bottle!

I was very contented and looked over at Barbara. In the dim light of the apartment she was very alluring. I felt an overwhelming desire to kiss her, so I did. The kiss had more intensity than our normal fare.

I still remember being somewhat confused by everything, except that I was quite animated, and I stopped questioning things.

Before I knew it my hand was touching her breast through her shirt and bra. To this day I don't remember doing that. But I must have done it, because I was touching skin and that is a feeling hard to feign—unless Barbara had placed my hand there.

I didn't need any more encouragement than this. Barbara was letting me touch her without resistance. I kept wondering why she didn't move my hands away. I must be overcoming her with passion for me. I started fumbling about. I did not know what I was doing.

"Get the light," she whispered. I obeyed.

*   *   *

It was about four o'clock when Barbara woke me. We were lying in the Murphy bed. I had a terrific headache. I remembered the hours before when she had almost guided me through the motions. It surprised me how much there was to learn about an action that I had always thought came naturally somehow. The man is supposed to take the lead, but in dim light and no roadmap, it was more daunting than I had dreamed. But she made everything work out fine. I did not consider that this skill might have been acquired from previous experience. I was a virgin and just assumed that she was. I would have been too embarrassed to ask. (I asked her once whether she had been a virgin just before I left for Europe and she had said, "yes," but then, knowing Barbara, what else would she have said? With Barbara, truth telling meant doing whatever was convenient.)

It was an understatement to say I was confused. Here it was very early in the morning—even for me, an early riser. I wanted very much to talk to Barbara about what had just happened and I wanted to get some aspirin for my headache.

Barbara had awoken me, but she now seemed to be in some sort of alternate universe.

What was she thinking about? Was it me? Was it what we had just done? Then it occurred to me that I didn't know what we had just done. I had no intuitions on this one. I was very confused. Once again, Barbara brought clarity to the situation.

"We've got to get me back to my room. They sometimes check who's not there in the morning. I know that it's very sporadic, but I cannot take that chance."

"Of course," I chimed in.

It was then that I realized that I could have just gotten Barbara into a whole lot of trouble.

What had I done to her? Could she be expelled for lascivious behavior? Was this moral turpitude? The time for speculation was over. It was time to act.

I started moving quickly, though I did not have the plan in mind. I should have asked Barbara. Barbara also seemed to be a little nervous as she got out of bed and began dressing. This arrested me. I wanted to watch her dress. The sight of a naked woman was unknown to me. I was frozen in awe. Just then, the cat tipped over a garbage can in the alley, the wind picked up and the lamp began to sway. This was getting surreal. For a moment I took the oscillating light to be a police car patrolling the alley. Barbara picked up on my agitation. But she was not deterred in the execution of her task.

At any rate she was returned safely. I went back to my room and awaited the morning as I watched the dying pattern made by the swinging beam of light across the floor.

CHAPTER SEVEN

THE SEXUAL EPISODES between Barbara and me were infrequent at first, but increased as the school year drew to an end. Now more than ever, she would play on my guilt over despoiling her. She exacted promises of marriage from me over and over. I wanted to have sex with her but I wasn't sure that she was really the girl that I wanted to marry. Why had I allowed our relationship to come to this? I had just wanted a casual friendship and now I would have to marry her. I knew this would have to be since I believed in responsibility. I could not risk ruining another's life just to satisfy my own animal lusts.

And so I was in a difficult situation. I wanted to be free to pursue the sort of life that I had planned for myself, but then I had this responsibility issue that I had created by my unforced actions. When I thought about Barbara I felt a certain tenderness for her, but I suppose that the thing I liked best about her was our newly discovered physical relationship. I reasoned to myself that many married couples had lots of trouble with sex and that we had none. It might not be a bad bet to marry someone who you know will be compatible in bed.

All of this made little impression on me. The only argument which carried any real weight was that I had a responsibility I owed to her. A responsibility was a morally sacred burden which must be accepted and carried out. It was this sense of duty that gave Barbara further power over me. She knew that she had me. She was just as good as Mrs. Andrew Viam and she used this knowledge to its full effect.

She became quite concerned when I explained that I was going to Britain for graduate studies until she graduated from college. She just expected me to hang around for her. But I had to go. I do not know if it was an unconscious desire to be rid of her (surely this was not unconscious—I felt it and recognized the emotion), but I told myself that when the time came I would marry her. She put up quite a battle with me, using all the guilt and strings she had attached to try and get me to change my mind, but for the last time in our relationship I stood up for something and won: I went to Cambridge while she completed her B.A. in New York. I think she gave up, really, deciding that if she pressed any harder she might lose, me for good. A man has a better bargaining position when he is single over such things than when he is married.

I went to Cambridge and in a year and a half came back, married Barbara, took her to Cambridge, and finished my studies. It was in Cambridge that Barbara finally decided that she could fulfil her dream of being a wife and a stock broker. At first she engaged in phantom investing. She pretended as if she were putting money into stocks and charted them in a ledger she bought at Heffers Bookshop. After a year of this, she showed me the accounts as proof that she knew her stuff. Now all she needed was some capital to invest. Guess where that was supposed to come from?

"No. I don't want to touch father's legacy. He made very exact plans for that money. I don't want to fool with it. We get a predicable 5 per cent per year."

Barbara pouted. The question turned to whether I trusted her enough and whether I thought that she was capable of handling the money. Now that she was my wife, she used all the powers at her disposal to win this war with me. If I didn't, then it showed that I was a bad husband. I was comfortable on $ 7,000 a year. She wanted more. I thought that you should adjust your desires to meet your income. She thought that desires were a given and that more income was necessary to satisfy a certain perceived *standard of living for someone of our class.* I didn't know what class that was. She was middle class and I was classless since I was a loner.

"It is criminal to let all that money sit earning a paltry 5% interest in those ultra-conservative stocks your broker has chosen. If you look at my practice ledger I was making 10 per cent — that's double. If I choose a higher risk plateau, I could move that up to 17 per cent easy. Then we'd have $14,000 in addition to your salary as a college professor."

"But I don't want to be a college professor."

"Pooh. You've got to earn a living somehow."

"What about that $14,000 you just mentioned."

"$14,000 is not a living."

"90 per cent of people in the United States earn less than that."

"Why not shoot for the top? You set your standards too low. You'll never amount to anything with that attitude. "

"Barbara, I want to travel; I want see the world. "

"We're traveling now. We're living in Cambridge. YOU travelled even before you married. It's time you settled down, Andrew Viam. You're a married man now. Act like one."

And so when I finished we moved back to the States. I get a job at Boston College and later went to Chicago University. Barbara invested our money in stocks she thought would bring us a better income. Her technique was faulty and she lost half of the money through poor investments. I suggested that we sink the rest of my father's legacy into a condominium in Hyde Park and a car. That took care of that. Barbara got an outside job at a brokerage firm that had upside potential. We also decided (at Barbara's suggestion) that we would establish separate bank accounts.

It was about this time that we began constructing various barriers around those parts of our personalities that we could not tolerate in the other. So it was that we went on for four years — happy, I thought, but apparently that was not so. We both had our jobs. Mine was rather repetitive: I taught five different classes over and over and over again. I went to the library on four designated work periods depending upon the day. Barbara was rising up in her job and was soon making more than I did. She showed signs that I should recognize that and render proper fealty. She was very jealous of her bank account. I suppose her vision of our life together changed drastically when she went through my father's legacy. Perhaps she did check up on my financial situation. Perhaps her vision of a *better life* had depended upon her parlaying that nest egg into something considerable. And if that was the measure of success and happiness, then she was deeply unhappy now. It was another stage of our drifting apart.

* * *

We finally arrived at the rather large state park. You had a choice of either driving on a dirt road to some designated camp sites with stakes driven in the ground and the numbers of the sites gouged out and painted with white paint. The second choice was a backpacking option where you walked on various trails and stopped where your fancy dictated. Anthea chose the latter.

"Are you kidding?" I asked. "Why not take the easy route and drive to your campsite?"

"Suit yourself, Andrew. But if you want to sleep in *my* tent tonight, you're going on a hike. That's real camping."

My only question is where to park our car so it isn't vandalized." She looked around and chose a spot behind some tall elm trees and next to some park ranger vehicles.

And then we were off. Now, it should never be said that I dislike walking. I walked all the time in Hyde Park (since Barbara took our car to work). But I generally carried only a couple of books and a pad of paper for notes. This was quite different from a heavy backpack and the water we would be using. (At the designated campsites they had potable water right on the spot, but for hikers you had to carry in your own.) Water is very heavy.

Anthea was in excellent shape for hiking. She kept up a steady pace. I struggled to keep up. Sometimes I would stop and she would scold me to keep up. The straps of my rucksack cut into my shoulders so that they became a sheet of pain. And then I fell down. I tripped on a tree root on the path. I had no desire to get up. But Anthea came back for me. "Get up you lazy head. Let's see what you are made of."

I wanted to say "Jello," but speaking the word was too much of an effort. "You've got to keep going until we get there."

"How do we know when we're there?" I moaned.

"Don't worry. I'll tell you." And so we went on further. I was in so much pain that I became very dizzy. There were three or four more roots that I tripped over but I managed to keep my balance this time.

And still we walked and walked and walked. I tried to hypnotize myself on her calf muscles. They were real and they weren't cramping like mine were.

It was almost dark when Anthea told me that we had come to the place. Had I energy I would have inquired how it was any different from a half-dozen spots that were miles back. I merely fell into a heap. I wanted to go to sleep right then, but Anthea did not permit me. Instead, she took off my pack and told me to clear some brush for our campsite while she went to gather some firewood.

I began clearing brush when I was overcome with fatigue and went to sleep. I don't know how long I was asleep (I had long since stopped looking at my watch), but when Anthea awoke me it was dark. I felt discomfort in my left leg and found numerous cockle burrs on my pants at the calf. I was laying on them. The path that we had taken was badly overgrown. I didn't know how Anthea had been able to follow it. Anthea had made a fire and was cooking something.

"Now we put up the tent," she said. "We've got to keep the tent away from the fire. The water-proofing they use on them makes them into instant infernos if they come into contact with a flame." I shuddered and made a mental note: keep tents and fire apart or it will be Fourth of July. I felt much better and obeyed her command. We got the tent up in no time. Then we threw down the ground cloth and our double-sized air mattress. "The ground is too hard to screw on," Anthea had said about the purchase. We zippered up our sleeping bags together and had some coffee.

"Dinner's almost ready, why don't you get some of that grass out of my pack and we'll have a few tokes."

"You brought marijuana?" I asked in surprise. I don't know why I was surprised. So many young people used the stuff that I ceased to wonder when I discovered some acquaintance was a user. "I don't indulge."

"You *what*? Come on, Andrew, and be a good boy."

"No, Anthea. I won't be bullied about this."

"But what's the matter? Afraid your hair will fall out? Look, grass is a harmless herb."

"Goes along with your vegetarian philosophy, eh?" I thought that she was a little surprised at my stand, but there are things that a person must believe in. It was dark now and the only vision I had of Anthea was via fire light. I was sitting on a rock that she had moved close to the fire for that express purpose. She was across the fire sitting seven or eight feet away. The shadows made her seem like a different person. They danced a mysterious rhythm across her visage.

"I don't see why you don't want any. It will make our sex more intense." There was an irritation in her voice, but she saw that I was not giving in on this.

"I don't use it because it is against the law."

"Against the law! That's the funniest thing I've ever heard. Who obeys the law? We *all* break the law *all* the time. If it isn't speeding in our car, it's cheating on our income taxes or jay walking. Don't give me that crap about obeying the law." She rattled these off as if she were saying her catechism. She wasn't particularly livid, though her words had a sharpness that seemed to portray something that was clear to her but was opaque to me. Her manner of delivery, as I have said, was mechanical. Her face seemed somewhat passive, and yet there was that edge. Was this a remnant of some emotion which had ceased to be associated with the words that had been repeated so many times? Was there really an underlying emotion to which this acrimonious undertone was projecting?

"I know that certain things you say are true. We don't all obey the law, but that does not speak to what we *ought*.to do. I know that

I have driven my car over the speed limit. But that does not mean I was right to do so. I do not habitually flaunt the law."

This little conversation was giving me a second wind. We philosophers like a verbal confrontation. It's mother's milk to us.

"But what if it is a stupid law? You don't have to obey stupid laws."

"I don't see how the stupidity of the law has any bearing on whether we should obey it. In Seattle there is still a law that requires men to remove their hats indoors. If I were in Seattle and I was aware of this law, I would feel under an obligation to obey it."

"But why? I can tell what is good and bad without any law telling me what to do.

The law can't legislate morality. That's what the marijuana laws are doing. It's just like Prohibition."

"You're right. It is just like Prohibition. It is a prohibition against an intoxicating drug. But then, I believe the government has the authority to prohibit alcohol if it wanted to."

"But Prohibition was a big failure. That shows that the law was dead wrong. And today millions are disobeying the marijuana laws in just the same way. This shows that the marijuana laws are also dead wrong." She was no longer reciting rote questions and answers. She was sitting up on her knees and gesturing animatedly. I had not changed my position on the rock. I pulled up my knees to my chest to relieve the pressure on my lower back. "So you believe that millions who disobey the drug laws render those laws invalid?"

"Sure, it's a democracy isn't it?" Anthea stood up.

"Yes, it is. We have three branches of government and it is the legislative branch which is the sovereign that makes all laws subject to our written Constitution."

"So you agree with me."

"Well, sort of. I agree we, in the United States, live in a federal democracy. Where we disagree is *who* makes the laws. I'm saying that only Congress and the State Legislatures have the right to make laws. You're saying that a few million pot users can stipulate the law for all 231 million Americans. That is inaccurate and even if it weren't, you'd have minority rule."

"What I wanted to say was that it was up to each person to think about the laws and then only obey the good laws."

"So everyone picks and chooses the laws to obey."

"Now you've got it," Anthea looked at me as if I were a moron.

"That would mean that personal values trump civil law. So that if I had a personal value about killing blond haired women, then I ought to be able to indulge my personal inclination."

"That's a stupid case. Of course murder is always wrong."

"So murder is different from smoking pot. It's all right for people to disobey the pot laws but not for them to disobey the murder laws. All murderers ought to be punished."

She rolled her eyes. The flickering light of the fire seemed to accentuate her irritation over my simple-minded questioning. "Of course they should. And they should throw away the key."

"But on what principle? You said earlier that each of us must decide what laws are right and just for ourselves. The law shouldn't legislate morality. Those were your very words, don't you remember?" She didn't answer.

"If killing is a moral issue, and I can hardly think of anything which is more of a moral issue, then the law has no right to tell me whether I should murder or not. By your own admission I may choose to ignore those laws and be perfectly justified in doing so. And the society should not punish people who do what they think is right. So if I think killing a particular person is the proper thing to do, then society should not punish me."

"But you can't equate murder with smoking grass."

"You're right. They are different sorts of cases. Smoking marijuana is a recreational activity that is victimless—unless you operate a car while stoned. I see the right to personal recreation to be a limited right. So if the government wants to say it's okay to drink alcohol or to smoke tobacco—even if alcohol and tobacco create a greater health risk, it is within the purview of the government to do so. Now it would be different if there were a single drug for cancer treatment and the government said I couldn't take it to save my life. That would be about the right to life and would be similar to the murder case."

I could tell that this argument was not to her liking. She turned her face away from the fire for a bit. I just sat there and wondered what she was going to do. It was a little difficult for her to go back to the car particularly over a trail that we could barely follow in the light. Finally she said, "Where do we draw the line? You say it's okay for the government to tell me whether or not I can smoke tobacco or whether or not I can smoke grass, but it cannot take a cancer drug from me. And that's because I'm not really *harmed* by losing the ability to toke a joint, but I'll die without the cancer drug." Anthea had regained her focused look.

"Yes."

"I agree to that. But I still think that the government is wrong in telling me I can't smoke pot. What's the harm?" She was genuinely asking me a question now.

I sensed somehow an authenticity in her voice which had not previously been there. "Just that it is against the law."

"But who does that harm?"

"You just admitted that the murderer should be locked up and made to obey the laws. And I suppose that there are quite a few others who you would agree ought to be locked up and made to obey the laws, such as the rapist, robber, embezzler and so on. Correct?" She didn't respond, but looked at me with open eyes staring intensely.

"Well, the only reason the government has to put them on trial is that they have broken laws that have been established by that government. Presumably the legislative branch passes laws which it thinks are right and just or at least in the best interests of its citizens. Now say that there is a silly law which says that men may not wear hats inside. It also is a law. It may deal with a trivial and stupid aspect of behavior, but it is still a law. As a law it must be obeyed in the same way as the murder laws are obeyed. This is because there is no way to create individual exceptions to the law without tearing down the whole idea of laws in the first place. Laws don't work unless they apply to everybody equally. And laws don't work unless people try to follow all of them. Whenever we break a law (especially when we aren't caught and punished) we weaken the fabric of law in general and undermine the government."

"But how can my smoking a little grass bring down the government?"

"It's accumulative. One person sees another doing something and getting away with it and so he tries to get away with it. This continues until there is widespread non-compliance with the law. When this happens, the ability other laws to protect people is diminished."

"You're saying that I'm hurting the law by smoking grass?"

"Yes. You're indirectly undermining all laws by disobeying even a silly law."

Anthea didn't like our conversation. We ate our entire dinner in silence. She probably thought that I was a prude, but I didn't care. There were some principles that I held to be important and morality was one of them. I admired the way that Anthea could act on her own and not care about what others thought. No, that wasn't it. What I found fascinating was her ability to tune other people out and not feel inextricably tied to them; that she put loyalty to herself first. This entailed a degree of selfishness, of course, but I was attracted to a certain sort of selfishness because it showed that she knew and accepted herself. I, on the other hand, was deficient in that area. Would that I had more of Anthea within me. Barbara manipulated me any way she wanted to. Barbara knew it and made me pay for my flaw.

*   *   *

After dinner I cleaned up the dishes and thought that it would be nice to take a little swim. We were only a hundred yards or so from a little lake. It was a beautiful night (a little nippy, but still tolerable for a swim). We were isolated. There were no other human souls within sight or sound. So I made for the water.

It was not the kind of water that one could get used to slowly. I knew that I had to either jump in or sit on the bank and throw pebbles. I opted for the former alternative. So with firm resolve I ran into the water and hurled myself into the cold depths. It was *unbelievably* cold. This frigid hydro mass engulfed me and instantly

I was gasping for air. It was as if my involuntary muscles had gotten out of control. I had to slow down my breathing, so I began doing some sidestrokes. The action of moving my muscles helped get my breathing under control. I moved through the water for a few minutes and then got out.

I had not completely gotten under control in the water, but considering my gasping state when I first entered, my feeling at exit was one of triumph. I felt as if I had really accomplished something. As I climbed back onto the bank I felt the mud slide through my toes. I was more tired than I realized. My little nap and my conversation with Anthea had fooled me into thinking that I was really more awake and strong than I was. It was a struggle to put my clothes back on. The cool air made my wet skin shiver, and the hundred yards back to our camp seemed three times as long.

When I returned, Anthea was sitting on my rock staring into the fire. She had a blank expression. I attributed it to the marijuana she had smoked.

"I'm pretty tired," I said. "I think I'll be going to bed."

Anthea didn't answer. I figured that she was still pretty mad about our conversation. I stripped down to my underwear and got into the double sleeping bag. It's a lucky thing that we zipped these two together before the argument, I thought. It wasn't long before I was sound asleep. There is nothing more pleasant than being tired to your every fiber and then settling down into a comfortable bed (and the sleeping bag with the air mattress was very comfortable) and falling to sleep quickly. There is something very satisfying about the entire process.

This brief pleasure was soon interrupted by Anthea as she entered the sleeping bag and preceded to wake me up. "Andrew," she shook my shoulder.

"W-w-what?" I managed in a half-awake tone that betrayed my desire to go back to the other side.

"Andrew, wake up."

"What is it?" I refused to open my eyes or to remove my mind from its sleeping mind-set. This way I would have no delay in getting back to sleep.

"How was the water?"

"What?" No other question could have perplexed me more. I was semi-prepared for her to rant about how unfair I was or what a rotten time she was having with me or some such prattle. I was prepared for something along those lines and could have put off such answers and fallen back to sleep without missing a blink, but this question was so out of character for Anthea (or at least my understanding of her character) that it caused me to displace, at least momentarily, my somnolent attitude.

"The water. You went swimming. I could hear you splash in."

"Oh yeah. The water. Very nice." I was ready to nod again.

"Do you want to go swimming now?"

"I want to sleep." My eyes wanted to close. The lids felt weighted.

Anthea put her hands on each of my shoulders and turned me around so that my body was on its side and facing her. Then she released the hand on the lower shoulder and brought it to my face and stroked it gently. This had more of an effect than her trying to jar me awake. "I know you're tired, but the moon will be going down soon. If we are going to swim together tonight, it will have to be now." *Swim tonight together*—I could feel myself getting more and more awake again. I could not help it. It was the force of her argument. One could not argue and hope to maintain that delicate equilibrium between this world and the realm of Hypnos. I wanted so much to return to that quiet and restful state and yet all her questions were making such a journey impossible. I felt the accessibility of that other world fade away despite my efforts to embrace its quiet unconsciousness.

"Anthea-a-a," I said in a final effort to regain that last state of peace. I intended for there to be an edge to my voice, but because I was concentrating on recovering my cherished Hypnos, I could not judge whether *intention* matched *execution*.

She didn't respond but grabbed my shoulders and gave them a tug. The other realm was gone. I made the final submission; I opened my eyes. There in front of me was Anthea. Her short hair was untidy. Our fire was dying down and so it was difficult to really catch the expression on her face, but it seemed to be one of great concern. I had never seen her so earnest (it was similar but not identical to the expression she had had on her face in the Marc Plaza when the goon show came to visit). For some reason she really felt it was important for us to go swimming. And of course, in accord with our respective personalities, she put her own needs above mine and I put mine out of mind. Here was someone who needed my help. What could I do?

We hurried down to the lake (or Anthea was hurrying and pulling me along with her). It had gotten colder. The moon was about to set. I must have been asleep for hours. Anthea quickly and effortlessly stripped off her clothes and then helped me as I fumbled for my shorts. I could not help admiring her beautiful body as it was presented to me in yet another light. There is a cool dull glow that moonlight gives (especially when reflected off of water). Anthea's skin took on a different hue. This gave a different presentation of her geography. Her eyes seemed to stand out and sparkle. I had the feeling as we stood and looked at each other naked in the moonlight that she was somehow genuine with me for the first time. She had somehow lost her swagger and was now before me with as few pretentions as she could have at that moment. I stretched out my arm and touched her shoulder. I was alive with a swelling passion, but I remained still. I let my hand slide down her smooth skin.

Then we were in the water. It seemed even colder than before. Both of us splashed around a bit, but we didn't really engage in swimming. It was merely water-play. But vigor of the cold caused us both to exit before very long.

I was lost in the mystery of it all. Our love making was amazing. There were no politics. There was no *you* or *I*—only *us.*

Then we ran back to camp. My body was no longer sore from our hiking. It was time to slow down to the pace of our environment— our cenacle of solitude with nary another human about. It was just Anthea and me as we scrambled into our double zipped sleeping bag. I was totally in that moment. No past or future—only the noise of the insects and the chill of the June night air. I wanted that moment to stretch out and hold me still. But nothing lasts forever.

My eyelids began getting heavier. As I breathed, each movement of my chest brought me closer to yet another dreamland. Soon the urge to go to sleep returned. Even as I lay down I felt myself quickly drifting away. But just as I was reaching a transition state, Anthea nudged me just as before.

"Andrew."

"What?" I was not in the mood to be disturbed again.

"I want to talk."

"Not now."

"Andrew."

"We'll talk in the morning." I rolled over, expecting to go right to sleep, but I kept waiting for Anthea to lay down; she was half sitting being propped up by her elbow. I knew that she was thinking. She wanted to talk to me, but I wanted to go to sleep. Surely there was a time for everything. Still I couldn't relax very well thinking about her brooding. I don't know how long she stayed awake since I did manage to fall asleep within the hanging conversation. We had had a long day, so when I awoke I anxiously looked at my watch. It said one o'clock, but then I also noticed that it wasn't running. I had forgotten to wind it. Anthea didn't have a watch, so we were without time.

Now I am usually the kind of guy who never pops out of bed in the morning to scurry toward his many tasks that await him. This morning was no different. I decided just to lie in bed and think. It was an interesting perspective, looking up through the walls of a small green tent. The birds were out (some of them were probably mating and establishing territories). Everything seemed alive to me. There were no blockbuster books that I had to read or projects I had to get done. For once I felt free. It was a feeling that I hadn't experienced since my Cambridge days. I remember vividly getting off the plane at Heathrow. I was going to be a student at one of the best universities in the world. I was thrilled at the prospective academic stimulation. I might get to hear all the great names in philosophy (I had not yet specialized in philosophy of science). The world was all before me and I looked not for a place of rest.

Barbara and the rest were all behind me. I hadn't given them a single thought since I got on the plane. I felt that that great mechanical monster was taking me away from the cares and obligations of marriage into that world that I had planned on from the start. I felt free even though I knew I was not.

The plane pulled up at the appropriate spot on the runway and we all got out. It had been a redeye flight and everyone was tired (or at least they all looked tired). I was no exception. I had a single bag with another case, a trunk, coming in the baggage compartment. Then there was waiting. We waited to get the luggage (my trunk was not there). Then we waited to go through customs. Finally we were out. But what was I then to do?

I was out; free to do whatever I pleased, but how to do it? I didn't know where to go. I changed some money at the airport (getting a terrible rate of exchange) and asked a fellow how one got to London.

He told me which busses to take and how much it would cost and how long it would take. I decided to spend a night at an airport motel until my trunk arrived. Checking a directory located in the air terminal, I hopped onto a courtesy van run by the hotel and in ten minutes was checking in. The room looked just as any motel room would look in America. I lay on the bed and put on the television. It was a horrid game show. The quality of daytime television in Britain was definitely lower than it was in the U.S. (and that's pretty bad). I quickly fell asleep for twenty hours.

I could not believe it when I awoke. It hadn't been a sound sleep but a fitful one punctuated by the television, which woke me up (until I finally turned it off), and numerous trips to the toilet.

I finally got up and felt like I had been hit in the head with a siege hammer. I paid my bill and took the van back to the airport. My trunk had still not arrived. I was a little upset. But it seemed the more I tried to let them know that I was upset, the more I was ignored. I believe that I was learning the first lesson in English customer relations. Whereas in America the customer is "always right" and businesses go out of their way to honor even dubious claims, in Britain it is not that way at all. One's claims are only occasionally honored and only then when the customer can prove that it was the store's fault. "Let the buyer beware" is the catch phrase. However, in this case I was completely in the right. I had every reason to expect that my case would come when expected. This was not an unreasonable demand on my part. I left after getting a promise that they would "look into it".

This time I was upset. I just started walking when I suddenly realized that I didn't know where I was going. I started hitch hiking. I had always heard about people hitch hiking in Europe, so why not here? It was not long before a delivery man stopped for me and took me into central London. He dropped me off near Grosvenor Square. He said that this was a good place for a "Yank." (I found out later that this remark probably referred to the U.S. embassy which is located there). I hailed a cab and asked him to take me to a rooming house near the University. We went through a maze of streets and I was finally dropped off at Gower Street. "There's lots of places 'round here, mate," he said as I paid him my last crown.

I went into the first place I saw. It was right next to the Goodge Street Underground Station. It was a cheap, mildly dirty place, and a lot different from the motel I had stayed at near the airport. For one thing, the bed was fixed on a slant so that one was always sleeping uphill or downhill (depending which end you set your pillow). There was a sink in the room which only ran cold water and there was no heat unless you fed sixpence into a gas heater near the end of the room. It was January and plenty cold. The toilet was at the end of the hall. There were only two toilets for all the lodgers—two floors with three rooms on each floor. The toilet was a dark and musty place which didn't exactly appeal to my sterile American sensibilities. The morning breakfast was greasy sausage, eggs cooked in lots of butter, a fried tomato, and six slices of bread served in a metal stand. You were suppose cover the toast in butter and marmalade, but I passed on that one.

I headed to a local bank and exchanged some more traveler's checks even though I wanted to go to sleep again. On the way back from the bank I happened into Dillon's (a prominent bookstore near University College London). I was amazed at how inexpensive the books were. They were 40% less than the same titles sold in America. I bought a couple of novels and went back to my room for some reading. It wasn't long before I had fallen asleep. I awoke around nine that evening with a great hunger. I hiked over to Southampton and found an inexpensive restaurant. (I knew it to be inexpensive by reading the menu posted outside the establishment—at least they did one thing like New York). It was a Greek place, and I had a filling meal for four shillings, eight. My meal put me in better spirits about my situation. I even felt like doing some exploring. I bought a plan of the city and walked downtown and gambled a little in the penny arcades in Soho. I broke even on the night and was feeling exhilarated at my new found freedom. I did not think about it at the time, but at that very instant I so wanted those moments to last forever.

The next morning at breakfast (included in the price of the room) I saw the other inhabitants of the smelly hole in which I was living. They were mostly Africans and Asians and had markedly different table manners. I got into a conversation with one and found out a little about the University area. They told me to go to the British Museum. That sounded like a good idea. Karl Marx studied there. I enjoyed my chat with the other foreign students. I felt a compelling sense of satisfaction over my situation and this spread to all that I did. The smell of the rooming house got more tolerable and I finally got my trunk. I had learned my way around the city and in only two weeks felt ready to travel to Cambridge.

I was doing some informal study at first so it made no difference (to some extent) when I arrived. But when I did arrive the first thing I noticed was that it was much colder than London, even though it was only seventy-five minutes away by train from King's Cross.

I wasted no time finding a temporary place to stay until I should be able to hunt around for something permanent. I wanted to settle in and start. I was excited by Cambridge in a different way than I had been excited by London. The entire set-up was different. The number of cultural centers was much different and the town as a whole seemed less of a hodge-podge than London. I had only been in Cambridge a month (I already had a cold from the lack of central heating) when I met Ronnie. Ronnie was in philosophy of logic and was working on his thesis. We hit it off from the first. It was Ronnie who took me to his favorite pubs and eating houses. It was Ronnie who took me to various societies and lectures, and it was Ronnie who offered to share his "digs" with me. I accepted.

Ronnie was the perfect friend for me. He was introspective and sensitive and yet fiercely independent and mildly disinterested. He was not the type of person who had ulterior motives for anything. Ronnie would answer various questions I had about the ways and customs of Cambridge (which in some respects is a country unto itself, totally distinct from other "countries" such as Oxford). There is a coldness about Cambridge in the scholars which matches the climate of the area perfectly. Each person (depending on his place in the dominance hierarchy) had a prescribed mode of social behavior which began with one's salutation (for example, never ask someone higher up on the scale how he or she is feeling and never proffer your hand to the same—if they want you to know how they feel, they'll tell you. If they want to shake hands, they'll offer theirs first). Ronnie was perhaps the first human being (I'm not counting Gambol here because he was a dog) that I had gotten close to—man or woman. He was not a demanding sort of person. I often thought to myself about the contrast between Ronnie and Barbara. Why could not she be more like him? Ronnie and I would often take long walks and he would discuss aspects of his thesis and ask me what fields I was becoming interested in. Often we would just walk in meditative silence. How different this silence was from silences that occurred between Barbara and me. With Barbara silence meant that something was wrong. One of us had to be mad or else troubled. The natural state was to talk (usually about our (odious for me) future). We could never simply *be*. We were always forced to be planning something, it was necessary to be always trying to get somewhere. With Ronnie it was different. Perhaps it was because there was nothing sexual involved that we were allowed to be freer, but when we took our walks, the silences denoted quiet contemplation, enjoying the scenery or simply relaxing. There was no pressure to be constantly probing the other's mind. His thoughts were his affair; mine were mine. We remained very separate and yet considerate at the same time.

One day I told him about Barbara. We were sitting in a pub over our drinks. "Are you going to marry her?" he asked.

"I don't know," I replied. I stared into my pint of half 'n half (bitter and lager). "In many ways I wish I didn't have to."

"Is she pregnant?"

"Of course not. She's a very careful girl." I half wondered to myself whether Barbara would have ever allowed herself to become pregnant in an effort to insure the success of her snares. I dismissed the thought since it would entail too great of a risk on her part and one thing that Barbara did not do was to take risks which would endanger herself.

"Then why don't you sing her *the long good-bye*?"

Marlowe himself was not made of hard enough stuff for that order. "I'm not sure whether it would be right. After all, in the U.S. sex is inextricably linked with marriage. Since I've slept with her I feel under an obligation."

"That's the stupidest thing I've ever heard of. Things aren't so different in Britain. She's just trying to use leverage on you. How do you know you were the first with her?"

"Oh really!" I felt as if he could not be serious.

"No, I'm serious. Did she bleed? Did she act clumsy? Did she show enormous waves of guilt over it? These are all signs, you know."

I was thrown into some confusion. No, I don't know if she bled. I was not paying attention. She didn't mention it. Did she act clumsy? No! It was I who acted clumsy. She helped me along. She seemed so sure of herself and there was certainly no wave of guilt. I wondered whether she'd another partner or partners before me? This would take me off the hook. But the problem was that I couldn't say for sure. But even if it were true, could I still leave her? She had constructed a model in which I had promised to marry her. Could I back down now?

"Well, look, even if I was not the first, could I back out of a promise to marry her?"

"You promised?" He looked worried. This was a new complication.

"Rather."

"But what were the circumstances of the promise?" His face lit up as a man whose knotty problem was straightening itself out.

"I've told you, when she finishes school I will come back and marry her." I decided to take a long drink.

"But she hasn't really been on the up and up with you, you know. A promise extracted under distress is not binding, elementary ethics in anyone's system." Ronnie was getting into the argument. He lit his pipe and was busily puffing away.

I took another drink.

"But I'm not sure if I really want her to go away. You see I do feel some sort of attachment towards her."

"Quite; you'd be a cad not to feel anything. But there's a considerable difference between having affection for someone you sleep with and wanting your bed-partner to be your wife."

He had a point. I was perhaps under no strict ethical obligation to marry Barbara. I could leave her in America and I'd not be engaging in some grave moral sin. But still this did not satisfy me. It wasn't as simple as I was describing it to Ronnie. There was a sense that I loved her. I don't know if I was using the word correctly, but I felt dependent upon her. My concern for her gave rise to a sense of loyalty. I felt I would be disloyal to her to give her the shove. I would be disloyal to her and perhaps to myself (that part of myself which made judgments and promises). Maybe it was because I had lost both of my parents and had been forced to move about in my youth (consequently having no real friends) that I put such a high premium on people being loyal to each other. Devotion meant sticking by the other chap even when it was not to your advantage to do so. Without devotion this whole social fabric would come apart. Leaving Barbara would be contradicting all of this. I would be going against some part of me that was beyond rational control. I felt compelled to return to Barbara, but knew that I could never let Ronnie understand how and why I felt this way.

"That's true, but it's so complicated. I can't see myself straight on this one."

"You sound like a bloody idiot, you know."

"I probably am not being rational, but I can't help it."

"We can all help it. Rationality must rule all. It's part of the Cambridge creed, you know." I nodded my head and finished my drink.

The next morning I was awake before Anthea. She was sleeping very late, I thought. The sun was already up and so I decided to get some fire wood. I plodded back in the woods past the latrine we had constructed and looked around for wood lying on the ground. I knew enough not to try and get green wood which would only burn very slowly, but there didn't seem to be much heavy wood around. I had figured that wood gathering would be an easy task, but it wasn't. It was necessary to search high and low for something that would do. After quite a while I did manage to get some good sized branches which I lugged back to camp.

When I returned, Anthea was still asleep. I decided to surprise her with a fire. I broke some of the sticks and set them up as I had seen her do. It wouldn't go. I tried lighting the bark, but the dew on it wouldn't allow it to light. I decided to cheat and got some paper to put under it all. It still wouldn't catch. The paper burned right enough, but it wouldn't ignite the thick branches which I had so diligently collected.

"You have to start with small sticks first," I heard. Turning around, I saw Anthea poking her head out of the tent.

"The big ones won't catch by themselves." I smiled and went over to her and threw her the matches.

"Here, you show me how to light a fire."

And she did.

CHAPTER EIGHT

IT WAS CHILLY in the morning so we huddled close together as we drank our tea and ate the hard roll which was our breakfast. Anthea was especially close to me. It was hard to believe that we had had a disagreement only the evening before.

When we were finished, Anthea suggested we make a stock pile of wood. "I think we should stay here. It's very nice and we're not going to get anything better."

I was not going to argue for more hiking so we sallied forth and gathered sticks. Anthea's theory for fire starting had to do with acquiring sticks of all sizes and large amounts of dried moss and lichen. The fire was built up from small to large with the moss and tiniest twigs acting as tinder to ignite the whole project. I was determined to light the next one to test my technique.

When we had gotten all the material together Anthea asked me, "You know your idea about laws has one serious defect: it does not allow anybody to do anything about bad laws. The people are all at the mercy of the government."

This was the last thing in the world that I expected her to say at that moment. Perhaps that was what she had been brooding about all that time. She had been thinking about our conversation and when she had come up with what she considered to be a strong objection, then she warmed up to me again. I tell you, philosophy is sexy. It gets you thinking. And thinking is very close to who you are. What could be more stimulating?

Anthea's proposition put everything into a new light. I'm always happy to talk about the good, the true, or the beautiful so I replied, "Bad laws or civil disobedience are not a problem at all. You see, if there is a bad law one has three options: first, one can try to change the law through Congress and the normal legislative process. This is the ideal model. But it does not always work.

"If that does not work, then one may try openly disobeying the law and making oneself or a large number of people examples of the law. If one can amass a large enough group to openly protest the law in this fashion, then it will bring attention to your viewpoint. If you are correct, hopefully, others will voice their accord and put pressure on their representatives to change the law.

"However, this second model is dangerous in that the individual runs the risk of going to jail. The final option involves leaving the country and renouncing one's citizenship. This is only for the individual who feels that there is no hope to change the law and/or feels that the state in which he had been residing is not worth saving."

"What if you don't have enough money to leave the country?"

"Well, you get a bus from Chicago and go north."

My reply came off like a prepared speech. This was because I had given it so many times before in my philosophy classes. She was perhaps thinking about this problem for the first time and I had ceased thinking about it years before. I had solved the problem to my satisfaction. But she wasn't yet convinced. We started taking a walk through the woods going west. They were full with new growth, yet were not too difficult to navigate. All of a sudden I felt not as this woman's lover but as her tutor. She, who had lorded over me, was now faced with a different role. And I was not sure how to handle myself or whether I even liked it.

"But what would happen if you lived in a country which was not a democracy?" she asked after we had walked slowly in silence for a half hour or so (remember I didn't have a working watch)

"Obviously the first option would be closed to you," I began with a little surprise at how much she was interested in this topic. "One would be forced to alter the law in another way, if they thought that such a law should be changed."

"But take Russia, for example. There they could not have the law changed. The government would shoot them down with machine guns."

I was a little surprised at the vigor with which she delivered this reply, but I continued, "I'm not so sure that is true. Remember the strikes that they had in Poland in 1980 and how they affected labor reform."

"Poland is not Russia."

"True. Let's imagine, for example, a state where reform within the existing government is impossible. In such a state one would, I suppose, have to work for the overthrow of the entire government. This would be done in the name of morality. The individual cannot abide by these immoral laws and yet he cannot simply covertly break them. He would have to disappear into the 'underground' and wage a campaign to topple the regime."

"Let me see if I have this straight," she started. "If I were living in Russia and they passed a law forbidding marijuana, then I should work to overthrow that government? Sounds a little *extreme.*"

"Ah, but you see, the use of any particular drug (except in cases where it is designed to save a life and it is the only drug which will do so) is not a moral issue. You would have no valid moral grounds for your objection."

"Marijuana smoking is not a moral issue?"

"No. It is a non-moral issue, because there is no moral right to a particular form of pharmaceutical recreation."

"How do you get that?"

"The realm of morals only deals with one's duties insofar as they affect the abilities of others to act and live freely."

"That's just what I said yesterday. My smoking a joint does not hurt anyone, so it isn't bad."

"Your smoking a joint is not in itself a moral issue. What *is* a moral issue is that the government has passed a law against it. The government has every right to pass laws governing non-moral issues. When they do, you must abide by their decision."

"I don't understand."

"Look. Take driving the car. There is nothing inherently moral about how fast you drive. There is nothing magical about 55 miles per hour. They could have set it at 60 or at 50. Where they set it is morally arbitrary. What isn't arbitrary is that once they set it you must obey it. The cases we were just discussing were concerning moral issues only."

"Well, then, what would count as a moral issue?"

"Take a country that systematically robbed a particular group of their rights. In Nazi Germany, the Jews were terrorized and murdered by law. Now if you understood this law to be immoral (and any moral agent should), then you are obliged *not* to obey it. If your option to change the law within the system is not open to you and you cannot escape the country, then you must work to overthrow the government. You cannot sit passively and support a system which is immoral." Anthea did not respond. The teaching impulse got ahold of me for a moment and I could not resist adding, "But if you were living in Nazi Germany and they had not done anything immoral yet and they passed a law forbidding you to eat hotdogs, or drink wine or smoke marijuana or drive an automobile, you would not be justified in trying to overthrow the government or practice civil disobedience since it is within the government's legitimate power to legislate on any non-moral matter it chooses."

Anthea pursed her lips. I did not like to take the tutor role. But it would be arrogant of me to ignore her arguments—especially when I refused to smoke dope with her. And that was that. She didn't pursue the matter. We walked for a while longer and came upon an open field. There we stood and watched the morning come into its full being. It was a glorious sight. The natural setting filled me with inspiration and it filled Anthea with lust (which is as good an object for one's inspiration as any other). We began kissing and were just about to get down to business when we heard some giggling.

You don't know how startling that can be to think that you are completely isolated and away from everyone and then to hear some high pitched giggling. We turned around and saw three little kids, two girls and a boy, spying on us.

"Where did you come from?" I asked, hoping that the sound of my voice would scare them away so that we could finish what we had begun.

"Over there," said the boy who appeared to be the oldest.

"Are you camped there?"

They nodded their heads vigorously. "Want to come see?" asked the youngest girl.

I was about to say no, since I had other things to attend to. But before I had the chance, Anthea had accepted.

"I thought that we were camping to get away from people, not to be making their acquaintances," I said under my breath as we followed the little beggars back to their camp. It was not far. They were located in another open area which had a number of stumps on it. This was an "official" camp ground with a stake in the ground that was numbered. The campsite was on one side of the dirt road that we had not taken. They had two motor campers and a tent.

"There must be more than one family," I said as we just got this sight into view. "Unless someone likes trailers," she returned lightheartedly.

Then a woman came into view. She was wearing blue jeans which were rolled up to mid-calf. She wore a red plaid shirt and had her black hair held up in a scarf. She was not particularly good looking, but then she wasn't ugly either. When she saw the children bringing us she brightened and waved.

"Howdy! Did the children find you?"

"They're very friendly," began Anthea (I could tell by the tone of her voice that she liked this other woman), "are they yours?"

"Two of them are. I claim Tad, the oldest and Cyndy, the youngest. My name is Martha Miller. We're camped for the week. We still have three days to go. It's nice camping this time of year; not so many people you know— oh I didn't mean to be rude—" Martha seemed to be truly embarrassed.

"—Not at all. We came for the same reason. I'm Anthea and this is Andrew."

"How do you do," I said, but the words were completely ignored as these two women were thoroughly engaged in a conversation before I had a chance to fix the introduction. They began talking about the area and the conditions and how nice it was to have a camper, but that one was limited to roads and public campgrounds. It was all very boring stuff for me. I decided that the best thing to do was to sit down in the sun and catch up on some sleep. This might be a commodity that I would be soon in need of (or hopefully I would be in need of it, if Anthea ever stopped talking to that woman).

I had just dozed off for a short time when I was brought to my senses by a cup of cold water in my face. Now I am sure that I am not peculiar in my aversion to this method of being awoken, but this did not seem to bother the burly fellow who administered this action.

"Hey there, how are ya?" came the voice of the barrel chested man who was bald from the forehead to the top of his crown. He looked like a friendly fellow. This could be because of his homely appearance and big ears. How could I get mad at a face like that?

"Well, I was sleeping," I said trying to impress on him that I was not to be my friendliest when I was splashed with water during my nap.

"Hey there, we got to get you to have some lunch with us. We haven't seen another soul all week."

"Oh?" was my weak reply. The other helped me to my feet and I came to the conclusion that, like it or not, I had better get used to the fact that the next three hours would be in the company of this jolly group. I walked over behind the camper to where a large portable table had been erected.

"Andrew," began Anthea, "this is Glen Miller—"

"Like the band leader," said Glen immediately, "only without the other 'n.'"

"—and Samuel and Judy Johns and their daughter Margo."

I mumbled something.

"And I see you've met Glen's brother, Ed."

Ed, I took, was the name of the jokester who poured water on my face.

I nodded and tried to keep my lips firm to show neither pleasure nor the real feelings I was experiencing (though I admit that this was probably due to my rather rude awakening).

I sat down with the others who were about to have a "bite to eat." This group was an interesting one. We began with some berries that Tad and Cyndy had picked.

"You know that Margo would have gone with them," Judy said to me, "but she had a terrible headache." Judy was the best looking of the two women, having auburn hair and very fair skin (though no freckles). She seemed to be a very delicate person who was painfully shy and very nervous. As we talked she had her hands in her lap with her shoulders hunched forward. Her left hand was a fist and her right hand was cupped around the fist and was turning it and twisting it.

"Oh she's just a big baby, like her mother," was Samuel's reply. "These women are all the same, you know. They carry on as if they were about to fall apart at any minute. Why just look at Judy here," he put his arm around his wife and gave her a powerful hug with his left arm that appeared to take all the breath out of her. I could see that white skin turn even paler as I was suddenly concerned that he might break one of her bones or was causing her serious harm. But then he let her go and laughed boisterously as she gasped for breath. Everyone was looking at Judy and she was more uncomfortable about that than the physical jolt she had just received.

I looked at Samuel and wondered to myself what could make such a coward out of a man. He sat there with his massive chest and muscular arms, which almost seemed to be accented by his red hair and ruddy complexion. When he laughed it was a mammoth affair. His bellowing lungs could really produce a loud sound which made me want to walk away.

"Samuel, please," protested Judy, who wanted to be anywhere doing anything than where she was just at that moment.

"Sammy, you stop picking on Judy," said Martha with half-seriousness. "You're stronger than you realize." Samuel liked this. He laughed again.

"You women are all alike. You want to be protected by us, and then you turn around and want to be our equals."

"We don't want to be beaten up, Sammy. No one likes that."

"A man's got to learn to stick up for himself in this world. There are people everywhere trying to knock you around. But when they run into Samuel T. Johns, they learn another thing. I can take care of them."

"Sam's right, Judy," began bald headed Ed, the jokester, "there is only so far a man can be pushed. Why when I was in Germany with the 44th Fighter Squadron: the Vampires—"

"C'mon Ed, not another army story," put in Glen, his brother.

"Army! Them is fighting words, Glen. I'm an Air Force man and proud of it."

"Well, flyboy can the stories, we've heard them all five or six times," said Martha, backing up her husband. But Ed was determined to tell us his little story about a mission that they almost flew into East Germany.

" . . . And we came this close to World War 3," finished Ed, putting his fingers together about a centimeter apart.

"Thanks to you, Ed, the world is a better place to live." Glen put out his hand in a mocking way as if to shake his brother's hand for the mission that they almost flew.

"You can laugh, Glen, but while you were playing around in high school and college I was out on the frontiers of the world protecting your right to make an ass out of yourself." Ed was a little perturbed with his brother and was having a hard time controlling himself. I looked at him in another light. On the side of his left temple there was the outline of a large blood vessel which was now bulging from his face. I thought that we might come to blows, but then Martha asked me. "Do you two have any children?"

I looked at Anthea for an instant. It may only have been a fraction of a second, but that brief instant conveyed countless interchanges between us. I saw in her eyes first a question about what she should say and then whether she should tell them that we weren't married and finally some real interest in whether I did have any children. All this I thought I saw in her eye, but a moment later she replied, "No, we haven't been as fortunate at you."

"Well, they aren't always little angels, but I think we're pretty satisfied with them, aren't we honey?" As she delivered these words, she put her hands on the heads of her children who were sitting next to her.

"Yeah, I think we'll keep them," was his loving reply as he smiled at his two children of whom he was very proud.

At the other end of the table, Ed was still hot. He had finished his chicken before the rest of us and was now getting restless.

"Let's throw the football around, eh Sam?"

"Just a minute, Ed, I haven't finished my eats yet."

"No need to hurry. I'll get the football. That'll take at least two minutes."

"Samuel has to eat so quickly when he works that he needs some time to slow down some," said Judy in a quiet but firm voice. She looked a little hurt that her husband hadn't bragged about their child the way that the Millers just had. It was obvious that she doted on her Margo who was, in truth, a little slow compared to Tad and Cyndy. But that didn't make any difference to her. Margo belonged to her and that made all the difference.

"Yes, Ed, you let Sammy eat in peace," said Martha. She and Ed did not appear to be on the very best of terms to me. "He'll play football with you later."

"What about it, Sam?" asked Ed, ignoring Martha.

"I'll be with you when I can," he said almost apologetically. He seemed to appreciate his wife's looking after his interest (though he did not show this in word or deed), but he also seemed to feel that there was something wrong with eating at a normal pace. There were no exact behaviors that signaled this. It was just my reading of events (very suspicious behavior, indeed, for a philosopher of science who was wedded to physical data).

"You see I'm a salesman," he said, "and I've got to be on the go from morning to night." Samuel's words to me were in the form of some sort of explanation, but I could not figure out what it was that he wanted to explain.

"Samuel sells office files. It is a very competitive field so he never gets a chance to eat or sleep right except for his week vacation. That's why I want him to have it. A week's not very much really."

Judy spoke to me and looked me straight in the eye. It had been the first time she had done that since I was introduced to her. I was amazed that even after he had abused her so publically and embarrassed her that she was still so eager to put her husband in the best possible light.

Samuel ignored what his wife said and considered that he would be fully justified in eating slowly. After all, he was not hustling after clients today. And yet, even after all of that, he bolted his remaining food and was ready to "play ball" when Ed returned with the football. Ed showed great enthusiasm. He held the football in his right hand and made several pretend passing movements and then brought his left hand over and slapped the ball a couple times. Each slap elicited a cry, "Yeah, baby, yeah!"

"Why don't you come with us, Andy?" I hated the name Andy. It sounded so weak and informal. I very much preferred 'Andrew' with its formality and strength. "I don't play football."

"Oh, come on. We now have four men. We can have a little game."

"Why don't you ask someone else I'm sure that I would not be good enough to make the game interesting." I didn't know why they were pressing the matter. Couldn't they see that I was averse to their little suggestion?

"That's all right. Glen's no good either. You don't want to sit here like a woman, do you?" I was not sure how sitting at the table made me a female—nor why that was such a bad thing. But I was sure that there was some kind of vague, non-logical connection somewhere which I didn't care to have explained to me.

"I'm still eating," I said.

"That's okay, take all the time you want. We won't be able to start for at least five minutes. That's how long it takes to get my arm warmed up." Ed was trying to be very persuasive, but it was Anthea who got me to agree. "Why don't you go, Andrew? It would do you good to get some exercise."

I decided that I would throw the thing around with them and they would quickly see that a game with me would not be any fun.

"Office-mate. It's a rather new company," she added, seeing as I didn't show visual recognition of the name. "He used to be with a company in Minneapolis, but things didn't work out there so we moved down to Glenview." Glenview is a suburb of Chicago on the north shore. It is a rather exclusive area generally, but which (though many people don't know it) has its share of poverty and anguish.

"And your husband sells in Chicago?"

"He has all of Illinois as his territory. He has to do a lot of traveling, especially when he is servicing his clients down state."

Judy was now looking elsewhere. She did not want to talk about her husband any longer, or maybe it was that she simply felt great anxiety about discussing his employment. This could be because he really was not bringing in the bacon like she claimed he was or because he had given her strict rules about discussion his work with others.

"I imagine that must be hard on you and Margo." I wanted to give her an exit ramp if she chose to take it.

"Oh well, Margo is a good girl. She never complains. Sometimes—" Her voice became low and she leaned over to me. "—Sometimes, I think that Samuel has a hard time understanding Margo." She bit her lip and looked again into my eyes with a pleading look which I could not understand—but I could *feel*. It was some sort of hidden pain.

"Sometimes a mother is the only one who really knows her children." It was all she had to say. Obviously she was reaching out to me and confiding something, and I did not know just how to respond. However, I must have said something right because she smiled a knowing half smile and nodded her head. We were now the only ones at the table as Anthea had gotten up to help Martha with the dishes and Glen had gone over to the only tent on the camp site in order to change his clothes to play some football.

It wouldn't be long before they'd be calling me, but for this brief instant I would be able to observe this timid creature and listen to her weighty complaint.

"He wants Margo to be the best student in her class and become an accomplished piano player. And though I love Margo with all my heart, I know that it isn't in her to do it. She is an average student and does not have the dexterity to be more than middling at the piano. Why, I love it when she plays little popular songs on our old upright piano, but Samuel fumes when he hears them. 'Not serious enough,' he declares, 'I want that girl playing Mozart or List,' I don't know why he wants her to play those difficult pieces when she struggles through the popular songs. She loves the popular songs that the kids sing along with the radio. Besides, we never listen to that kind of music. Why should he expect Margo to? I've no more knowledge of that kind of music than that Beethoven's song, the one that goes da, da, da, daaaaaaa." I nodded.

She was whispering desperately, trying to get all of this out of her soul before I would be called away. But why had she picked me? Why not talk to Martha or Glen? They seemed like sympathetic people. Perhaps it was because they were her friends. Sometimes it is easier to talk to a stranger, especially one who you know you will never see again.

"He always says, 'Why doesn't she play Mozart or List?' But you know something? I don't think he's ever heard any of their songs, either. They were just the favorites of Benny McPherson, a friend of his in Minneapolis. Benny used to be an electrician at a concert hall in St. Paul, so he knew all about that stuff."

"Maybe he wants for Margo the things he never had," I put in. "It isn't an unusual reaction."

"Don't you think I want what's best for my Margo?" She raised her voice somewhat and pulled away. There was indignation in her tone.

"I didn't mean to imply—"

"But how is it good for Margo to constantly feel the pressure that she isn't good enough? Is that helping my daughter?"

"Certainly not," I said. I didn't mean to offend her, but had only been trying to offer to her an explanation for her husband's conduct. It was an explanation that she apparently didn't understand or one she didn't want to hear.

"Samuel was not scholar and I was never more than a 'C' student in school. Why should he expect his daughter to be any different? But still she tries, bless her little heart. She tries to please her father by working so hard that I have to tell her to stop at night and have some play so that she can sleep. You know it isn't good for a nine year old girl to work so much. I think it stunts their growth." She made her conclusions forcefully. No longer was she the timid Judy, but she was now the Judy who knew what she wanted and could express it with ease. She thought her daughter was working too hard and she wanted something done about it. Unfortunately, I was not the person to effect the change.

A new look came over her face as she sat there looking up in the sky. It was a peaceful look. Her visage changed and she looked radiant. "She so wants to please her father, bless her soul," she said about her little Margo. The discussion had brought a little color to her cheeks and this showed off her complexion to its full advantage. It was a picture that I will not soon forget. How my heart went out to this woman who was so tied to her husband's dominant character. She so wanted to be a good person and to do the right thing that she allowed herself to fall under the sway of his authority. Being a mother did not help matters any. She wanted to establish the best possible home for her Margo. But need that be with such an ogre as Samuel? Shouldn't people make the break when the situation warrants it? By devoting herself to her husband and child she was putting other people's happiness above her own. That was an admirable thing, but the vicious consequence was that it made her susceptible to being conquered and ruled by another. Once that happens a person is no longer able to make firm decisions and is easily led by that strong personality. A person in that situation becomes a slave.

This conclusion personally made me feel extremely uneasy. I could not think of this any longer. I felt like Judy and actually cupped one hand in the other and started to twist it even as she had done.

But then I was called over to play some football.

"Don't try to hide over there," said Ed who was very keyed up. "Here, let's see how you can catch," he said throwing the ball in my direction. I put out my hands to catch the ball, but it was thrown so hard that it bounced off my hands and onto the ground. It felt as if one of my fingers was bent back from trying to make the catch. The finger really hurt.

When I missed the pass Ed and Samuel really laughed loudly, "You catch like a woman," chided Samuel.

"C'mon fellas," said Glen, "you really burned that one in and you know it."

"I threw him a tough one, sure. I wanted to see what kind of stuff he had. Instead, it appears that I knocked the 'stuffing' out of him." Ed replied as Samuel laughed at his response.

"I never said I could play," I replied. "If you don't mind, I'll just watch you *men* play."

"Oh, don't let them get to you," said Glen walking over to me and putting his hand on my shoulder. "Look, I'm not much better than you are. You just have to ignore them."

And so I played and came to realize that my dislike of athletics was not the result of a childhood whim. However, I am not sure whether the game playing was distasteful because I hate football, or because of my dislike of the presence of Ed and Samuel. While we played I kept thinking about Samuel and how he must have treated Judy to make her the way she was. I speculated about whether he beat her or merely used psychological cruelty.

We played on the dirt road which connected the campground to the ranger station and the highway. We were probably three miles in or so and it was impossible to tell how far north the road extended. This charade lasted a couple of hours until Samuel hit his knee on a tree stump. He was cursing us all and blaming everyone except himself for his injury. The group broke up and I got Anthea to go back to our camp. We promised to return the next day for supper.

"That was an odd bunch," I said when we had gotten a ways away from the clearing.

"I liked Martha very much," responded Anthea.

"And how about Ed? Did you like him very much?"

"I didn't pay much attention to Ed. Do you like him?" Her sarcasm was not lost on me.

"Rather. He was really tip top."

We walked in silence for a while and I was learning the route back (as I had not been paying much attention when we had left). It was quite a ways. I hadn't realized that it was so far. We had to go through several fields and then through a very dense section of forest and then through a long section of new growth. Finally, we returned after what must have been over a mile.

"You know, Martha says that Ed's brother, Glen, is gay."

"Oh?" I replied. "So what?"

"Nothing. But Martha says that's why he sleeps in that tent by himself."

"Why, do they think it's *catching*?"

"No, of course not. Martha was just letting me know some of the back story behind the rest of the group." We walked another long stretch without talking.

"I didn't realize that it was so far," I said when we had gone about two thirds of the way back.

"You had your mind on other things this morning."

I smiled. Anthea had a different look to her. She was changed from the woman with whom I had been traveling. There was a quiet about her and I thought I sensed a real longing that she had for me.

"You seemed to be having quite a talk with Judy," she said, breaking my train of thought.

"Yes, she is a lonely woman."

"I don't like her."

"Why not?" I inquired.

"She lets herself be pushed around by her husband. I can't respect a woman who allows herself to be used in that way." Anthea was sincere in her point, but she was not as vehement as she had been in our last discussion. She was not acting defensively, but rather bitterly.

"I think that it all occurs because of her love for Samuel, though I agree with you that it is hard to understand what she sees in him."

"But that is not a reason at all," began Anthea, "If it were, then everyone who was in love would act like that."

"I'm not suggesting that it hast to be that way, but merely that it can. I think that because she is so sensitive and concerned about her husband that she loses some of her own aggressiveness."

"Fine," began Anthea, who stopped me and put both of her hands on my shoulder so that she could confront me head on. "But what I'm saying is that it is sick. No one should be so dependent upon another. People should lead their own lives and be their own people. This loyalty that you claim she feels is toxic because it has drained her of her individuality. She's a nothing and he's made her that way. But worst of all, she's allowed it to happen."

There was truth in Anthea's words. I didn't respond but merely thought about Barbara and me. Weren't Barbara and I really Samuel and Judy in reverse? But this thought was interrupted by Anthea who asked me, "What did you think when they asked us if we had any kids? I almost died."

"Yes, I was a little embarrassed myself."

"That's not what I mean. I almost split my sides laughing. They didn't even realize that we were campers in love and not married people."

I smiled at the disjunction which Anthea had constructed. Were these really mutually exclusive entities—lovers and married people?"

"I know that you gave me quite a look." I gave Anthea a little poke with my elbow.

"Me! What about you?"

"It was a mutual tête à tête, or rather yeux à yeux."

"What?"

"A conversation of the eyes."

Anthea didn't respond. I probably shouldn't have made such an obscure joke. Now she might
not talk until we returned to camp. But I was wrong, for we hadn't gone a hundred yards when she asked me, "Well what about it, do you have any children?"

This question coming out of the air took me by surprise. Certainly I had read such a direction in her eyes as we broached the subject.

First, she had brought it up as humor extraordinaire. Then there was the unsaid dialog and now it was the time for truth. I was happy that she asked me this question. I did not expect such a direct query, but this information request carried an uncharacteristic air of attachment to it. Why should Anthea care about whether I had any children unless she planned to use this information to alter her behavior? And what possible behavior modifications would be significant? What else except her continued attachment to me? She wanted to know whether I had any children because she wanted to form an internal exploratory session on whether to form a strong attachment to me, and because of this she wanted to know what might get in the way.

But couldn't this question be merely idle curiosity? In some people I'd say yes, but Anthea did not like to collect random bits of personal information about others. She had stayed so far away from my other life that it had been conspicuous. It was as if she didn't want to become involved. That was the key to Anthea's behavior: she didn't become involved. It was this that allowed her the freedom which she guarded so fiercely. By only dealing with me on one level, she was able to retain all her own power and capacity to do just exactly as she pleased. Multi-level involvement implied losing some of yourself in the other person which, in turn, meant that one was not entirely autonomous anymore. This was what she despised in Judy (and, by extension, probably also in me). Judy and I had lost large portions of ourselves, which had caused us to become pawns to another's will. It was this, more than anything else, that Anthea feared most.

I looked at her again. I had really become quite fond of Anthea. Her short hair was in need of washing and she was a little grimy from our hike, but there was a familiar feeling that I was already getting from gazing into her eyes. What was this feeling? I didn't bother to analyze it, but merely enjoyed the calm emendations which it conveyed.

"Why do you ask?" I responded. I don't know why I hadn't just told her. It would have been so simple, but my curiosity had gotten the better of me. Even before I had finished the words I sensed that she was closing up on me again. This young woman who had so fiercely resisted the onslaughts of other lovers was showing the faintest hint of weakness in her inviolable fortress. By asking the question that I did, I was making it appear that I didn't want to participate in her display of shared intimacy.

I took her and kissed her. "I'm sorry. It was a perfectly natural question. And the answer is that I don't have any." She pretended as if she didn't care a straw about my reply. She wanted to return to the Anthea of old—Anthea the Bold, but though she probably didn't realize it, at that moment, her projected retreat was doomed to failure. I could see that her feigned indifference to my reply did, nevertheless, strike a chord within her. What this chord was and how exactly it was affecting her I could not be sure. But I did notice the effect.

We returned to our camp and even though she didn't talk to me I felt that she was mulling over what had happened between us in her mind. I thought about it too. I recalled how Barbara and I had wanted children. At least Barbara had wanted children; I wasn't quite so sure. I had grown up as most people in the baby-boom generation, thinking that having children was the most natural thing.

All of this was rather jarring. You know the British call the fetus the "little stranger". This is because one gets used to a routine. Routines are what make life bearable. Just ask Aristotle or Thomas Aquinas.

"Don't I get a say in all of this?"

"You already have," she replied. I thought that it was interesting that she could make such a major announcement without breaking her normal rhythm of meal preparation and enjoyment. She had moved at her normal pace as she opened the package of hotdogs and tossed four wieners into the boiling water and emptied the can of Boston baked beans into the companion pan. No one ever accused Barbara of being a gormandizer.

"Before we got married, I asked you if you wanted children, and I distinctly remember you saying, 'sure, one day.'" The fateful words had been uttered. I owned up to them and so there was nothing really to do. I had made an agreement and there was no backing out of it now. But the whole idea of having children once you've been married awhile is not an easy one for the father (at least it wasn't easy for me). I had had plans of returning to Europe when I could, and we would have enough money to go all of next summer, and if I could get a sabbatical term from teaching we could have six months. But this would all have to be thrown out the window now. A baby was big money. A baby would tie us down so that we could no longer travel. Paying for two is bad enough when you are on the road, but with my salary, paying for three would not be possible.

You might say that I was not thoroughly excited at the prospect of beginning a family, but I went along with Barbara and we tried during September and October with no results.

"I think we should go see a doctor and see why we cannot have children," said Barbara after we found out that our October try was unsuccessful.

"It has only been two months," I said. "Don't you think we should give it another few months?"

But Barbara was adamant so we went to a doctor who told us that there was nothing wrong with either of us. He said that we were just being too impatient. "You have to relax if you want to get pregnant. It isn't something that tension and anxiety will help."

So Barbara interpreted this as the doctor saying that I was too tense. She tried everything to make me relax. We explored various ways for me to relax. I tried yoga from a book she bought second-hand at Reynolds Club. We also tried to create "quiet spaces" in our condominium where I was supposed to sit, but not to read. You see, reading is my work. By that measure whenever I am reading, I'm really working! I didn't buy it. But Barbara had her hypothesis. To counter this would mean that I was backing out of my promise to have children.

Six months went by and still nothing happened. Now Barbara openly talked of me as being infertile even though the sperm count taken at the doctor's office showed that to be an untrue statement.

At the beginning, Barbara had purchased some baby clothes so that "everything wouldn't have to come all at once." But now there was none of that. Our sex life, which had been more active than it had been in three years, began to taper off again to its normal inactive level.

Then one day after another eight months had passed, Barbara announced at the dinner table, "I'm pregnant."

And so she was. It must have happened by accident (I'm sure that she was not seeing other men at this time, so I was the father). We hadn't thought about children for some time. Barbara was ecstatic and I must admit that I was carried into the enthusiasm. We went out and bought a bottle of champagne. Then Barbara came home with several boxes of stationery which she intended to use for the purpose of informing all of her friends and relatives of the news. By now I had returned to my rather neutral feelings about the matter and decided to just leave it all up to her. If it was going to be, I had better get used to the fact. Barbara made so many plans in those days. She decided that my study would become the nursery. After all, I could always work in the library. I didn't relish that, but then it was common sense that a baby needed space, time, and attention. It was all very logical. And above all else, I maintained a commitment to logic.

Sometimes I felt very guilty about my ambivalent feelings. Babies are supposed to bring such happy times. Why did I feel so uncertain about it all? Was there something wrong with me that I didn't jump up and down like the proverbial expectant father? One hears so many stories about how protective and close couples grow during pregnancy, but that first month I felt none of these feelings. All that I felt was extremely introspective about what a change this event was about to bring into my life.

I would spend hours trying to convince myself that this was the greatest thing that ever happened to me, but then just when I felt that I had done the trick, some new reflection would bring all of this tumbling down again. I felt morose both because of what the baby would mean in terms of sacrifice (I never thought of getting anything in return) and because I was depressed about what should be one of the happiest events in a man's life. (Next to getting married it was supposed to be the happiest part of life, but with that as its comparison, you can see why I was not doing handstands.) Why was I feeling this way? Wasn't it wrong? Wasn't I being immoral or at least dumb? The guilt I felt about all of this, compounded with my natural feelings which I could not discuss with Barbara, made me want to spend increasingly more and more time away from home. I began writing papers like I had never written before. I spent hours on research on Saturday and Sunday in the library. I would walk around and around the card catalog. It was an exercise in and of itself. I'd get my books in the stacks and then read or skim as the material directed. I took reams of notes and was beginning to develop my own position. No longer was I simply writing articles about where others had messed up. I was now saying something positive about theoretical biology and the direction of cutting edge research. I felt driven to work, for at least when I worked I could live with myself.

Then it happened. Barbara had only been pregnant for three months when she miscarried. It happened in bed. She got terrible cramps, which must have been contractions. Barbara yelled my name. I could tell something was wrong, so I led Barbara into the car and drove her two blocks to the hospital.

We went to emergency. They put her onto a gurney. I parked the car and made my way to the designated lounge. It must have been a couple of hours when the doctor came in and told me the bitter truth: Barbara had miscarried. I went to Barbara and held her as we both wept from the depths of our beings.

*   *   *

We never became pregnant again. We tried three years later, but the effort was not the same. Something had gone out of Barbara that night which would never return. She reacted in a myriad of ways to the event. Sometimes she would claim that it was a cosmic sign against our marriage. At other times she would claim that it was my fault for not being more supportive. At other times she might just sit down and cry.

The loss of that child changed our relationship. I almost think that it was at that point that we gradually began moving apart. Somehow the plan which Barbara had laid out for herself was not working out, so she decided to change her plan. She began working more hours and angling for a management position. I had a suspicion that she would be excellent in management. She had been managing me all our married life.

After a brief interval, she made her way to sales manager. With that she had more salary, her same client commissions, and an override on the commissions of those under her—she made money on *their sales!* Since we owned our condominium free and clear (because of my father's legacy) and we had no auto loan, all that money went straight into her bank account. In a short time she was making 3.5 times what I was. But this didn't satisfy Barbara. She wanted us to pay for everything separately out of our private accounts. This meant that I would buy myself macaroni and cheese and she would eat out at a restaurant in the Loop after work.

We began acquiring our own friends and doing many things without the other. This occurred over a period of time; until perhaps six months ago. Then she began being sweet again, and I thought that she was finally ready to make a try again. What had most likely happened is that she had started her affair.

Well, Barbara got over the miscarriage in the sense that she ceased talking about it. That happened very quickly. But other things came up. She acquired a phobia about traveling. Barbara didn't want to leave the Chicago area. It was lucky for her that Chicago was a hub in her company and she didn't have to travel to New York—as many do in her line of work. This was especially hard on me, one who likes to travel. I wanted to help her overcome this, but she refused any of my help or any professional counseling. Instead, she dug in and launched assault after assault against me in numerous ways: all very subtle and all designed to tell me that she had contempt for my very being. All this harassment began to change six months ago, but as I was to find out, it wasn't because of a renewed interest in me.

* * *

The evening was rather unusual for us. Anthea began telling me stories about her childhood. I listened, eagerly conscious of the fact that she was doing something contrary to her basic instincts. She was a person who liked to ask questions of others and collect this information to use or not to use as she saw fit. She did not like to give any but the most general answers to questions about herself. Tonight I was not questioning her, but she was revealing secrets about herself which I doubt she had ever revealed to anyone before.

The woods did strange things to me. I felt a deep inner relaxation to the very depths of my being. There was rarely much to do except be with yourself so that one couldn't hide behind piles of paper to grade or essays to write. All that one had was the ever present environment and one's natural needs. I felt close to Anthea and yet at the same time there were great periods of time when I was totally by myself. For example, after Anthea and I finished our long dinner and conversation, I took the pots and plates to the lake to wash them. While I was there, I stopped and became enraptured by the water and the ripples playing on its surface in the moonlight. The coolness of the June air would have normally made me shiver or at least tense my entire body, but now I consciously relaxed and tried to let everything in. I found that my interest in leaves and plants was also being renewed. It was not Central Park or Prospect Park, but it was even more special. The years hadn't taken all that much away (except the proper names for many of the specimens). But even though I didn't remember all the names, I recognized numerous leaves and stem patterns almost as old friends. This made the setting seem ever so familiar to me—one who had never been camping before in my life.

When I returned to Anthea I found her burning something. It had an awful smell. Then it suddenly hit me that it must be marijuana. Her face was intense and concentrated. It was an expression that I had witnessed more and more lately.

"What are you doing?" I asked.

"What does it look like?" was her response. She didn't look up.

"It looks like you are destroying some marijuana."

"Good guess." She looked up and gave me a sarcastic grin.

"That must be worth quite a lot of money." I didn't know how to take what she was doing. Why was she burning this stuff?

"Yes, about two hundred dollars' worth."

"Two hundred dollars for that?" I never knew that marijuana could be that expensive. No wonder the drug lords drove Cadillacs.

"The stuff is valuable." Then she looked up at me. "You know, when we stopped in Eau Claire I had about twice as much as this, but I sold a bunch for ready cash."

"You sold drugs?" I must admit that I was taken aback. It was one thing to possess it for personal use and another thing to sell to others.

"Don't be so surprised. Most people who smoke dope also deal at one time or another. And don't get me wrong, I'm not saying that there is anything harmful in it either. I wouldn't have ever done it if I thought so. I believe this stuff to be a harmless herb."

"Then why are you destroying it?" I half expected her to say that she was getting rid of it because I disapproved of it. But this would be so out of character for Anthea that I could not really buy it myself.

She did not answer at first but set herself to finishing the work she had begun. She wanted every last trace of the dried leaves eradicated. When it was finished she looked at me. "Let's go to bed."

I took this to be a signal that she didn't want to talk about it anymore so I simply followed her into the tent. We got into bed, but before I could kiss her she put her finger to my lips as if to stay me. "I didn't do it for you either." The fire outside was flickering and I could barely see the shadowed relief of her visage. "I did it for myself. I did it because I had to do it."

She didn't say another word.

Chapter Nine

THE NEXT DAY was the best day of our trip. We got up leisurely and took our time about preparing something to eat. Then we took a long hike. We went along the water and stopped for a long swim. It was a warm day and the water was a few degrees warmer than it had been two days before.

Nothing much happened during the day time. We took a nap. I vainly attempted to skip some stones. In the late afternoon we went to the Millers & Co. for dinner. Ed was more restrained than usual (perhaps Martha had said something to him). Anthea had a very good time and so we made plans to bring some food for the next night's dinner. It was supposed to be a big affair since it would be the last full day that they would be camping there. I had no trouble finding our way back to camp this time as the general lay of things was beginning to be impressed upon my mind.

* * *

The next day was spent leisurely again, though I could tell that Anthea was thinking about her new friend, Martha. This was their last day and she would be sad to see Martha go.

"I have not met a woman I liked so much since I was in grammar school," Anthea said. "I usually like men more than women, but Martha is so different. She is someone who isn't at the extremes. She's not the moral pillar of the community nor is she a bitch. She's my kind of woman."

"Well, she certainly has a lot to live with having Ed around."

"That's just the point. Martha is so sure of herself that she doesn't have to bother with the likes of Ed. She can let him do whatever foolish things he will do and go about her affairs just the same."

"That's quite a feat," I replied.

"And she does it with ease. "

"There is nothing easy about Ed. His brother, Glen is much more to my taste." Anthea was not interested in talking about the men. She was taken with Martha.

"She is not ruled by men. They are not overly important to her. She just is herself and says to hell with the rest of the world." Anthea's eyes were full. I'm sure that she was reading into her new found acquaintance all the things that she, Anthea, found admirable. Who was I to start an argument? I was in no mood for an argument (even if I had one); the calm of the woods had exorcised me of my irascibility.

"I hope that she doesn't send me to hell with the rest of the world. I don't think that I'd find it quite to my liking," I said.

Anthea turned at this comment, looked at me a moment and then smiled, "You goon. You know that I like you very very much?"

"I should hope so," was my reply which led to a kiss and a playful hug. There wasn't time for more since we had a hike ahead of us for dinner.

"I could find their camp blindfolded," I contended as we trudged with our food over to their location. "I just don't know why they didn't move closer. This walk is getting boring."

"They couldn't move any closer. They are tied to the road, remember?"

"Yes, yes and we wouldn't want to move away from our lake, but isn't there something you can do about this walk?"

"Do you want me to carry you?"

"Oh yes, please do," I replied lightly.

It wasn't long before we were fully amidst the group once again. Ed had been hitting the bottle and so was a little tight. "Here is Anny and her little Andy pandy," he tried to give Anthea a pat on the butt but she avoided him and he got me instead.

"Watch it, Ed," said Glen. "This is our last full day. We don't want any fuss."

"Who's making a fuss? What am I anyway? I'm just your older brother who helped put you through college so that you could become a hot shot engineer."

"Let's not go through that again, okay?"

Ed walked over to his brother who was standing in front of their trailer. I wasn't sure how angry Ed really was. With a person like Ed it is always hard to tell for sure.

"That's easy for you to say. You didn't give up Holly Hoffmann just because you had to go into the Armed Forces. You didn't give up a life of eternal happiness that that little woman would have brought me just so you could put your lousy kid brother through school." Ed delivered these words as he moved over to Glen. Ed accented his points with his index finger, which was jabbed in the air in the direction of Glen's sternum. And yet Glen took all of it. After his brother's little speech was finished, he merely said, "C'mon Ed. Why don't you have some coffee? You've had too much to drink."

"Too much to drink? Why I can out drink any of you. Why when I was in the Air Force you should have seen the drinking contests we used to have. There was one time when I was stationed in Germany that I went through a full bottle of some local hard stuff. And I mean it was hard. Damn, we were something." Ed seemed to have lost his aggressiveness for the moment and Glen managed to slide out of the predicament.

I stepped over to help Anthea, but Anthea and Martha were already deep in a conversation. " — You see he has nothing to do anymore. He can't get a commercial license because of that and he doesn't like to do anything except fly."

"He was really giving Glen a hard time," put in Anthea as the two were preparing some of the dishes we were to eat that night.

"It's all a lot of bull and sibling rivalry. That girl who he claims he wanted to marry was a run-around. She didn't want to marry Ed.

She just wanted to sleep with everyone. You know she was a free spirit. Do you think she'd ever allow Ed to try and brand her?"

"I know what you mean. Men can be the pits."

"You know what they say, Anthea: 'can't live *with* 'em, and can't live *without* 'em'."

Then Tad came running up and was very angry.

"Mrs. Johns is cheating so that Margo can win." Tad was bouncing up and down.

"Now Tad, what's the matter?"

"Mrs. Johns is helping her daughter. That's not fair!" Martha put her hands on Tad's shoulders and stopped him from hopping up and down. Then she stroked his back and smiled at him.

"Go on back and play, Tad. Margo doesn't win many games, surely you can let her win this one."

Tad looked at his mother in surprise for a moment and then looked down as if he were ashamed. He had a general idea of what his mother meant and it was beginning to sink in. Then he smiled, turned around, and went back to the others.

I watched Tad return to his group. Glen came over and sat next to me at the picnic table. "Looking for something to do?" he inquired.

I nodded, even though I was thoroughly amused at catching bits and pieces of Anthea's and Martha's conversation.

"Why don't you come out with me and get some firewood for the bonfire tonight."

Since the Millers and Johns had trailers, they had no need for making cooking fires. Inside each unit was a complete stove and oven. It was sort of having every modern convenience transplanted to the wilds. There was something about that which had rubbed me the wrong way. I much preferred Glen's idea of sleeping in a tent (but then that is what Anthea had chosen for us so I was a bit biased). I nodded. "Let's go!"

*   *   *

Samuel was taking a nap, but wanted to be awoken for a final game of football to be played before it got dark. I was not really in the mood and so relished the opportunity to get out of camp for as long as I could. But soon all of this was over and we were all around the pull-out table that folded down from the back of Ed's camper. All of us were squeezed in to an area designed for eight while there were ten of us. The children were very tired, but instead of nodding off as you or I might have done in such a circumstance, they used their fatigue as an occasion for pulling all sorts of horseplay which they normally wouldn't do. Cyndy would pull Margo's hair and Margo would think that Tad did it and so punch him in the kidney. Then all would be scolded by their parents and things would quiet down again for a time until Tad, who thought that he had gotten the worst of it and could not forget it, took one of his peas and put it in his spoon and used this device as a catapult for propelling said pea into Margo's left eye. This occasioned a shriek from Margo, who was a very nervous girl and hated to be startled. Then there was a shriek from Judy who began furiously rubbing her hands together. Samuel had his solution. He reached over and slapped Tad across the face.

Now Glen was sitting some distance away, but he arose and told Tad and Cyndy to go into their trailer for a time out. Margo also got up as if to go to her trailer, but Samuel told her to stay. Poor Margo knew that the children were being sent away for a reason, but she was now not sure what to do.

"Go on in," prompted Judy to her daughter.

"I tell you, stay here," roared Samuel as he slammed his mug of beer down on the table, making the flimsy structure tremble considerably and spilling a portion of his beverage.

Margo looked from one parent to the other. Then she began to cry. Now Margo was a child who didn't just quietly sniffle, but she really bawled out her complaint to the world. Judy couldn't stand the noise and so got up herself and took her child forcibly into the trailer.

"Bring that child back here this instant!" commanded Samuel, but Judy, who obeyed in all things, was too shaken from all the commotion to be in any kind of control of herself. She had to follow her instinct which said to get away.

Samuel was almost beside himself because he was disobeyed. He started after her

But he was checked by Ed's hand. Ed had moved around from the far corner of the other table so that he could block Samuel's progress.

"Don't you ever hit my boy again. I'll discipline my own children."

Samuel didn't answer for he was too busy trying to get to his disobedient wife. But Ed successfully interposed himself. "Do you understand, Sam?"

"Yeah, yeah," replied Samuel. It was as much of an admission as Ed was likely to get, and he knew it. So with that he let Samuel go. Samuel went to his trailer. We could hear him yelling at Judy and also the sound of items being thrown around.

"Is he hitting her?" asked Anthea in alarm.

"He hits her sometimes, I think, but what can we do? We have no proof. And Judy is certainly not the kind of person to say anything." Glen seemed apologetic at this admission. Martha held her head down almost in shame at their impotence to act. We heard a groan and I decided that if I heard one more sound that I was going to go into the trailer myself. But we heard nothing more. Neither Samuel nor Judy re-emerged from their camper. We all felt very uncomfortable. It was finally Ed, who had been quiet through all of this, who broke the silence with a political comment on school desegregation in Chicago. "You know the world's upside down when those *darkies* are calling all the shots."

"Don't give our guests the wrong opinion, Ed," began Martha as she put her hand on his arm and gave him soft pats. "They'll think you're a bigot."

"You don't have to be a bigot to be against this bussing stuff." Ed inhaled deeply so that his chest puffed up.

"But you don't have anything against integration," said Martha.

"Of course not. In the Air Force we had lots of Negros. I even used to chow with one or two of them sometimes." Ed started cleaning the dirt from under his fingernails with the thumbnail of his opposite hand. Then he said, "I'm not against it, by itself, it's only when it's forced that I'm against it." Ed talked in a conversational tone.

This was clearly not the kind of discussion that appeared to get him mad, or perhaps he sensed that one outburst of anger an hour was the group's quota and that we had fifty minutes to go.

"But Ed, that's the only way we'll get desegregation. If we depend upon the natural integration of the neighborhoods it will take forever." Martha was a little more adamant about this topic than Ed was. She had the ring of idealistic fervor in her voice and manner. I watched Anthea look on admiringly.

"So what? What is the harm in going to an all-black school? Especially now that they are spending more per student than they are spending in the white schools." The alcohol must have been wearing off, or perhaps Ed was getting a second wind because he was extremely lucid in his speech and was no longer slurring words as he had been only hours before. Martha shook her head as if she were talking with a child who simply did not understand the basic truths she was uttering, "Ed, it's people like you who set social progress back fifty years." Anthea and Glen smiled, though I thought that I could detect some preoccupation on Glen's part. Perhaps he was still thinking about Judy and Samuel and what had happened to his nephew. Glen seemed to be only a partial listener. "You see, Ed, we live in a pluralistic society, one which has many races and ethnic backgrounds. Now if blacks only go to school with blacks they are not getting the advantage of contact with other groups in society, and their education will automatically be inferior." Martha was in form. Clearly, from Ed's demeanor, this was role playing that was not novel.

I was a little unclear on what she had said. I had vowed to stay out of the conversation. But I could not help asking one clarifying question, "You mean that for a person to go to school with people of only their same race (like blacks in the South and West sides of Chicago) that they are doomed to an inferior education."

"That's right," said Martha, a little surprised at my intervention, but happy to have someone inquire after her position.

"I think my sister-in-law would go even farther," said Glen, feeling himself drawn into the conversation more and more, though still (I felt) with part of him worrying about what had just happened. "It is wrong for our society to let a group of children go to schools like that with only one group represented—especially when the two groups have such disparate economic and social opportunities."

Martha nodded her approval of this sentiment.

"But is bussing the answer?" asked Ed. "When they move into the neighborhoods, then let them come to the schools."

"You haven't heard a word I said," responded Martha in despair.

"But I have another question, if I may," I added once more. "If it is immoral to send one's children to segregated schools—that is schools of only one racial type—aren't the parents in the suburbs being immoral? They send their children to such schools. And hasn't the so-called suburban flight by whites been a way of trying to distance themselves from the problem? If there were equal housing opportunity, then we wouldn't have a problem." I knew that this was a dangerous approach because the two families and Glen all lived in the suburbs.

"And by your own argument the children are getting inferior educations and the parents are immoral for letting it happen," added Ed quickly. He thoroughly enjoyed the new dimension to the argument. But Martha and Glen didn't.

Anthea shot an angry look at me. It was as if I had gone over to the enemy. I had not, but I was puzzled at two people living in the suburbs making speeches about how Chicago should integrate its schools. If they were really for integration, it seemed to me that they should move into an integrated neighborhood like Hyde Park or Rodgers Park and send their own children to such schools.

"I said a variety of ethnic and social groups. This doesn't require all multi-racial schools," said Martha. "After all, there are only so many blacks to go around! Besides there aren't any blacks living in Glenview (or at most only a few). If there were, they'd be welcome to come to our schools."

"Why not bus them in from the south side of Chicago?" asked Ed, now eager at the prospect of having Martha on the defensive.

"Come on Ed," put in Glen, "that would be impractical and too costly. It would mean a two hour bus trip."

"If you bussed them from the North and the Northwest side it would only be thirty to forty minutes. Some of the proposed bus routes for the city integration already take an hour. You'd save twenty minutes bussing to the suburbs."

"You don't mean that, Ed, and you know it," said Martha.

"Okay, but I'm just trying to show that bussing is silly."

"Perhaps it's better to say that bussing across school districts is impractical and wouldn't accomplish much. We're still for intra-district bussing, but bussing to the suburbs would cause too many problems," put Martha.

And that was that. We talked over their plans for tomorrow and then the dishes were cleared and washed while Glen and I made the campfire. I was an expert now (thanks to Anthea) and in very little time we had a blazing fire. As we gathered around the fire, Samuel and Judy came out of their camper. I strained my eyes to see whether Judy had any marks on her face which might indicate that she had been beaten. But there were none.

The conversation around the warm comfortable blaze turned to discussion of old movies. Ed went into his camper to look for some whiskey he was saving. When he stepped from his trailer he turned his head.

"Hear that?"

"Sounds like some motorcycles," said Anthea.

Suddenly a shiver of fear swept over me. I could sense it in the others as well. It was partially the disruption of our false sense of isolation which we had enjoyed. With no other campers in the area it had seemed to us that we were a community unto ourselves. We were far away from the ordinary crowd: we had found a place to privately rest. I remember an analogous feeling that I had upon being discovered by Margo, Tad and Cyndy. They brought a similar sense that nothing was really private. People were everywhere.

But there was something different about motorcycles. They were so loud and threatening. All of us hoped that they would not come down the road as far as the campers. That was the real drawback to this easy variety of spending time in the woods. If they had packed it in as we had done they would not be faced with the same problem. No one could find us in a motorized vehicle unless it was a boat. And even then we were far enough inland that it would be difficult for someone to come and invade our privacy.

"Bunch of punks," said Samuel. "Probably blowing off steam."

"Do you think they're high school kids?" asked Martha in a thin, shaky voice.

"Who knows," replied Samuel, "but they better not have their loud radios along with them. I left the city to get away from the noise of teenage music."

But the engine noise was getting closer. No one did anything; we just all sat and watched and waited. The road through the woods must have been a winding one for the noise sometimes seemed to move to one side and then to the other. Soon we saw the bobbing glow of the headlights from the cycles through the trees. We had been silent when Glen said, "It looks like a group of them."

"You don't suppose they like riding alone, do you?" asked Samuel in a sharp tone. It was clear that he was edgy just like the rest of us. Judy was grabbing her own arm. Her shoulders were shaking. Martha was a statue staring at the lights coming through the trees while Glen was reaching for a stick to hold. Ed went for something in his trailer which he brought out to Glen's tent. I sat there in a state of disbelief. Here was Samuel trying to sound authoritative while others like Anthea were eying an escape route. And what if it were just some harmless group of people out for an evening drive with their motor bikes? How foolish we all would look: a bunch of suspicious cowards. That's what we were at that moment. I tried to convince myself that there was no more to it than that. But inductive logic said I didn't have adequate evidence.

But then we could see them: three, four, six—there were six bikes. The riders didn't look all that menacing. They were dressed much as any college kid dresses these days: jeans, wife beaters, and bandanas. I clung to my hope that these six fellows were harmless young people out for an evening ride. Two things struck me: no one wore helmets (though two wore said bandanas) and the lead driver (who was older than the cohort) had a swastika tattoo on his right arm at the bicep.

"Hey, Sail, looksee here, a campfire!" said one of the bikers as they all stopped at the head of the clearing.

Ed poked his head out of Glen's tent for an instant and then pulled it back inside. The others in the group laughed at this rather astute observation. "Hey Pigman, doesn't that fire there turn you on?" queried the one called Sail (short for Salvador?). The one called Pigman nodded and grinned at Sail (the lead driver) as he pulled up near to the fire and dismounted.

Glen got up holding his stick and slapping it against the open palm of his hand, "What do you boys want?"

Glen's voice was firm and it stopped the laughter among the people on the motorcycles.

"What do we want?" repeated Sail to Glen's question.

But he did not reply, instead speeding up his cycle in the direction of Glen. The bike was coming right at him. Would the bike veer at the last second or would Glen jump out of the way? It was a battle of nerves between the two of them. Somehow I felt that there was more at stake than merely a game of chicken between the two. The cycle sped nearer—ten feet, five feet, at the same rate of acceleration. Then Glen jumped out of the way. If he hadn't, Sail's bike would have hit him. There was no doubt about that; he couldn't have stopped his cycle in time. After he buzzed past, he turned his cycle 360 with his stiff left leg as the fulcrum and sent a spray of dirt up in the air at all of us. We quickly moved out of the way. Anthea decided to make a break for it. But one of the boys on the motorcycles went after her and caught her within a couple of seconds.

"That-a-boy, Marco," said Pigman. Marco was one of the younger riders. He had bushy curly hair which came away from his head as a white afro. He appeared to be Italian-American. The others were too far away to tell, but there were no riders who appeared to be over thirty-five (except maybe Sail, who was probably in his forties) and none under eighteen. Between this span was a wide range: Sail was the oldest and was spinning around and coming back at Glen who had fallen to the ground. Glen rolled out of the way and Sail turned around and came at him again. This time he hit Glen's shoulder as he passed.

I could hear the dull thud even over the roar of the machine. Glen grabbed his shoulder in pain. Sail got off of his bike in an instant, turning off the motor and raising the bike on its natural stand. He ran at Glen and took the arm which was injured and pulled it up while sticking his foot in Glen's chest. This had the effect of stretching the injured arm past its limits. Glen screamed out in pain.

Marco was dragging back Anthea, who was kicking and scratching and cursing her head off. The others, still on their bikes, were cheering on Sail and Marco.

"Listen *big boy,* you aren't too hospitable is you?" Sail pulled Glen's arm again and Glen screamed out. "Now we can be nice or we can be fuckin' bastards, and frankly I don't give a shit what we do. Get it?" Glen moaned. This was all Sail wanted and he threw Glen over, kicking him in the kidneys as he did so. This caused another spasm of pain in Glen. I wondered whether any internal organs were damaged. I tried to think what I could do, when Ed emerged from his brother's tent with a rifle. He didn't give any warning, but simply stood tall and fired off a shot at Sail. The leader hit the ground and blood began to pour onto the dirt around him. Marco let out a shriek and threw Anthea onto the ground. She hit the earth, senseless, laying there without moving.

Ed turned to the rest of the cyclists and fired one more shot at one of them when a return volley glanced Ed in the face. He fell backwards to the ground, wounded, but not seriously hurt, it appeared. The other cyclists jumped off their bikes and rushed over. Marco got to Ed in an instant and began beating him with his fist.

"Stop it," I cried. "Can't you see the man is hurt?" But they ignored me. Martha was bent over Glen but now ran to defend her husband. She was intercepted by another cyclist who grabbed her and slapped her in the face. This froze Martha who most likely had never been hit in the face in her life.

One of the men said, "Get them Billy," and "Take care of him, Grunt." Grunt came over to me and Billy went to Samuel and Judy.

We got up at their rude request and they pulled us over to the fire. Marco was still hitting Ed in the face. I was sure that Ed was dead by now.

Then frightened little Margo ran from her trailer.

"Mommy, what's all the noise?" was her question in her small high voice. Judy let out a scream. "Go back in the trailer, Margo," shouted Samuel. But Margo knew that something was wrong. She wanted to stay outside and see what was happening. I looked at the other trailer and thought I saw a curtain moving, indicating that Tad and Cyndy were watching the proceedings also, but from a safer perspective.

"Take care of the girl, Kid, and check the other campers for any more wise guys with guns." The Kid was by no means the youngest of the gang (I thought that Marco fit that role with Billy coming next), but he was the least involved in what was going on. It was as if he was miscast into the role he was required to play. He lifted up Margo and carried her to her trailer. "What have you done with Mommy and Daddy? What is all the noise about?" The Kid didn't answer, but merely carried her to her camper and then went inside. In a few minutes he went inside the other trailer. There was some shouting, but I took it that the Kid was merely tying the children up.

Meanwhile, the Pigman got Marco to stop punching Ed, or what was left of Ed, and they followed Billy over to their fallen Sail who was lying, badly wounded in the stomach, on the ground. Sail was having a difficult time breathing, but with every gasp he was cursing all of us and the entire universe for putting him into this situation. The five of us, Glen (who had been dragged over), Martha, Samuel, Judy and I were sitting with our backs to the fire. Sail was lying five or six feet in front of us. We were facing the trailers. Behind us fifty feet or so lay Anthea, still motionless on the ground. I wanted to go to her, but then I also was looking for an opening in their modus operandi which would allow me to make my move. I was also studying their faces and relative heights so that I could identify them later in a police station (if I lived that long). Sail was the tallest at maybe six foot, two inches with Pigman just an inch shorter.

Marco was the shortest at about five foot five or so. The Kid was around five foot ten. They all had tattoos, but only Sail (with the swastika) and Marco (with the Stars and Bars dripping blood) had violent tattoos.

Glen was starting to come around now, though he was obviously in tremendous pain. He could barely move. I thought that they might have injured his back when they dragged him over to us. That kick by Sail hadn't helped matters any either. The Kid came back from the trailers and four of them huddled over their fallen leader. Grunt pointed a hand gun at us. They clearly didn't know what they wanted to do. Sail appeared to be going fast. They were split between trying to get help for Sail and taking care of us. Marco and Pigman seemed most intent on staying and having some sadistic thrills while the Kid wanted the group to leave with Sail. It was decided that the Kid would take Sail on a bike to a hospital. However, Sail was in pretty bad shape to be riding on a bike. It was decided that they would load Sail into a camper and drive him to a doctor they knew. While they busied themselves, Grunt, the one with the gun, was watching us and waving his weapon as if he might shoot the rest of us.

"Can I look at Ed over there?" I asked Grunt.

"Go ahead. He ain't going to be doing any more talkin'."

I moved over to Ed and saw that he was indeed dead. As I was doing this I wanted to check Anthea, but did not want to draw attention to her, hoping that when she came to she might be able to make a break for it again. And so after looking Ed over I walked back to the others.

They had gotten Sail into the Johns' camper (after depositing Margo in the Miller's). The camper pulled out with the Kid driving. The image of Sail being carried away was graphic. Here was the leader, a man dressed in the style of a young thug—even though he was probably in his forties (or more).

That left four of them: Grunt (with the handgun), Billy (who seemed overwhelmed), and Pigman and Marco who were itching for more. I gave Sail little chance to live even if we had been close to a hospital. I should have been glad at the justice of the situation, but I was only sickened by it. I felt no happiness that Sail was being carried away. There was no time for any reflection, only nausea at the entire spectacle that was Sail.

Now they were coming for *us*. Pigman seemed to be the next in authority. He ordered Billy to get Anthea, who it seems had been just lying there feigning unconsciousness and waiting for another chance to make a break. So we were together there, all six of us. Glen was half sitting up. I had advised him not to exert himself in case he had a back injury. But Glen was outraged and was desperately trying to move his body around in case he might get another chance at these animals.

"Well, Marco," began Pigman when they had gathered us all together again. "What do you think we should do with these pricks?" Marco only laughed and then made some peculiar animal sounds.

"That's what I think too, how 'bout you, Grunt?"

Grunt merely blew his nose into his hand and flung the mucus away with a flick of his arm so that it landed on Samuel. Samuel hadn't said much, but then neither had I. I supposed that he was waiting for his opening to make a move. If we did it in concert we might be able to overpower the one with the gun and so gain control of this group.

Samuel wiped the mucus off his shoulder with a look of disgust which made Grunt laugh. Judy was huddled next to her husband, gripping his arm with all her might.

"Do you want to start with the pretty one?" asked Billy. "Why not?" said Pigman. "Or we could do them all at once," suggested Grunt. They wanted to rape the women. "I like the one with the black hair," said Pigman, pointing to Martha.

Martha seemed to be in a daze ever since she had been slapped. It was all too unbelievable for the suburban woman from Glenview. They seemed to enjoy her terror; it excited them. Pigman reached for Martha. Glen tried to make a move to stop them but he was in too much pain and weakly fell down in the effort. All that he could do was stare up from the ground.

"You impotent bastards," said Anthea. Her words weren't unnoticed. Grunt went over to her. Even the Pigman stopped what he was doing.

"What did you call me?" asked Grunt.

"I called you all impotent bastards. You couldn't get it up if your life depended on it." Anthea's eyes were shining in defiance.

"Oh yeah, you bitch. I'll show you who's an impotent bastard. I'll make you eat me here and now." Grunt handed off his gun to Billy and started to unzip his fly and make good his claim when Anthea responded in the same tone, "You try, and I'll bite it off. So help me; I'll chew up your balls and spit them out." Grunt didn't like the thought of that. He took his hands away from his half-unzipped fly. This woman was threatening to him. He didn't like it. Then Marco stepped forward.

"You talk pretty tough, don't you?" He laughed. "But I know what you're afraid of." He took out his knife and grabbed Anthea's hair and pulled her head back by her hair. "You fancy your good looks, don't you?" Then he took the knife and made a small cut in Anthea's face. I could tell by her expression that he had her. She was terrified of that even more than death. She shivered in his grasp.

"Now that was only an inch," he said quietly. "But the next one I have to make will go the length of your face until I so disfigure you that no plastic surgeon will ever be able to make you right again." With that he tightened his grasp on her hair for an instant, smiled at her obvious discomfort and his clear victory, and threw her to the ground again. There Anthea stayed, shocked in her own way just as Martha had been affronted earlier. All the fight seemed gone from her as she lay there looking up from the ground, holding her cheek which was crimson with blood.

Then Pigman and Marco made Martha get down on her knees and sit up before them. She was situated so that her profile was three quarters and turned toward us. Before her stood Pigman and Marco. Grunt was watching the rest of us along with Billy (who was now holding the gun). Martha was shivering. It was a little chilly, but she shook with terror and mortification. She began to whimper and cry. It was not loud, but it was clearly audible.

"Take off your shirt," said Pigman. Martha looked at them with pleading eyes. Her hands were pushed together in front of her chest. "Take off your shirt, I said," he demanded again. She lowered her head and grasped her top button with both hands and began to unfasten it with quivering unsteadiness.

Of course it was this pain and human degradation which seemed to excite the rapists. As each button was undone they thrilled not so much at her body/which was being exposed as by the pain and anguish it was causing her. I felt tremendous empathy for Martha and wanted to do something.

Billy had the gun and perhaps if he began to watch Martha, his attention might be diverted so that I might gain control of the weapon. It was a low probability scenario, but then that was all we had.

"Now the pants," barked Marco. Martha was shaking violently. Her husband was on the ground dead. Her brother-in-law was crying at his pain and frustration at not being able to move to help his sister-in-law. He might already be paralyzed for life, I thought, by these foul excuses for homo sapiens infected with their anti-social sickness. But there Glen lay. He was helpless; a spectator to his dead brother's wife's degradation and humiliation.

Martha, who had had her hands and arms about her breasts to cover them as best she could, now had to stand up and completely expose herself to those beasts by the bright light of the bonfire that was now at its peak.

She haltingly slid down her pants and her underpants and began sobbing loudly. She closed her eyes and covered her face with her hands as she fell to her knees and then to her side onto the ground. Pigman and Marco were laughing with delight as Pigman knelt down to the ground and turned Martha over on her back so that her body was in plain view to all of us. It was then that I leapt for Billy's gun. He had turned his head to watch when she was lying on her back, completely naked on the ground. I thought that would be our best chance. Besides, even if it turned out to be futile, I couldn't sit by passively and watch Martha get raped.

I reached for the butt of the gun and tried to tackle Billy, but my angle of attack was slightly off and I didn't get the kind of mechanical advantage that I had planned on. Billy staggered back, but merely swung the other end of the gun around and banged me in the head. I went down instantly. I hit the earth hard and rolled near the fire. I remember opening one eye to see Glen vainly trying to lift up his hand as Pigman began to rape Martha.

I was unconscious for a short time. When I awoke (with a hard lump on the side of my head that made my ears ring with pain) Martha was lying face down in the dirt. She was no longer crying, but seemed exhausted. Judy was now being summoned for her turn. It was sad to watch her being pulled away from Samuel. (The vision is still very hazy because I was just regaining consciousness at the time.) She clung to his arm and had to be pried free. Samuel did nothing to resist. Seeing this I felt a strong surge of anger and energy. Why hadn't Samuel helped me when I went after Billy? Together we might have been able to do something. Why . . . questions were for later. I had to do something now.

But what?

Judy was taking the role of total passivity. She would neither kiss him nor would she fight him. This made her a less desirable victim than Martha had been. For it seems that these thugs feed on fear and suffering. When one appears not to be suffering, but completely passive, then much of the excitement is absent.

Billy put the pistol in his pocket and began feeling Judy's breasts and started taking off her dress. Then I had an idea: the fire bucket. If I moved it into the fire it would get very hot. Then I could throw it at Billy and stop him. He would get burned and we'd have enough commotion to fight back. I put my hand behind my back and tried to slide the fire bucket toward me. But the bucket had been too close to the fire and was scalding. I didn't make a sound at my instantaneous second-degree burn. Martha was lying on the ground next to Glen. Anthea was watching me.

Billy was taking his time. He wanted Judy to cry and show him her misery. But Judy was still passive. The other three: Pigman, Marco, and Grunt were getting impatient. I sensed an opening.

I was lying close to the fire. Ten yards away from me was Glen's tent and two of their motorcycles. Samuel was fifteen yards away, sitting on a rock watching Billy rape his wife.

Then it hit me: the Fourth of July. I grabbed the unburnt bottom of one of the large burning branches that constituted our fire. In one movement I scurried over to Glen's tent and set it on fire. Anthea had been correct about it being a flammable combination. Almost instantly I had a torch. I pulled up the tent by the ridge pole. I was supercharged so that the ground pegs came up without a notice. In three paces I had covered the two motorcycles that were already decorated with flammable paraphernalia.

I didn't calculate; I just moved. And now I had to escape the impending explosion.

In a matter of moments Billy let out a scream, "That's my bike!" Pigman also turned and tried to run toward the sacred motor bikes. He didn't even take the time to pull up his pants. In five steps he fell to the ground. It probably saved his life.

Marco and Grunt were indecisive. On the one hand they saw Martha, Judy, and Samuel running toward the field. Anthea was also headed in that direction, as was I. But they also saw Billy and Pigman running to save their sacred bikes. Billy was trying to put out the flames with his shirt, but it was in vain. Where should they choose to go? Should they help their gang members or save themselves? Both decided together, without talking, to head towards the meadow. It was then that the bikes exploded. I hadn't imagined that the sight would be so spectacular.

There was a tremendous pillar of flames that extended thirty feet into the air. I knew that there would be a compressive force, but I didn't realize that I'd feel it as I did almost seventy yards away. The flames subsided almost as quickly as they came as there was nothing combustible within range. The children were safe in their camper and the other bikes were at the far edge of the campsite.

Billy was killed instantly. Pigman was hit with shrapnel in the head and didn't move a muscle for a considerable time. By a miracle Glen was spared further injury.

I caught sight of Anthea, Martha, and Judy. They were fifty yards in front of me. Marco and Grunt were fast approaching from the right. Then I came upon a number of tree stumps so I had to slow down and turn my attention to making it through this section. I heard a scream. They must have caught the women, I thought.

Then I saw the clearing. By the light of the moon I saw Grunt's knife glint as he held it over his head. I reached for a stone which I hurled at him with a yell. I badly missed my target with the stone, but it hit a tree behind him and ricocheted once. That ricochet along with my yell put them into another moment of decision (a trait that was definitely not their strong suit—Sail did all the thinking for them and Sail was headed for hospital).

I kept coming and they saw my shadowy form approaching.

I groped for something to wield as a weapon, but could find nothing handy. Then Grunt was upon me and Marco was close behind. I didn't think but dropped to the ground and rolled to the side just like the fire drills in elementary school: stop, drop, and roll! I rolled into Marco and grabbed his legs to try and tackle him. What I didn't know was that Marco also had a knife.

I brought Marco down on top of me, but as he fell he reached for his knife and slashed my right shoulder blade. I reacted to the pain and rolled back the other way which changed the trajectory of Marco's fall. When he hit the ground I instantly felt him grow limp. He must have hit his head on the way down. I didn't stop to analyze it, but rolled over to grab his knife. It was then that Grunt came down. He had started his dive when I was atop of Marco. I continued my momentum and rolled under the limp Marco. It was then that Grunt crashed down atop his gang member, sticking his knife in *him* instead of *me*.

This infuriated Grunt even more. He pulled his knife out and raised it above his head, ready to do me in. It was only the shortest instant, but at that moment I felt how wrong my life had been. How senseless it was to die out here in northern Wisconsin in a part of the country that I didn't care for. There was nothing I could do but accept my fate. But then from out of the shadows (even as the knife was descending) a branch struck Grunt squarely on the side of the head, causing him to miss me with his knife. I didn't hesitate, but immediately rolled on top of Grunt and delivered a blow with both my hands tightly grasped to the base of his skull. He didn't move.

"Get out of the way; he's mine to kill." The voice was hardly recognizable for the raw emotion it evinced.

I knew the voice, but I had never heard it infused with such a bestial, wild quality. I turned and saw Martha standing with the stick in her hand. It had been she who had saved my life. Just when Grunt was about to deliver the lethal blow, she had struck him against the side of his head and allowed me a chance to help subdue the sadistic criminal.

"He raped me and now it's time to give it back to him," she said in a shrill tone which was beginning to break. I felt the primitive desire for revenge that she felt, but I also knew that it was better if the killing and violence were to end. There she stood before me: scratched, dirty, and naked. All of her trappings of civilization had been removed and we were down to the basics: life, death, and struggling for what is ours.

"Martha," I said as I rose and took the branch from her hands. "It's all over now Martha. We have to start over again." I held Martha who was tense, and then relaxed, and then sobbing. I held her and tried to comfort her as Anthea came forward and the three of us held each other against the cold and the darkness of the night.

CHAPTER TEN

"I THINK YOU MISSED your turn off," said Anthea, suddenly lifting up her head from the map. I was driving the Miller's van on the access road.

"No, I didn't. I remember the way *we* came and then I triangulated our position."

"This isn't math class. I'm looking at a map here."

"I cannot look at the map. I'm driving. Look, we've got to stop for gas in a half-hour or so. If we are on the wrong track, we'll find out then."

"Great. I'm in the car with a fellow who looks at the gas gauge and says we have a half hour of gas in the tank. I didn't know they calibrated by time these days." She stopped momentarily. I didn't know whether she had finished or whether she was trying to summon up another charge. It turned out to be the latter, "And another thing, you can't follow directions."

I continued south along the road. What a different feeling I had from the time before when were first going north. How many things had happened to Anthea and me. And I don't just mean our nightmare in the woods, but somehow it seemed that a change had come over me and over the two of us and our relationship as well.

When we had secured Marco and Grunt, we dragged them back one-by-one to the trailer. Pigman was coming around (he had sustained a concussion from a flying piece of metal from the bike), so we bound him too. Martha put on some clothes, but I cautioned her not to clean up since certain tests would be required for material police evidence. Glen, luckily, was not injured further. We decided that it would be best not to move him, but to wait for an ambulance which could dispatch him properly. Samuel agreed to stay with him (Samuel was in no mood to disagree). In fact, Samuel didn't say much of anything. He seemed afraid to look his wife, Judy, in the eye. Her attitude about Mr. Superman also seemed altered. There was a great cloud of disillusionment that hung over Judy and one could feel that a large part of it lay not only in what had happened to her, though that had certainly been bad enough, but rather in her husband's lack of support. When it had come down to a crisis, he had opted for his self-preservation over her protection. I wondered whether they would ever again be able to enter the same kind of relationship that they had enjoyed before. It seemed doubtful.

Anthea made Martha lie down on their couch inside their trailer and wrapped her up in blankets. She was in shock. I rounded up the children and gave them directions for care. Soon Samuel and Judy came in, too. When the situation in the trailer was stable, we then drove out until we got to a pay phone where we called the police.

They gave us directions and we took our camper first to the jail (dropping off our group and filling out forms on the stolen camper and the two still at large) and then we went to the hospital so that Martha and Judy might be examined.

Anthea and I rode back in the ambulance which picked up Ed and Glen. We, of course, had to go back to our camp and get our things. It was an especially long hike that night, which was quickly turning into dawn.

Somehow when we had gone half-way, a tremendous surge of fatigue came over me. I could barely move my tired body. How foreign this way back seemed after the evening's events. It all seemed to be so unreal. Neither one of did any talking. There was nothing to say. We knew that we would have to go back and get some sleep and then pack it in to our car and finish up our work at the police station.

How different the forest seemed that evening. The quiet innocence that had pervaded everything, even hours before, now seemed to be replaced by a valueless veil of nothingness which could embrace the sinister just as well as the pure and noble. How false an ideal I had held about this forest. It was no different than uptown Manhattan or the Wentworth district in Chicago. It could be peaceful or it could be destructive. The blackness, that stark absence of color, was morally neutral for it contained within it everything. We both fell asleep, but when the morning came Anthea was already cooking something over the fire.

"I thought we should have a proper sendoff."

I smiled. Anthea had, during our stay, altered her behavior toward me. I could not put my finger on it exactly, but the change was clearly there. I went down to the lake to bring back some water. We ate slowly, feeling saddened by what had happened and that we were about to leave our sylvan retreat.

After we had lingered over our coffee for a time Anthea asked, "Why did you come after us?"

Her eyes looked at me directly. There was an expression of sincerity and simplicity that I had never seen in her visage so completely. The professionally cut hair which had so attracted me when I first had seen her was a mess, but somehow at that moment I felt a tremendous love for this woman. We were communicating on a level that Barbara and I had never achieved. There was no posturing nor angling for leverage, but rather there was an atmosphere of trust and openness.

"What do you mean?"

"After you had ignited the tent and caused the diversion, why didn't you simply take off into the woods? Why come after us?"

The question had me stunned. Was she serious? Why come after them? Why protect Anthea? I could not reply. Anthea read my reaction correctly and replied, "You couldn't think of anything else to do, could you?"

"You needed help."

"So what?"

"I couldn't very well let you get cut up by those thugs."

"Why not?"

"You should know the answer to that."

Anthea paused and thought a moment. "Because you sleep with me?"

"That's part of it, I suppose. But we're not a couple of dogs, you know. There's something else that goes along with sleeping with someone. At least that's my opinion."

Anthea poured herself some more coffee. It was a beautiful morning. I could tell that it would be a rather warm day for hiking. Anthea was in thought as she sipped her coffee. She was intense as I had only seen her the night we had our discussion about marijuana.

"There doesn't have to be," she said out of the blue.

"How's that?"

"Sleeping—screwing—having sex: it doesn't have to have any more to it than a pleasant feeling." This appeared to be an important point with her.

"I suppose not. I suppose it is harder in one way, but I'd rather go about doing meaningful things than meaningless ones."

"But suppose pure pleasure was the meaning."

"I don't believe in pure pleasure. Pleasure is a construction of humans to make us eternally frustrated. It's a goal that none of us will ever reach."

"If there's no pleasure, what is there?"

"I don't know."

Anthea did not like this final response. I suppose she thought that I had a quick neat answer to everything (or at least pretended to). She threw out the rest of her coffee and started to gather up the dishes. As we walked down to the water she suddenly said, "You put a great stock in loyalty, don't you?"

The question took me by surprise. I was trying to experience our environment (which I know would soon change and which I might never see again) so I was not expecting any dialogue.

"How's that; oh sorry ... What was that? 'Loyalty', you surprised me."

"You do, don't you? That's why you saved me last night. You felt a sense of loyalty and that's why you came after us and did not simply take off to save yourself."

The question was so damn specific that I did not know just how to answer. Who knows why one does something? I certainly don't. In a situation like that, one just acts. That's all there is to it. You don't say: now here are all the things I believe in, how can I best actualize the utility of each of the various coefficients? No. One acts. That's the whole story. "I believe in loyalty, sure, why not? But I didn't take out a scale and weigh everything up. The light was too bad. I wouldn't have been able to read the calibrations."

Anthea looked at me as if I were holding something back (from some kindly motive) and then she hugged me.

"These pans will wait," she said playfully, "let's take a final swim before we trudge on back."

"It's daylight. Might'n someone see us?"

"Unlikely way *up* here, but who cares? I have a passion for your body." She delivered these lines in a carefree way that made me marvel at the beauty of youth. For no sooner had she made her proposal than she had dropped all the pans where she stood (one fell on my left foot) and began to run to the lake without waiting for a response from me. As she ran she was peeling off her clothes. I did not want to be left behind so I took a deep breath and went off after her. The water was very cold from the night before, but the running approach had gotten my blood moving so I didn't feel all that bad. We played a kind of unofficial game of mutual pursuit in the water till we finally caught each other and indulged ourselves with a passionate (built up from all the tension and anxiety of the day before and what lay before us), though rather short session of love making.

Then it was time to return. We methodically packed up camp. It was not a happy time for either of us. We both wanted to stay in our little glen, but events required otherwise. We packed up and started on the long trip back. This was the part that I dreaded most in anticipation. I could remember how I had just barely made it on the way up, and I felt that with such a short sleep that I would be in worse shape going back. However, I was surprised. After an hour or so Anthea asked me if I wanted to rest and I said that I could keep going. Perhaps the past few days in the woods had gotten me into better condition or perhaps I was just getting used to the whole idea of walking about in the woods. I don't know. But I do know that I was not as fatigued as I thought I would be.

We didn't really talk until we stopped for a rest. I picked some berries and handed some to Anthea.

"How do you know those are all right to eat?" she asked.

"I used to study plants. They're from the raspberry family if my memory serves me correctly, *rubus idaeus.*"

"My, my we do have fancy names for things, don't we."

"Quite."

We had our berry lunch and went on our way again. In a couple more hours we were back at the car.

"Well, it's still here," I remarked.

"Not stolen or vandalized. Amazing!"

*   *   *

We went to the police station to sign our depositions and took a room at the hotel/motel. It was one of those one story affairs with about six rooms and you wonder who the last person was to stay there.

"Do you think," I began aloud, "that they ever change the sheets in this place?" I walked over to the bed and pulled back the blanket. The sheets were a light gray.

"Sure they change the sheets," replied Anthea. "The only problem is that they merely change them from bed to bed: a continuous six room rotation."

I laughed and decided that we could stand it until we were sure that everything had been well taken care of. At least it wasn't the Bates Motel. Our next stop was the hospital to visit our friends Martha, Glen and Judy were staying. Samuel was looking after the children in a park nearby. I thought about those poor children going through the shock of seeing their parents assaulted. I could still picture vividly the little curtain being pulled back so that they could witness what was going on. And then little Margo bravely coming out to discover what the trouble was. Poor little Margo. She was not the smartest of the three children, but surely she was the most loyal as she risked putting herself into a situation she knew nothing about to find out what was happening to her mother and father. She put others above herself. This was a noble thing to do and I admired her for it. Yet at the same time I was beginning to realize that there was something to the outlook that one had to assert his own entitlements, too. Not in the simple-minded selfish way that Samuel had, but rather in another way. There had to be compromise between the two. There had to be a way to live for others and yet maintain one's own goals and personal desires as well. And what did one do when there were conflicts between the two?

Oddly enough Glen seemed to be doing the best of all three. His condition was painful, but not serious. He would be able to get around normally in a month or two. The emotional scars, however, were more difficult to heal.

"I tell you, Andrew," he began from his supine posture in the hospital bed with three needles sticking out of his arm, "when Ed came out with that gun I thought for a moment, 'You're going to get hurt.' Then I thought, 'You've got them, 'atta boy.' Then, 'Oh my God they've killed you.' I felt so helpless. Apparently a number of my motor nerves were damaged when they kicked me about. But they are going to be repaired as much as they can tomorrow in surgery."

"And then there is Martha." He began to cry. I knew we weren't supposed to overexcite him so I tried to sooth him by stroking his brow.

"You can't let yourself get so excited," I said. "Martha is being looked after and they will let you see her when it won't do either of you medical damage."

Glen looked so helpless in his white gown with all the tubes coming out of his arm. He was sedated, but still I could read the savage trauma of that night's events in his every facial expression. Here had been an easy going fellow turned inwards upon himself with recriminations at his physical impotence during the episode of terrorism. I wanted to help him to somehow provide him with hope and strength, but there was no way to do that which I could see. All I could do was to stroke his brow and tell him everything would work out.

I knew how acutely fortunate I had been in the evening's activities. Not only had I not been physically injured, but neither had Anthea (that is, to say beyond the superficial cut on her face and a minor knife wound in the shoulder).

I wasn't allowed in to see Martha or Judy, but Anthea reported to me that they were just now beginning to enter into the trauma of what had happened to them. Though their physical conditions seemed relatively stable (even though the night before I had been very afraid that Martha would catch pneumonia due to her prolonged exposure), their mental conditions were far less favorable. They were both on anti-depressants and were going through intensive psychiatric therapy based upon the five steps of grief which would have to be continued once they returned home.

All this had been done by a handful of destructive people riding about on motorcycles.

* * *

We stayed for a couple of days to oversee the preparation of Ed's body in the mortuary. After the autopsy and police records, Martha was able to give us the name of a local mortician who would handle things in Glenview (where Samuel and Judy also lived). Glen's successful operation allowed him to assist the police investigation. Then there were the confession of the Kid and Pigman. After these events: *Marco* was charged with 2nd degree murder, rape (2 counts), aggravated assault (7 counts); *Pigman* was charged with rape (1count), accessory to murder, aggravated assault (7 counts); *Grunt* was charged with rape (2 counts), accessory to murder, aggravated assault (7 counts); the Kid was charged with accessory to murder and accessory to aggravated assault (7 counts). Sail and Billy were dead and so could not be tried. As it turned out, (the trial was held three months later and because they pleaded guilty, sentencing occurred a week later) because of previous convictions, Pigman and Grunt got sentences which didn't allow them to be eligible for parole for fifteen years while Marco was sentenced to life without the possibility of parole. The Kid got a suspended sentence of five years.

*   *   *

It became apparent to me that we had to leave. This put Anthea and me into a rather awkward position. What were we to do? We were coming back from dinner. It was evening, but the sun was still up. Anthea was wearing a purple scarf about her hair.

"There isn't much more we can do here, you know."

She looked at me out of the corner of her eye without moving her head. It was apparently a conversation that she also had in mind, but didn't know how to broach the subject.

"Yes, I know."

"Where do you think you'll go?" I asked immediately. She didn't respond as quickly, but walked along slowly. We were next to each other, but we weren't in contact with each other.

"I don't know. I'm not sure."

"Well, I think I'm going back to Chicago."

She didn't reply to this. Instead she folded her arms and walked off to a little stone wall and sat on it. I followed her.

"Are you going back to your wife?" she asked in a soft voice without looking at me.

"No. We're getting a divorce. She decided not to contest it when I indicated that she could have our condominium and our car. It was all my money to begin with, but that was always the problem between us. Now she's got it and if it makes her happy I say 'so be it.'"

"Then why are you going back there?" This time she looked up, though not directly into my eyes.

"Well, for one thing that's where I have my job. I can't very well work where I please, you know."

"You could do other things. Teaching is not the only thing there is." I smiled and sat down next to her. It was a beautiful summer evening. I wanted her to know that I cared for her, but then I was not full of any illusions either.

"That's true, but I have to go back to it for a while to see where I am. So many things have been happening to me and I need a chance to sift them out."

Anthea began untying her purple scarf and rearranging it. It seemed like a ridiculous thing to do considering it had been perfectly arranged before she started fooling with it.

"So you're going back to Chicago?"

"Yes."

"Ah—and how will you go?"

It was the kind of leading question that I was hoping she'd make. I hadn't really known if I would have been up to asking her myself, but when she gave me the chance I naturally said, "Well, I was hoping that we'd go together in that old car of yours."

"Back to Chicago?"

"Why not?"

She seemed genuinely nervous at this suggestion. I wondered whether she didn't want to go with me and was upset at how she would tell me.

"Well, there is Clay."

"So what?"

"He does have some muscle." She looked at me and spoke as if I were too naive to know about such things, living there in Hyde Park.

"He's a punk. You may find that he has—no offense—several other girlfriends by now. If he was really that attracted to you, why didn't he follow us up here?"

"He tried. Don't you remember Milwaukee?"

"But you told me yourself that you often went to Milwaukee and always stayed at the Marc Plaza. You weren't too hard to find. He probably just told a few of his loyal workers at the 'messenger' service to go up to the Marc Plaza and fetch you. When they saw you were serious about going, they probably went back and told the boss. Clay probably threw up his hands and said, 'Another broad, eh?' And that was that."

Anthea didn't like this scenario. She thought that I was undervaluing her. "I'm not depreciating you, Anthea, I'm just making a judgment about Clay. I think that I'm saying more about him than about you."

She said we'd see, and we made plans to go back together and tentatively to set up house together. One of the first orders of business was to see this Clay McDonald and get a few things straightened out. And so it was that we were driving back. How different it was than the ride up had been. At that time I felt that I was passionately drawn to Anthea and that she had no real attachment to me at all. I didn't like to admit it at the time, for such an admission would have lowered my self-esteem, but it was true nonetheless. She was just having a fling. After Clay she wanted variety and had been on the lookout for a pleasing little interlude which would hold her attention for a time. There was no way that I could have kidded myself into thinking that she really cared for me. If it had come down to it, she would have dropped me like a hot rock. As evidence, take her behavior in Milwaukee when she knowingly deserted me for her flight to freedom. She was quite willing to sacrifice me to the apes who thought that I was 'making time' on their boss's girl. She was willing to leave me to possible hospital bills for her own happiness. This was because I didn't mean a thing to her. I cared for her, but she had not cared for me.

This attitude of hers persisted up to and including our setting up camp. Then after a time, I sensed a refocusing of my image in her eyes. Maybe it was all in my imagination, but I felt that she was really beginning to care for me. And certainly after our ordeal I felt a warm closeness from her so that when we talked about what our courses could be next, she seemed genuinely to want to be with me. And yet, I was feeling things about myself and my own self-knowledge which made me less dependent than I had previously been. It was an ironic turn of events.

And so we drove back to the city. I made only one wrong turn the entire way and she turned out to be a less than successful navigator. But all in all we made it into Chicago a few days later— almost three weeks to the day since I had left. We put up in the Drake and decided to look for a place on the north side. After only a day of looking we found a one bedroom place in Rodgers Park and grabbed it. It was semi-furnished (since we had no furniture and didn't want to buy any), with a bed, couch, and some assorted kitchen utensils. We didn't feel a need for anything too fancy (especially since we had been doing just fine on hardly anything when we were camping).

That evening Anthea and I had a kind of celebration of sorts. We bought a bottle of medium-priced champagne and she cooked us some chicken in a white wine sauce on rice with first growth string beans cooked in butter and served with shredded New York cheddar. The meal was great and afterwards we sat together on the couch and looked out the window that overlooked a park. It was really an ugly little place and my thoughts momentarily turned to that apartment that I had had as a senior in college. However, there was a much better view and there was no swinging light outside.

Anthea was sitting next to me wearing a new outfit that she had purchased in the afternoon. It was a sleekly styled yellow sun dress (strapless) with two sharp tucks on each side. She also wore a new pair of leather sandals which were the latest fashion. Her hair was not up to what it was when I met her, but she was going to have it set in a day or two. She was quite striking. I looked at her and tried to imagine what I would think looking at her *now* for the first time. I decided that I would be very impressed. It wasn't that Anthea was the most beautiful woman I had ever seen (for real beauty may take on innumerous guises and still proclaim itself. Anthea's guises were limited, but then she knew these limits) for she would probably be rated by most as merely above average, but to me she represented a particular look which drew me. I was captivated by her face and body so that I could sit and study them for hours. They seemed uniquely formed as if to tell me something.

We had turned off the overhead light (our only lights were overhead since we owned no lamps) so that we could recreate the kind of setting we had at night in the forest. How different she looked now in her beautiful new clothes than in her casual attire. And yet, it was the same woman.

"I sometimes wished that I had gone on in school," she said. "It was just that I hated sitting there and listening to a teacher drag on and on."

"Then you were correct to leave," I replied. She had her foot up on the couch and was sitting on one side with her back against the arm of the sofa, while I was in the same posture on the opposite side. I began playing with her sandal.

"But I have nothing I can do."

"You were an airlines stewardess once."

"Terrible job."

"Supermarket checker?"

"I've hated all my jobs. I don't know why I ever took any of them. Well, I know why I took the supermarket job. That was strictly for the money. But the others I went into for no real reason at all." She paused and turned her gaze out the window. "There were so many things I did without any reason."

"I'm sure we all do." My response was really more than just a reassuring statement, but a personal confession as well (though she was unaware of this other meaning).

"Yes, but that's not right. I don't want to live that way. It's the way I've lived my whole life. I've always acted without thinking it out. I've never taken the time to think it out."

I took off her sandal. I was getting in the mood for Anthea. I wanted to try out our new bed.

But Anthea wanted to get her thought out. "It's so important to think about the consequences. It's so easy to ignore them." Then she turned to me. "You know—I think I've learned that from you. You've taught me that."

"Me?"

"I mean I knew it before, but I never thought it was of much value. I never really practiced it."

I didn't know why she wanted to give me all this credit. I hardly deserved any of it. I was actually thinking that moment of something else. And it was not a contemplation of philosophy. I brought her other leg up and kissed her knee. Her long leg was so smooth as I stroked it with my fingers. I took off her other sandal. I looked at her and smiled. Most decidedly, I was not in the mood for philosophy.

*   *   *

The next morning I awoke and found that Anthea was gone. She had gotten up some time before, but I had just assumed that she was going running or something like that. Instead I found a piece of paper on the sofa. It was a picture that she had drawn. It was a figure study of me! I was amazed. She was actually quite a gifted artist. She didn't seem to have all the anatomy correct (for some features were slightly exaggerated), but for a naive artist it was excellent. She must have drawn it in the early hours of the morning (I looked at my watch; it was nine o'clock). Well, perhaps it was not too early in the morning after all. I liked getting up later. I had always had Barbara waking me up so early for years for her job that I had become accustomed to rising around six. But this never went very well with me. I would always go through the days tired. I could never tell this to anyone for they would just say, "Oh, poor fellow. You have to get up like the rest of us. Do you think we like getting up at six o'clock either?" I could get no sympathy from anyone (perhaps I deserved none). But since I had left Barbara, I had gotten long, sound sleeps. Unlike Barbara, Anthea did not insist on staying up late (the combination of "late to bed and early to rise" I am sure makes the undertaker wealthy and wise). We went to bed whenever it pleased us.

I was taken by her drawing and wanted to show it to a friend who might be able to tell me whether it demonstrated any real talent or not. I was certainly no expert, but it seemed like good quality to me. However, when I turned it over I saw that there was a note on the reverse side.

> —*I decided to confront Clay myself. I have to do it. I'm a little scared about the whole thing, but I couldn't consent to putting you into any more danger on my account. I hope and trust that he will let me come back to you. Until then,*
>
> *All my love,*
> *Anthea*

This letter bothered me to say the least. What was I to do? I wanted to run after her. What did she mean, "if he will let me come back to you"? How could he stop her? I thought for a moment. She couldn't mean that he would hold her by force. That kind of thing could not happen. Who was this Clay McDonald, anyway? He was just a punk. He couldn't do anything to us. He didn't have any connections at City Hall or the police. But perhaps he paid protection money to people who did have such influence? Then I would have no legal recourse to tracking her down. I would fill out forms and nothing would be gained. Could this really happen?

I couldn't take the chance. I had to get to Clay before he put the squeeze on Anthea. I mean what did I know about this character? He was a *nobody* as far as I was concerned. Did he have any muscle? Could he really make his will into de facto law? Or was he all bluff? Was he (as I had suggested to Anthea) really a two bit operator who liked to talk big? A man with a few apes to do his bidding, but beyond that was as powerless as the next fellow. Chicago was full of types like this. These overinflated egos walked around thinking that they would be the next Bugsy Malone. They really didn't have any mob connections (or at best it was only the fringe of the fringe) and so they were actually amateurs in big league costumes. They were only dangerous because they often didn't realize that they were so insignificant. As a result they might take on some job of harassment themselves and might do an excessive amount of damage or get themselves and/or innocent people hurt/killed in the process.

I don't know what it is about Chicago that seems to attract all these flakes, but they are there nonetheless. Other cities like New York, Los Angeles, Detroit, Philadelphia, Boston etc. all have an orderly crime organization which keeps the amateurs out of action. Crime works outside the law and the two have their traditional adversary relationship. But in Chicago where crime is integrated into the city government so closely, the situation is different. The organized crime bosses spend so much time running the city government that they have no time to keep the small time operators off the streets. Consequently every ward (barring a few) has their pod of little Caesars swaggering around and making money on small time ventures. They are so incompetent that many of them go bankrupt and have to become city policemen.

This McDonald was different to one degree: he was not struggling to make ends meet. Anthea described him as having lots of money which he made from selling little plastic washers (how a person can make a fortune manufacturing and selling so limited a commodity is mysterious to me). Perhaps he had used his money to make himself more than a little toy criminal which one winds up and puts on the floor to either destroy the other toys or break itself by walking into a wall. There was little to be gained by such speculation (though anxiety never does that which will bring forth the most gain). I had to find this Clay myself.

This proved to be not the easiest task. There are lots of messenger services in Chicago. These establishments operate on the principle that there are many people who want to bet on horses who don't have time to go to the track. For a small commission, the messenger service supposedly will send a messenger with the customer's money to the track to place the bet for the customer. For only tracks (which are taxed by the state) are allowed to take betting.

But there are very few messenger services which operate in this way. Some make use of the principle that if the messenger does not get to the track on time so that the bet could not be placed and the customer would have won, then the messenger pays the customer out of his own pocket for the inconvenience. But in those cases in which the customer would have lost, no one is the wiser. The suspicion, of course, is that the messengers never make track bets, but pocket the money on the losing horses and refund the money on most of the winners saying that they didn't make it to the track on time. This method makes the messenger service a mere front for an illegal bookmaking operation.

I didn't speculate on what type of operation this Clay was probably running. What I did concentrate on was the location of the place. Lacking the name, I tried to remember where Anthea had told me it was located. I strained my memory and seemed to recall something about the Diversey "el". It was not much to go on but it was all I had.

I hiked down to the Morse station of the Howard "el" and boarded a "B" train going south.

I asked the conductor about the Diversey Street "el". He said that what I wanted was the Ravenswood. I had to get out at Belmont and switch trains for Diversey. I thanked him and bided my time on the old noisy train going around that terrible corner at Sheridan and then forward to my destination. It was slow going. There are no express trains like there are in Manhattan (except the Evanston express, but then who lives in Evanston?), so the progress was uncomfortably poky.

I finally detrained and waited fifteen minutes for my connection. This ride was quite short and by 10:30 I was descending the steps to Diversey. I looked around me for a messenger service. I do not know what I was looking for except some sign with a horse on it as are always displayed on the South Side on such occasions. There were no such signs. I walked into a furniture store, New Town Interiors, and walked up to a rather queer looking character. He wore tight pants and cowboy boots and an open necked Hawaiian shirt which made his very small head look even smaller. Behind his one inch thick wire rimmed glasses he squinted and said, "Anything I can do for you pal? A little trundle bed or a sleeper sofa?"

A trundle bed? This guy had to be kidding. "Do you know where there's a messenger service around here?"

The man smacked his lips several times and shook his head. "No, no, little buddy, them's not for you. They take your money and lick you clean. Just like a mama cat; clean as a whistle. Take my advice, buy furniture. After your money's gone at least you can sit on it."

What was I going to say to this idiot? I could go on into an explanation of how I didn't want to place a bet, but only wanted to speak to the owner of the establishment, but that would have gotten me into more trouble (if I were even believed) than the intention that my question implied. I decided that perseverance would be my best ploy so I said, "A messenger service. I want to know where there's a messenger service around here. I was told that there was one on this block, but I cannot find it."

"You're going to be sorry. Those places are nothing but trouble. Let me tell you, I've made a few wagers in my time and I've only won once. They let you win once, you know, just so you keep coming back. It's all part of the business and what a dirty business it is too. Take my advice and buy furniture."

"Look, I'm not interested in furniture. Can you tell me where there is a messenger service around here? If not, then I'll go my way."

The fellow squinted again at me. He was trying to figure me out. I wondered why it seemed that every person that I happened to meet in order to interrogate about something important had a screw loose. "Well, since you are so intent on losing your money, I'll tell you. It's across the street on top of the little store there." He pointed to a building only fifty feet away. I thanked him and went to the building. There was no sign anywhere to indicate that this was a messenger service. That didn't look good to me.

A place that tries to keep such a low profile must be a little bigger time than I had anticipated.

I knocked at the door atop the wooden staircase. A man answered; it was Joey. He didn't recognize me from our brief interlude in Milwaukee.

"What does ya want?"

"I want to see Clay."

"Oh yeah? And who are you?"

"My name is Viam. Could I see Mr. McDonald?"

"I don't know no Veeam, why don't you get lost?"

I could see that Joey would not be an easy one to convince. "Look, Mr. McDonald would like to see me, I'm sure. I want to talk with him about Anthea Brevist." I could see that the name made Joey's eyes alter in their expression toward me. I now had his complete attention.

"What do you got to say?"

"I want to talk with your boss. Can I see him now?" I pushed my way inside and Joey was so surprised at the whole thing that he didn't offer any resistance. He was unsure about what he should do. He called over to someone in another room.

"Hey Mark, beat it in here."

In came a very short man with pencil thin arms and legs and a suit with padded shoulders. He wore elevated shoes.

"Mark, this guy wants to see Clay. Says he has information on Miss Brevist. What should I do, Mark?"

Mark scratched his nose and looked me up and down. "Does not look like no lieutenant to me. Think he might be a fed, but looks too stupid to me.

"Say, I think he is just some jerk who might be after a buck. I can't knock that, ain't we all after that? Say, I think he'll be all right." Mark checked what appeared to be a shoulder gun and then turned to Joey. "I'll be back in a few minutes. I'll just run this jerk to Clay's and I'll be right back."

I was getting a little nervous. I had pictured Clay McDonald as a two bit little guy without any real power at all; I was judging by the quality of strongmen he employed. But the little waiting room to the messenger service which was so clandestine made me nervous. There had been a quiet buzzing of noise in another room and I wondered to myself how many of these were customers and how many were Clay's men.

We climbed into an old Buick (from when they were still making those huge tank-like machines) and sped away. Mark thought it was fun to drive with all eight of his cylinders going at peak efficiency. We drove to a house on the Gold Coast. It was a turn-of-the-century mansion (eight or nine bedrooms) which had that quiet elegant look of all the houses in that neighborhood.

Mark took me in and seated me in a little room by myself. After a ten minute wait or so, Mark took me upstairs into a large Victorian bedroom. There must have been four couches and a large desk and chair along with an adjoining dressing room and bath. On the couch was a fat middle aged fellow with a receding hairline which he tried to hide by combing his hair forward Italian style and cutting it off straight at the forehead. He was a powerfully built man who seemed capable of holding his own in any fight he might get into. Clay was dressed in a red satin smoking jacket over a pair of black, pin-striped pants. He was smoking a fat cigar. Seated next to him and holding his free hand was Anthea. I looked at her, amazed that she was so friendly to this man she disliked and no longer wanted to be with.

"Yes," said Clay as he knocked off a few ashes from his cigar into a large cut-glass ashtray that was already half-full. "What do you want?"

What could I say? I didn't want to sound like an idiot arguing for something that was before my eyes a living contradiction to what I was about to say. No, this would not do at all. On the other hand, I did not want to stammer like a dolt, and it was certain that this little fellow would not like to take unnecessarily long in his deliberations.

"I came to talk to you about Anthea, there."

"Yes, yes, my run-away song bird. I understand that it was you who found her. I am grateful to you. Let me show my appreciation by offering you a little reward for your good work." He reached into his smoking jacket and immediately pulled out a clip of hundred dollar bills.

"I am not here for a reward," I replied.

"I like a man who shuns the glitter of money and likes doing a good turn for its own sake. Kind of reminds me of a boy scout. Are you a boy scout?"

'Mr. McDonald—"

"I did not think so. Since you are not a boy scout, let me give you a reward and compliment you on your sincerity."

"What I want to know sir… is Anthea her own woman or will you continue to keep her here as a prisoner?"

The smile passed from his face. He was no longer the jovial, benevolent man doling out goodies for all to keep and enjoy. As his mask dropped, I saw the image of a small-time prima donna who does not like his will to be opposed. He was king of-the-hill even though his hill was only an ant heap. Clay McDonald would not allow me to talk that way to him within his own little castle. Clay put down his cigar gently and brushed some ash off of his hand. "You are a rude fellow and I do not like rudeness within my house. It shows poor breeding and one thing I will not abide is such impropriety here. However, you have leveled a serious charge here. You claim that I am keeping this little song bird in a locked cage so that I can admire her and listen to her beautiful songs. But I tell you this is not true. She is free to go whenever she likes. I will not hold her back."

"Is that why you had your apes follow her to Milwaukee a month ago?"

This charge seemed to enrage Clay, but he was one not to let his emotions show when he was trying to be impressive as he was at this moment before Anthea. He did not like to get caught up in his little lies. The pressure was clearly growing within him. He stood and walked over to his empty fireplace. "I don't know what business that is of yours."

"I'll tell you. I had had dinner the night before with Anthea and the next morning your monkeys beat me up for it. Does that betoken that your little song bird is free? It sounds to me like you intend to clip her wings."

Clay laughed nervously and then ran over to me and pressed me against the wall, but before he could utter his little threat I spun away and pushed him backwards. Instantly Mark ran over and pushed a gun in my ribs. Clay staggered backwards and almost fell down. He was clearly surprised that I would not cower to him (even perhaps when it would have been the most prudent thing to do). Clay was breathless for a moment and then righted himself and straightened his smoking jacket.

"Let him go, Mark," he said. "You've got quite a bit of spirit, young man. But let me tell you a thing or two: I can crush you whenever I want to and don't you forget it."

"That doesn't make you right. Power can't purchase morality."

He laughed, and smoothed back his hair as he walked to the other end of the room. "Perhaps you *are* a boy scout after all." He continued to smooth his hair even though it did not need it. "What is it you want with me, boy scout? All this is very interesting, but I have to work for a living and time is rather a limited commodity."

He had changed his course once more. This man was a pragmatist to the core. "I want you to agree to let Anthea go."

"Let her go?"

"That's right. I want you to unlock your gilded cage and let her fly away."

He laughed. "What makes you think that she isn't free to go anytime she likes?"

"Well, the last time she tried it she was hunted down by your boys." I made a slight gesture to Mark who seemed more than eager to have a go at me for any reason whatsoever.

"You don't have all the information about that incident. I had reasons to check out where she had gone and whether she was all right. You see, she left in rather a great hurry suddenly without telling anyone. I naturally was worried. You notice that we didn't pursue her. No, Anthea is free to go any time she chooses, but I was under the impression that she was not ready to leave just yet. Is not that true, Anthea?"

Anthea was seated all this time on the couch where she had been sitting when I entered the room. She had not made any overt signs to me about anything. She sat staring and occasionally rubbing her new facial scar. In fact, the only time that she had acknowledged my presence was when I entered. She appeared very shocked at this intrusion, but aside from that she was silent and brooding over on the couch. "Yes, Clay. Whatever you say."

"See, what did I tell you? Now if that's all you came here for, I'm sure you will excuse us." His manner was smug. He knew with confidence what she would say. I thought that I also knew what her reply would be. I was astonished. How could this woman who professed to be so close to me now and to loathe this Clay McDonald turn on me so suddenly? There seemed to be no explanation. I tried to establish eye contact with her, but she wouldn't.

There was nothing more that I could say. I turned and walked away.

Had he bewitched her somehow? Was there some area to which she was sensitive that he had exploited? I could not understand any of it. The whole thing had me bewildered. I did not know whether to be suspicious or simply hurt at her attitude. In so many ways she was so different than I was. How had I been so stupid to form an attachment to such a woman?

*   *   *

After my visit to Clay's I decided to see a friend of mine at Chicago University. I had called him earlier in the day because I wanted some time with him to obtain his opinion about Anthea's drawing. Perhaps the point was moot now. Especially if she had changed so completely as the scene in his house had suggested. But still I went to see Preston McNeil because I liked talking with him even if it didn't make any difference anymore with Anthea.

Preston was a quiet man who had bursts of energy. He would often go eight to nine months without doing anything and then he would polish off a few paintings in a month! Preston was the sole full-time faculty member at Chicago University's studio art department. This great university that prided itself on the number of Nobel Prize winners on its faculty did not even have a respectable studio art department. I was always reminded of this sad fact each time I saw Preston. As a result of this situation, the closest thing to a colleague that Preston had was in the Art History Department. However, there is a great distance between these two disciplines. Art History was always trying to categorize Preston into some group or other, and this irritated my friend. As a result, McNeil's friends came from people either not associated with the University at all, or people from departments which had nothing to do with art. For example, Ted Simms, the football coach, was a good friend of Preston. (Though football was certainly an anomaly at our school since the university had resigned from the Big Ten and Division 1 football in 1939—though it was reinstated years later as a casual affair in Division III.)

Preston stood about 6' 2" with blue eyes and curly brown hair which had the slightest highlight of red in it. He was a good looking man who attracted the ladies (though since he had turned fifty, by his own admission, he had moderated his activities in this area substantially). When one caught Preston at the right time (during one of his bursts of energy), he was jovial and full of good humor. It was in just such a mood that I found him when I entered his studio next to the Smart Gallery on University and 56th.

"What ho there, Da Vinci?" I said as I entered his domain.

"Hey ho, who's there, eh?"

"Andrew Viam, maestro."

"Ah, Andrew. I thought you'd have made it over here sooner by your call."

Preston was sitting at an easel with a tray of supplies at his elbow. There were an array of brushes and materials on a little desk-like projection that he had invented for his own ease of execution. At his back was a large window which allowed him to get a maximum amount of natural light. "I never paint in anything except natural light," he had once told me. "One cannot see what colors look like unless one has sunlight." Since his window faced east, he usually painted in the morning and early afternoon.

"I'm not living in Hyde Park anymore," I said.

"Oh? How's that, if I may be so forward to inquire."

"Divorce."

"Really? Best thing for you, you know—though I've never tried it myself, as I've never been married. But I think I've experienced things that were close to that with various alliances that I have made, though they were all on a rather less official nature, you know."

"What are you working on there?" I looked at the painting and I was fascinated. At the middle top of the painting was an explosion of color—like fireworks. On the right was some confusion: men in combat. On the left was a lone figure running into the woods in what appeared to be a terrifying void of ambuscading dangers.

"Oh it's just a little thing that was inspired by a conversation I had with Ted Simms, the football coach, the other day."

"You got an idea for a painting from a football coach?"

"It's not so strange, you know. At Chicago, all the coaches also teach on the regular faculty. They give you three or four thousand extra to take on a sport. So it's not as if he's devoted full-time to athletics only." Then he cocked his head. "You know, I can get an artistic impulse from anything. Football is a part of life too, you know."

"I wonder. But anyway, how does this have to do with football? Is this part of a football game?"

"No. This isn't a sports picture. I didn't say that, if you remember, but merely that my idea got its genesis from Ted. He told me about a particular play that he's been working up for the team this fall. It's called a naked reverse."

"A naked reverse?"

"Yes, it's when the team blocks one way and tries to fool the opposition that the ball carrier is going that particular direction when actually the ball carrier goes the opposite way. He goes around and has to face anything that he encounters there *all alone,* all by himself."

"I'm afraid I'm not much of a sports fan."

"But it's just a metaphor, don't you see? A person goes his own way and must face the world alone. He can't rely on anyone's blocking, but must make his own way."

I looked again at the painting. Something had struck me about it from the very moment that I had looked at it. At present, Preston was painting a light area.

"If you'll excuse me for a bit, Andrew. I have this one glaze coat that I'm applying and there is an optimal time for getting it on."

"What do you mean, a glaze coat? Is that like varnish or something?"

"No," he said, now engaged again in what he was doing. "It is when you mix paint with this glaze medium (there are several) and the paint becomes translucent so that you can paint over other colors and you can leave just a hint that you've been there. Of course, if you put this stuff on in layers as I'm doing you can achieve very subtle effects. Rembrandt was a great master of glazes. Unfortunately, the varnish he used was not as first rate so that when one of his paintings is cleaned (the varnish removed) one often has to take off ten to twenty layers of finely wrought glazes as well."

I was fascinated by what he was doing. His light glazes must have been put on in great quantities since there was a noticeable white stream in the middle of the picture. It was like a waterfall in form, but in actual projection it seemed to be closer to refracted light.

Soon he was done. "The picture's almost complete. It has taken me a long time because I'm working in oils. With oils you have to wait until each layer is completely dry before applying the other layer. Well, actually that isn't exactly true, since oil never *completely* dries, but there is a minimal period required."

Preston washed up and wanted to take me to see the house that he had bought and was renovating. We started walking east along 55th. Apparently the place was located on Woodlawn and 52nd. "I bought it at one of these auctions because I just happened to see this poster pasted on the front door of the place when I was going to the A&P grocery store one evening. I love the design of the house and had a contractor friend appraise the basic structure for me. Apparently it was very sound, but needed extensive renovations."

As we walked along I marveled at the vitality of this man who seemed to be engaged in so many projects at the same time. I had always had my hands full with just one. I could never quite understand how a man could compartmentalize his mind so that he could be working on so many different projects simultaneously. He had students that were working with him on the house (as well as professional contractors for the various difficult tasks).

"I thought that I could go as high as five thousand dollars as I figured that I'd have to put in twenty five thousand into the house itself. Well it turned out that I got the house for seven hundred bucks and that my renovations (which are nearing completion) have only cost me twenty thousand. I have been very happy, and may take the extra money and do something crazy with it."

It seemed like a steal to me. The house was a three story brownstone. It had a certain character to it. I liked the house. We went inside and the place was a mess.

"They've just finished on the ceilings. They were in terrible shape. I had to put in new ceilings and floors almost everywhere. I've got new wiring and some new plumbing. I've kept the old height to the rooms since we've done such a good job insulating the place. The place is virtually air tight. And you ought to see what we've got upstairs."

We went up to the third floor. It was an attic of sorts which had large sections of roofing replaced by glass.

"This is my garret. I'll make it into a studio. Some graduate students are working on a federal grant for solar energy. They have constructed a model system here in my roof. Not only will it provide 20 percent of my heating and 5 percent of my electricity, but it also gives me all the natural light I'll ever need for my work—and from both sides too. I'm very excited about it."

"How much did it cost you for this little experiment?"

"Nothing. They were happy to find someone who would let them tear open his house. The whole thing would have probably come to another seven thousand alone if I had to foot the bill."

We talked for a while about the house. He had really done a very nice job on it. Then I took out Anthea's sketch. "I have a drawing that I'd like you to look at."

He held it up and examined it for a few minutes and then said, "It's hard to say from a single drawing, you know, but I'd say that this person is talented. Not *gifted*, mind you, I don't think that he or she will ever be a great painter or artist per se, even after he or she perfects some of the fundamentals of drawing. But I do see a good possibility in commercial art for this person."

"Commercial art?"

"Yes, you know, advertising, fashion, consumer retail—that sort of thing."

"Sounds a little dull."

"What isn't dull? Do you call lecturing to a class of students all semester on material that you've done and solved years before anything but dull? If I could make an adequate living at painting, I'd give up teaching tomorrow."

"But you do pretty well, don't you? I know that you sell most of your pictures."

"So what? Do you know what a moderately good picture sells for? If the artist is not nationally famous, it generally pulls in four to five hundred to a thousand dollars tops. An excellent picture gets the same price. At that rate I'd have to turn out twenty to thirty paintings a year just to maintain my present standard of living. Imagine thirty paintings a year! That's over two a month or more accurately one every week and a half. One couldn't do that working in oils and do the kind of job that I like to do. I'm lucky to turn out five paintings a year. I am satisfied with them and I can do them the way I like. All things considered, I think that I'd rather do five paintings and be happy with them than turn them out like toothpaste."

I smiled at Preston. I suppose I really admired a man who was so involved in seemingly high quality projects as he was. He must really have a sense of fulfillment that I had not experienced since I had written my series of articles on understanding feedback systems in hormonal secretions. I longed to get back into my writing and try to finish something again. Perhaps I'd write a book? Perhaps I could keep a diary about all the things that had happened to me? There were projects that I could get involved in and it was important that I do so. I hadn't been active in research for several years and it was time to return to it.

"So you think that this woman whose picture I showed you ought to consider commercial art?"

We were downstairs again and sitting on saw horses used by the workmen.

"Yes. She owes it to herself to give it a go. That is, if she likes drawing."

"How would one get into that sort of thing?"

"Only one way these days. You must go to a first-rate commercial art school and get contacts. That means somewhere like Bellomy's in Manhattan."

"New York? Isn't there something in Chicago?"

"Of course there is. But if one wants to make it into a competitive field in a decent position he has to go to New York. It's as simple as that."

"But aren't there plenty of advertisers in Chicago? Wouldn't they want to hire local talent?"

"There aren't *plenty* of agencies that are any good that originate here that would hire local stuff. I'm telling you that the action is in New York and L.A —and L.A. is full of New Yorkers who have decided that they want a tan."

We talked a while longer and then I left. When I got home, Anthea was there. I opened the door and saw her sitting on the couch reading.

"Well, well," I said, "I'm kind of surprised to see you here."

Anthea looked up. There was nothing angry in her motions, but then she was not ashamed either. "I don't know why you had to come by there today."

"I was trying to help you out of a jam."

"I don't need it."

"I should say not. You seem to like things just fine."

"That's not fair."

"Oh it isn't, isn't it?" She was not as aggressive as usual, and I could not detect the reason why. Was she ashamed of something? Had she had sex with Clay after I left? I pretended to myself that I didn't care.

"No."

"Well, when Clay gave you the choice of staying with him or leaving with me you chose to stay."

"Do you really think that I had a choice?" she said standing up and walking over to our refrigerator. "He would have come after me and taken me back by force. You don't know Clay. I am getting rid of him, but I have to do it in my way. If I had stayed out of Chicago, things would have been fine. But since *you* had to come back you're going to have to trust me that I can do it my way."

I did not respond, but then I did not completely believe all that she was telling me. It did seem odd that she was so paralytic about demonstrating her feelings in front of the very man she claimed that she wished to be rid of. But then, perhaps she was just weak. Perhaps she said the same things to Clay that she was saying to me. She might have been saying that she wanted to get rid of me, but that the time was not yet ripe. The bond of trust that had formed between us was being severely tested.

I was haunted by the possibility that she might be trying to see us both at the same time. Now this might not have bothered me if she had been open about her relationship with Clay (though I never cared for the triangle as a geometric figure), but as it was, I felt as if she were selling us each 100 percent of her. And as a consequence, each of us got none of her. Again, the question haunted me: was she having sex with Clay? I suppose that I had no right to worry about this. After all, there was nothing that I could do about it either way. The only thing that entertaining such a thought could do to me would be to tantalize: to dangle such images of infidelity before my eyes as to make me retire into the lonely corner of my childhood closet. That scenario was almost more than I could stand.

As we sat there in silence eating our dinners I tried to imagine her in his arms that afternoon and making love. I tried to imagine it, and yet I did not want to do it at all. I exerted all my will to extinguish such images, but the more I fought them, the stronger they came back and the more vivid they were. Anthea sat in silence. She did not share any of her thoughts with me. I wondered what she could possibly be brooding about except, perhaps, a bout with her conscience? I decided that I would go to a movie that evening to get away from the oppressive atmosphere that I felt around the place.

I went alone.

When I returned, Anthea was already asleep. This was fine with me for I knew that after what had happened that day I could not have sexual relations with her. I might have been able to at the beginning of our relationship when the main attraction was physical, but now that I infused meaning into our embraces and gentle fondling, such behavior would degrade all that we had had previously. And so it was that for the first time in our relationship we went to bed separately and remained completely apart.

CHAPTER ELEVEN

ANTHEA WAS GONE when I awoke the next morning. Her jogging things were missing so I assumed that she was taking her morning constitutional. I had a cup of coffee and got dressed, for this morning I had an appointment with Barbara and her lawyer.

I hadn't talked with Barbara since I left her. I understood that she was seeing Giles all the time (some think that he has moved in with her). I didn't know what to expect with Barbara. From her behavior when I found them together in bed, I had expected her to put up more of a fuss to have me back. Apparently she had taken that tack at first, for when I called from Wisconsin just after I left, she wanted me home and had communicated through the mutual friend who I had talked to that she wanted me back. But I didn't want her back. It is funny. One decides to get married and this one little decision colors his whole life. The little decisions and the big decisions put us into certain positions vis-à-vis our life possibilities. When we choose one thing, then a myriad of other future possibilities are closed to us later on. It's funny that I had never considered how much choosing Barbara (or accepting her choice of me—which is more accurate) would so alter and limit the kind of life I was to lead. For if I hadn't married her, I would have travelled around Europe and lived off the modest interest on the money my father had left me. I would have taken on no real profession and would have devoted myself to the fine arts and the life of a gentleman. But as it was, Barbara threw away a good part of that money on her poor investments and then most of what was left we sunk into the condominium and a car. How could such a comfortable little sum have slipped through my fingers? How could such a comfortable little life have passed me by? It had been my fault. I had been manipulated through my inexperience. I knew so little about women while conversely Barbara knew so much about men. Imagine my thinking that I had been the first real love in her life (either emotionally or sexually)? I just assumed that what had been so new to me, must be novel to her also. She had played on my strongest points which were conversely also my weakest. I allowed loyalty and devotion to permute into abnegation and subjection.

There was a good deal of hostility that I felt for Barbara, and yet— there was a tenderness too. She was the first woman who showed me tenderness. And there had been some genuine affection on her side. The years at Cambridge (when she could not stand England) could only have been endured through a feeling of love. There was a part of me which wanted to tell her to forget about Giles and return to me. Even though we had grown apart over the years since we lost the child, there still might be something that we could salvage from the marriage. People cannot live together for thirteen years and have nothing for it. A part of me wanted to confront Barbara right there in the lawyer's chambers and get outthe things that had been bothering her about me all these years. We could talk and perhaps work things out. Yes, perhaps there could be another chance. I did not really believe this when I walked into the wood paneled office on La Salle, but the hope was there, and I so *wanted* to believe it.

When I opened the door I saw my lawyer and Barbara's lawyer and Barbara all seated in a circle before one of those large floor length windows that revealed the lushness of Lincoln Park outside. I was only a few minutes late, and yet they appeared to be deep in the middle of some long conversation. I looked at Barbara and felt an uneasiness at how she would react. She looked unusually pretty sitting there in a new outfit which I had never seen. Her hair was carefully set and her nails were painted in a soft red. Sometimes one forgets what a woman looks like when you look at her for so long. One begins focusing on the odd parts of her face and, without too much trouble, distorting the features out of proportion. In addition to this one infuses one's feelings and moods into a face so that after a time, it is no longer the same face to the eyes as it once was. I looked at Barbara and got a hint of what it was like when I had first looked at her many years ago at NYU. And yet, it was not exactly the same—how could it be? The experience left me speechless as I entered the room.

Everyone turned and looked at me. But my eyes were only for Barbara. "Hello, Barbara," I said softly. What was I doing here in a divorce office? I wanted Barbara back.

"You're late, Andrew." Her voice was crisp. I instantly froze. All my warm feelings began to jumble themselves. I sat down. My lawyer began talking to me, but I did not listen. Instead I looked at Barbara. She was imperious. Here I was, almost at the point of conceding to her and willing to accept any blame if she would return to me, when she decided to act just like Barbara. That was the problem. The lawyers began talking among themselves, so I turned to her and said, "How are you doing?"

"As well as might be expected from a woman who has been deserted by her husband. They tell me that Illinois is a 'no-fault' divorce state so I won't be able to collect just damages for your inexcusable actions."

She was her same old self. She covered up for everything with a good offense. She would never allow herself to be put on the defensive. I smiled. Barbara was a person who would always be right and justified in her own eyes.

I wondered whether this was a fact or whether she merely did this to dupe others. Either explanation would order the same behavior. In one sense it did not make any difference. She would act the way she would act. But I was curious about Barbara. She had always domineered over me to such an extent that I never had sufficient distance to ask such a question. I was too busy reacting to her. In times past if she had made such an argumentative statement, I would have been sucked into the argument which would have been fought on her terms, insuring that no matter what I did she would remain the winner and still champion.

But now I did not snap at the argument bait. I could resist her snares and sit dispassionately, (well, relatively dispassionately) and ask myself why she was acting this way.

"How are you and Giles getting on?"

This response to her assertive jibe took her aback. She was not used to my posing directions of my own. It was not my style to be able to avoid her poisoned darts and deliver a repartee of my own. Barbara became confused and began straightening up her clothes. They were in perfect condition, of course, but she needed time to think.

"Giles?" she managed. "I'm not sure what you mean."

It was a very weak reply. This was not vintage Barbara. She must have gotten rusty in the last few years due to lack of exertion on my part.

"Come now, Barbara, you know exactly what I mean: Giles Coughlin—" She still was not responding. I braced myself for a strong punch, "—the one I found you in bed with the day I left." She was spinning, but I knew her better than that. Barbara could take the best punch that anyone could deliver and come back with a flurry of her own. She lifted her eyebrow and replied, "It's no use trying to hide the facts. The law holds you as the guilty party. There's no denying it. It was you who left me. You left me after all I had sacrificed for you."

I wanted to applaud as she lifted up her hand to wipe away the tear on cue. There was no one who would ever K.O. this game little lady. But it was then that I realized that as much as I enjoyed this banter, I was able to do nothing else with her. We had become locked into tight constricting roles from which we could not escape. As much as I wanted to say to her, "Barbara, let's try again. Let's stop measuring our territory and let's begin reacting naturally and honestly with each other," I knew that I couldn't. Barbara would never allow it. She was a person who played a game of power and was never comfortable unless she believed that she had the upper hand. There was no way that she would accept a situation of parity; it did not allow her adequate security.

Then her lawyer, dressed in his navy blue Brooks Brothers three-piece suit, turned and addressed her. "I think that we have come to a very good arrangement for us."

"That was quick," she said. "I didn't think they'd give in so quickly."

"Well, the agreement is that you both keep your bank accounts and personal possessions according to a list you both agree upon and that you get the condominium and car."

Barbara pursed her lips. She didn't like it. "You mean he gets all his bank account?"

"It is paltry compared to yours," said the lawyer.

"That's because I make more money than he does. I deserve to have more."

"That may be, but you'd only have a case against his bank account if it were larger than your own. As it is, if anyone had a case, it would be him against us and not the other way around." Barbara did not like this. It was clear that she somehow wanted to "clean me out."

"But I should get *something*? Doesn't he have to pay alimony or something?"

This time it was my lawyer who responded. "In cases involving no children and a wife who is self-supporting and earning more than her husband there is no provision for alimony—unless, as we have seen in a few cases recently, it is the *wife* who pays the *husband* alimony. But my client is not pressing for that. He is not even pressing for half of the condominium which is rightly his. He has, against my advice, offered you his half—a very generous amount—considering that the condominium and automobile came exclusively from a legacy given by his late father." My lawyer talked calmly, but I could tell that he was agitated with Barbara. "I suggest you accept this offer, for it is more than generous. It is an outright *gift* on his part."

Barbara did not like the word "gift." She felt she was entitled to it all. And well she might be. Just because the condominium was purchased with money given to me before I was married did not signify a thing. She married me to get at that cash and had lived with me for thirteen years. I guess that I felt that she earned it.

"But doesn't the injured party get anything?"

Her question made my lawyer even hotter, though he was remarkable for his ability to suppress his anger and not to let it get in the way of his ability to offer precise refutation. "Unfortunately, not in Illinois. If you cared to declare your official residence elsewhere you might be able to find a state that does judge according to traditional standards. However, I must warn you that in this case it would be your husband who would be judged by the court as the injured party and he could most likely get the condominium, half of *your* bank account and perhaps alimony to boot until the time of his re-marriage."

Barbara did not have the ability to remain calm when she became infuriated beyond a certain point. She was just about to reach for something to throw at my attorney when her attorney stepped in and said, "We've gotten an offer which is more than fair, Barbara. We have written the terms all up here. As your attorney I advise you to sign. You won't get anything more in court."

This defused Barbara, who acted as if she felt the world was conspiring against her. She looked at her lawyer for a long interval without speaking and then she turned and looked at me. It was not easy for her to end it like this. But there was nothing that she could do. The business woman in her said take the money and get out while you can. The proud general in her wanted to vanquish me completely. The business woman won. Our hearing was scheduled for July 22 and then it would be over. How my feelings had soared when I came to the office and thought about a possible reconciliation with her, and how they had plummeted when I saw that it would never be of any use. We were two people who, if we should ever have gotten married in the first place, were certainly not fit to live with each other anymore.

* * *

I travelled to Hyde Park by the 'el'. I was surprised at how well I was able to get around Chicago by public transportation. How strange it was that I had lived here for eight years and had only taken public transportation once or twice and now I was using it all the time. I felt like a different person as I returned to my office in the Classics Building. My mind had been thinking about a philosophy problem that I had begun and dropped again several years before. I had dropped the question partly because I saw no way to offer any original solutions to it, and partly because I was losing my interest in research all together. But now I had a new slant on it that I had not considered before. I began to work on it. There would be about three months of research involved, but I might just have discovered a solution to the whole thing.

I worked in the library the rest of the afternoon, came home and spent another evening with Anthea, but in another sense, not with her. I stayed at home, but read most of the evening, even after she went to bed. The next day was spent in the same way. Finally on Friday when I came home from my work at the library I smelled something cooking in the oven as I opened the door. It was something sweet.

"Hello," I said. "What are you making?"

Anthea ran to me. She put her arms around my neck and kissed me. I was not overly responsive. "I'm free.

"What?"

"I'm free. Clay told me to get lost and not to come back."

"But why?" Things were happening so fast that I didn't even notice that Anthea had purchased a new dress and earrings. Her hair was done and she looked stunning.

"I told you I had to do it my way."

She walked away from me and went over to the couch. Now that she had my interest piqued she knew that I would follow her anywhere. I sat next to her and cocked my head to the side as I studied her face which was half filled with sunlight.

"Well, you cannot just keep me in suspense," I said. "Tell me how you did it." At this point I was of several minds. On the one hand I was happy that she had gotten rid of Clay. On the other hand, I wondered why she had taken so long. And thirdly, I wondered why she had to wait for Clay to say good-bye. Couldn't she have made the move herself? Why all the intrigue? During the past few days our relations had been far from close. Now she was coming to me as if she had been desiring me every minute while she was away with Clay.

"Well, I knew how Clay acted to his former girlfriends. I mean, that he liked to keep them hanging on so that he could degrade them. That was a streak in Clay. He seemed at one time to hate everybody and wanted to push everyone's face in their own excrement. All this to the exultation of god-Clay. I mean it was ridiculous. Well, I didn't want to be one of those—"

"But how could he do that to someone?" I asked. "Why couldn't someone say good-bye and that would be that?"

"You saw some of his boys."

"So they bring you back? So you leave again."

"It's not that simple. You see that in the first time they bring you back and Clay warns you. The next time he brings you back in front of his new girlfriend and he lets his boys rough you up a bit. Then if you still don't get into line, he lets his boys do whatever they want with you while he and his new plaything laugh and eat grapes."

"Can't someone report him to the police?"

"They could, but it wouldn't do any good. He spreads his money around and is part of a pool which cannot be touched for its resources."

"I see." It was just as I had suspected. This little man was king of his hill.

"So you see, I didn't want to be treated like the others. He'd keep them around and assign them to lowly tasks around the house. Occasionally when he had company over and needed some women for his guests they would be secured for the task."

"That sounds like slavery."

"Well, it never happened when I was there, but it was said to have happened by friends of his (though I suppose *friends* are often exaggerators). Anyway, I thought that the only reason why Clay might put up a fuss was if he could get a kick out of it. You know, if he could show what a big man he was by forcing me come back to him."

She looked out the window. I didn't buy the story about his ex-girlfriends. Anthea can be a little gullible at times and I was sure that this was one of those times. Perhaps he might have hit one or two a bit or made them give back their presents, but surely this was too much to swallow.

"So I told him that I was coming back, but that I didn't want any favors nor would I accept any money or clothes from him. He thought that it was a rather dumb idea. After giving it the once over in that animal brain of his, he told me to get lost. So here I am."

"You mean you just hung around and he told you to leave?"

"Well, I wasn't fitting into the scene the way he wanted, so he told me to leave."

This seemed very odd to me. Why would a man who sent several men after a woman all the way to Milwaukee, simply tell her to leave? The scenario didn't make any sense. "But why did he tell you to leave?"

"I don't know. He had another girl, I guess."

This surely couldn't have been the reason, for by my estimation Clay had always had other women. He was a man who could not be tied down to one mistress. "I don't buy it."

"What difference does it make? I'm here. Isn't that all that counts?"

I smiled, "Of course." But the truth was that I was very curious about why she had been

allowed to leave. Perhaps it was that Clay could not trust anyone around him who he couldn't buy. When Anthea said that she would not accept any more money from him, he could no longer trust her. Perhaps that made sense? I don't know. It might be no more than Clay had indeed lost his taste for Anthea. A man in his line of work often goes through many girls in a year. At any rate, she was right, I should just be happy that I had Anthea back for myself.

She made me a very tasty dinner and we celebrated her return long into the night.

*   *   *

The next day I went down to Chicago University and ran into Preston. He was scurrying about with his hands full of all sorts of

folders. It was a windy day and I was afraid that he might let everything fly out of his hands. But somehow it didn't and he made his
way up 57th street on his way to his studio.

"Looks like you have your hands full there," I said.

"Andrew, just the person I wanted to see. Well, what do you say?"

I didn't know how to respond to Preston. Was he asking me a
question or merely passing the time of day? I decided it must be the
latter, "Fine thank you, and yourself?"

"You ninny, I didn't ask you how you were. I asked you to give
me an answer."

I was still unclear about what he was talking about. "An answer
to what, Preston?"

"Look, I'm not losing my mind, am I? Did I or did I not ask you
what you thought of my house?"

"You did."

"And don't you remember me asking you to move in with me?"

I turned my head. This really startled me. Preston's hat blew off
and I ran and got it. "It's a pretty windy day for all those papers,"
I followed.

"But the house, man—the house."

"Preston, I'm flattered that you're asking me to move in with you,
but you never asked me before."

"Well how about it?"

"It's a lovely house."

"Good, then. It's settled."

"Wait a minute, Preston," I said. I was not sure whether I liked
this manipulation. But coming from Preston, I really believe that he
thought he had asked me. He was a very absent minded fellow. The
only thing about which he could maintain his concentration was his
painting. But even if I did consent to move in with Preston, there was
the question of Anthea. I would not desert her. But even as I thought
about his offer, I recognized that the prospect of being separated
from Anthea did not seem all that frightening to me. I could remember that when I had first started having sex with Barbara the thought
of leaving her, at first, had been very difficult. I couldn't do it. Sure,

I went to Europe, but always with the intention of coming back to her. And that was the way it had been when I first met Anthea. She captivated me. But sometime—I don't know when—perhaps it was after the incident in the woods or perhaps it was after seeing her with Clay, I don't know—things were different for me. I no longer felt quite the same. I had a sense of independence.

"Look, Preston. I'm living with a woman just now. Wouldn't that be sort of awkward?"

"Why?" he said as his hat blew off again. I picked up his hat and motioned in the direction of the studio. I was heading for the library, but I decided that I would make a detour for the sake of saving those folders which seemed as if they would fall down at any moment and send their precious contents blowing in the wind. It wasn't far to his studio—only a block—and we made it without mishap. When we had gotten inside and I unlocked his studio for him (he fumbled around for a key, almost dropping his folders again—they were in such a precarious state that I did not know how they physically were still in his arms). We went inside and he walked over to a table to put them down, and almost a yard in front of the table they dropped.

"Wouldn't you know it? I walk a mile with these things in the gale outside and I end up dropping them just when I get to my office. It's crazy."

I sat down in a chair and stared at the painting that I had seen days before. It had affected me deeply. There was something about the painting which struck some kind of chord of truth within me. Now I'm not one who owns very many photographic prints of famous paintings (not to mention not a single original oil painting) so you have to understand that I am no expert on painting. Neither am I an expert on aesthetics. Philosophy of science is my field. But I underwent a developing tangible aesthetic experience with that picture in front of me. I enjoyed it for itself only—and not as some object of art that might have some commercial value. That is, I looked at that picture and it seemed to be stating something which seemed very correct to me. Not only did it seem correct, but somehow I felt oddly justified in the things that I had been doing since I left Barbara.

It is hard to explain, but the "new" me felt strong empathy and rein-forcement from that painting. I do not know what about the picture elicited that response from me or why, but when I looked at it and became immersed in its subtleties of shape and colors and design, I was strongly affected.

Then Preston came over. "I see you are admiring my work. It's done. I'm just putting on the various coats of varnish now. I have my own formula which tends not to collect dust, but even so, it is a good idea to cover it."

He took a sheet and brought it over with two arms so that it cov-ered the picture without really touching it. When he had finished his task, he sat down in the middle of the floor. There was no formality with Preston. When he wanted to do something or act in a particular way, then voila! It was a *fait accompli.*

"So you like it, do you?"

"I'd like to buy it."

"Oh really? Are you sure you can afford it?"

"I'm not sure about that. All I know is that I've been thinking about it at odd times. I don't recall ever being struck in such a way by a work of art."

Preston chuckled. It obviously amused him to hear someone praising his work in that way. He leaned back, took a deep breath and then rocked forward. "Well, are you going to move in or not?"

"You wouldn't mind my having a woman with me?"

"Not unless you do."

"How much would it cost? What rooms would we have?"

Then Preston told me all about his final plans for the house. He wanted to occupy the bottom and the top floors. He wanted to rent out the middle floor. It would have three bedrooms and a sitting room. He was also installing a kitchen (though we would be wel-come to eat occasionally with him if we desired). Off of the kitchen would be a little eating area. The whole thing sounded great to me. I could convert one of the rooms into a study. Preston offered to put in book shelves for me. The price was really very moderate and well within what I could afford. The whole thing sounded great to me.

His projected date of occupancy would be September first. I told him that I'd talk it over with Anthea, but that I thought that we would most certainly love it.

That being settled, Preston took out a bottle of wine and we drank to the proposal.

We made arrangements to come by in a week so that Anthea could see the place. Everything was agreed upon—unless Anthea acquired serious objections to it (though I did not see how that would be possible).

I took a couple busses back home (I was now able to travel by subway or by bus virtually anywhere in the city). There was something soothing about riding the bus. One did not have to get involved with the traffic and could just sit back and think or read, or better yet, watch other people on the bus. There were many varieties of people on the bus and I wanted to watch each in their own worlds. What a heterogeneous group—all incomes, races, and intelligences sitting together for a time on their ways to here and there.

When I arrived, Anthea was not there. I took out a book and began to read, but soon I fell asleep. When I awoke I smelled dinner cooking. Anthea was busy moving around putting this and that on the table. Next to me on the table was a large drawing she had made. It was of the lake shore. She must have spent the day at the beach.

"You're awake, are you? You must not have gotten much work done."

It was true. I had only worked a couple of hours. My interview with Preston had tired me out. My mind had raced at the possibility of living in Hyde Park again, but this time under different circumstances. I had to tell Anthea about it.

"Anthea, how would you like to live in Hyde Park?"

"What?" She was distracted by something on the stove that needed her attention.

"Hyde Park. Would you like to live there?"

"I like it here well enough, I guess."

"But you see I have this friend at the University who is renovating a house which is really quite attractive. It-s a three story and we would have the second story." She was still moving to and fro in the kitchen. Her attention was only partly on what I was saying. She was most attentive to what she was creating for me.

"Well, dinner is ready."

We sat down to a very good meal. She had pan seared veal with a garlic butter sauce coated with eggs and breadcrumbs. It reminded me of Chicken Kiev only with veal. She had picked out a nice Bordeaux and everything was beautiful. Mid-way into the meal I touched on the move again.

"Sure," she said without another word. "Just name the time and place."

She was very agreeable tonight. Perhaps it was because the dinner had turned out so well, or perhaps it was because she was rid of Clay. She lay down on the sofa after dinner while I did up the dishes.

"How did you like my picture?" she asked.

"I have admired both of the pictures you have drawn. Have you ever, had any training?"

She laughed. This was a compliment that she seemed to take to heart, for there was no banter following it.

"Have you ever thought of taking it up as a trade?"

"Are you kidding? People who can draw like this are a dime a dozen. There's not much money for the average person like me. You have to be famous."

"The friend of mine at the University is a practicing artist. He makes a good deal of money selling his work. But you know that there are other ways to make money at drawing besides selling your drawings and paintings at galleries or on the street corner."

"Oh really?" Her tone was sarcastic. I think that in the back of her mind she thought that I might be playing some kind of joke on her. This woman had never shown me her drawings before. I think that this was because they represented a very private part of her. They were that aspect of her soul which sought its own expression in something exterior to itself. Most of us experience this in something—a favorite hobby or avocation. A few of us are even lucky enough to be hired in the area that we love. This is indeed extraordinary since then one is getting paid to do what he enjoys doing anyway.

The very prospect of this latter condition (something which we all aspire to at one time or another I think) was very attractive to Anthea—if she could take what I was saying seriously. That was the problem. She had been around so many people in her life and had built up so many self-protection systems that it was often hard for her to actually open herself up to pain. Now, none of us want to be hurt, but there are times when opening one's self up to an unknown future is the only way to realize tremendous treasures. Most of us instinctively know this. But with Anthea, because of her experiences with men, she was less able than most to be able to open up in this way. It might just be a trap or it may be a delusion on my part. From her vantage point, it was impossible to say. So she waited: ambivalent and tentative.

"Yes, Preston, my friend, tells me that there are a number of fields for someone with artistic talent. But in your case—you see I showed him the figure sketch you did of me—he thinks that you would be well suited for commercial art."

"You had no right to show that picture. I gave it to you." Anthea was a mixture of emotions. I could tell that she half felt that I had somehow betrayed her by displaying something private to the public. And yet I thought that I also sensed a hint of pride that I had thought so highly of her sketch that I would show it to a professional.

"How can you see what I did as anything except a compliment? I was so taken by what you did that I wanted an expert opinion of whether you might have a future doing just what you seem to enjoy doing? What could be wrong about that?"

"But I gave the picture to *you*."

"When one gives a gift," I said, "then the receiving party is free to do with it what he wishes unless some previous conditions had been set."

"I thought the conditions had been implied," she said.

"Conditions are not conditions unless they are made explicit."

Then she broke down crying. "Do you have to be such a damn philosopher all the time? Don't you ever get off it?"

I didn't know what she meant. I was rather stiff in my words with her, but then I was defending myself. But if I was a philosopher and acted like a philosopher, then where lies the fault? It was beyond me. I went to her and comforted her. She sobbed like a child. I felt as if I were in a new role with Anthea. For so long she had been the one who had domineered over and protected me, but now I felt as if it was my time to assume the role of comforter. How odd it all was, I thought. How much my life had changed in only a month. It became dark, and Anthea fell asleep. I carried her to bed and lay her down. I sat up reading next to her. I was looking out the window at the lights. The night seemed intriguing to me. My fancy carried me over many thoughts, but somehow it always returned to the shapes and colors of Preston's painting. It seemed to call out to me even as I watched lonely figures moving into the mid-summer shadows.

CHAPTER TWELVE

INSTEAD OF SLEEPING, my mind went back to the Fourth of July. There had been a big celebration in Lincoln Park so Anthea and I packed a meal in a shopping bag and hiked to the proposed picnic. It was about a three mile walk, but since there were not too many people out yet it was very enjoyable.

The city of Chicago always puts a lot of money into its July Fourth festivities. There are numerous activities around the city culminating in a band concert and a fireworks display over Lake Michigan.

Anthea and I had a quiet day as we watched several soft ball games and people throwing Frisbees and other such items back and forth for hours. We didn't drink too much because it was a hot day and alcohol and heat together gives me a headache. But we found a tree for ourselves and our blanket and just did nothing for fifteen hours. How good it felt to be out with someone like Anthea who was so full of life; it was easily the happiest day we had spent since coming back to Chicago.

* * *

The next morning we had a fight. It was over how critical I was. I suppose Anthea was right, but at the time I left the place in a rage. As I rode the "el" all I could think about was how I wanted to be rid of her. I went to the library and put in a good day of work. This helped me to cool off and I went to the art store and bought her a large sketch pad. I thought that it would be an appropriate peace offering to make. But when I got there Anthea took my gift as yet another insult.

"So you don't think that my drawings are good enough as they are, do you? You think that I need all that fancy paper to make my stuff more professional like your friend who wants me to go into commercial art."

"Anthea, listen to yourself. You are being simply ridiculous. This is a nice gift. I don't know how you can construe it as anything else. If anything, it shows an interest in your talents. That's all."

Anthea did not have any rejoinders, but took the pad and dropped it on the floor near her things (we didn't have any dressers). She then went to the other side of the apartment and began sketching on her old paper as if to show me what she thought of the gift. We ate Chinese that night and were very uncommunicative. Several more days passed in the same way. Something was wrong. I thought about it and decided to confront Anthea.

"Things have not been going well these past few days."

"What's the matter? We've been having sex."

"So what? Sex is nice and I like being close to you, but the kind of relationship we've been having is not very healthy. You're not talking with me. We are not relating on more than one level. This is going to stagnate very quickly unless we do something about it."

"What do you suggest, doctor?" Her tone was sarcastic. She had become increasingly defensive about my academic status lately. She would make remarks that signified an apparent glorification of my intellect to the degradation of hers: 'Well you must know . . .', 'you're so smart . . .'' 'why does someone with your head hang around with someone like me', and 'I wouldn't know, but I'm sure you do.' I wondered to myself whether things were indeed failing apart. I felt that Anthea was closing up again. She was becoming the same woman who ate dinner with me in Milwaukee. There was something about Anthea which belied my powers of explanation. She needed something and was feeling terribly inferior about something. It could not be my academic degree, because I never talked about those sorts of things with her. In fact, we had talked more "philosophy" in the woods than we had since coming back to the city—and it was in the woods that we had formed our closest bond.

I looked at Anthea. She was letting her hair grow. She informed me that she was tired of the "cute" look and wanted something that was a little "older" looking. Was this the problem? Was I too old for her? I could find no other explanation for it. And yet, if that were true, how could we have gotten on before? One explanation was that the woods provided an artificial setting for a relationship. Now it is odd to think of the city as natural and the woods as the opposite, but that was the way it was. In the woods certain myths could be created and we might be able to live in a dream world of our own creation. But now we were back in the world in which we would have to live. If this world was less accepting of dreams, then perhaps we would be less likely to get along. All of this was terribly pessimistic. I wondered whether I was pessimistic because I was just going through divorce proceeding with my wife, Barbara, or because the relationship was turning in that direction.

But behind it all lay the fact that she was feeling inferior. Was I doomed to having only relationships with women of a similar background, just because I was a college professor? I genuinely liked Anthea. We could relate, I thought, on a very pleasant and perfectly acceptable level. There was no need to have a mate who could belch the worthless platitudes required of undergraduates with a college education who have gone through their intellectual repast so quickly that it has caused cerebral indigestion. I had had enough of such sorts having lived in a university community for so long. No, Anthea did represent for me a welcomed relief from that. She was so different from anyone I had known. But was that difference anything upon which one could build a lasting relationship? Or was there something about the two of us that was destined to remain (in this sense) eternally unfulfilled?

"Why do you use that tone with me? What have I done to deserve it?"

Anthea looked at me. It was the look of a teenager who has just been beaten in an argument by her parent, but still does not wish to admit defeat. "Why do you always want to 'talk things out'? There are other ways of communicating, you know."

"And are there other ways of resolving problems? Let's see, what might those be? There is force, diversion and ignoring it—oh, and I almost forgot, we could throw in there a sign from the gods. I think that about covers it. If those are the alternatives, then I think I will stick with rational discussion, thank you."

"You're welcome," she replied with derision in her voice.

I went to her and grabbed her by the shoulders. "What's the matter with you for heaven's sake? Why are you being this way?" There was a strain in my voice for I could not take her cool, detached attitude any longer. She looked at me and started to say something and then broke down and sobbed. She put her head to my breast and sobbed freely. She was very distraught, but even in the midst of this she lifted her face and said, "Why do you stay with me when you know that all I am is a cheap little whore who can't do anything except spread her legs apart?"

And there it was.

"What the hell are you talking about?" I replied, "You can do many things."

"Sure, I can suck and I can—"

I grabbed her shoulders and cried, "Stop it!" I had never shaken her before. I could not stand there and let her degrade herself. I was angered at her attitude of self-complacent defeat. Her self-pity was too easy. Anyone can give up.

It does not take any internal strength to do that. And I knew that Anthea had strength. When we were hiking in the woods there were so many times when I was too exhausted to continue, but her gentle encouragement kept me going when left on my own I would have given up. I was not going to let her stop now.

"Now you listen to me, Ms. Brevist. You are a coward and a quitter. Here you have a chance to make something out of yourself by developing a wonderful gift of being able to draw. Not many people have it, and you have it to an extraordinary degree. You could make a living at it and become fulfilled with some useful labor. But what do you do? You moan and groan. You take jobs that have nothing to do with your skills. Now if you liked serving people and the small talk that goes with it, you would have made a fine stewardess. The same holds true for your other jobs. You picked things that were merely available. Now these jobs are fine for people who have aptitudes for those occupations, but you don't. You have your own special talent and all you do is run away from it. You are a coward because you are afraid of taking on a challenge. You are a quitter because you want to give up on your best hope toward happiness."

I delivered this speech with a fluency which is not normal with me. The words came from my heart, and I wanted at that moment to let Anthea know that I cared about what she did with her life. She had come to become very important to me and I could not be happy unless she also was happy.

There was a long pause while Anthea pulled back and circled about the room. She was thinking about what I said, I could see that, but in her fashion, she had to have time to think it over. I respected her feelings and went outside for a cup of coffee. I don't mind admitting that I was more than a little uneasy. Had I said the right things? Was I too rough on her? My words had not been planned. Often this indicates thoughts that are not carefully wrought. Was that the case now?

When I went back to the apartment Anthea was gone. She had drawn me a cartoon of a woman with two heads. On the bottom was a note saying that she would be back in time for dinner. I would have to wait.

*   *   *

Anthea returned and we had dinner at the regular time. All was very quiet until after dinner while we were doing the dishes together she said to me, "Tell me Andrew, is that what it is all about? Is happiness really finding a job that you are qualified to do?"

Was this what I had said? Was I guilty of such over simplification? Certainly, I did not believe this. Somehow she had turned my words to mean something which I had not originally intended. "No,

I don't think that work alone is sufficient for anything. And even remunerative labor is not necessary. I just feel that somehow the self needs various modes of expression. And I suppose that one of those modes is through work—paid or otherwise—and the fulfillment of some discipline."

"Is it discipline then? What about my running?"

"What about it?"

"Doesn't that count for something?"

"It does if you want it to. Do you express yourself in it?"

"Yes."

Her answer was firm and definite.

"Then you don't think that you need anything else?"

"No."

"Then I'm happy for you." It was hollow. She didn't mean what she was saying and neither did I. But that was that. No more could be said about it that evening.

The next day Anthea was out running when I got up. So I fixed myself a couple of cups of coffee and chewed on a heel of bread. Today I would need my energy. I was beginning to clean my things out of the condominium that I had shared with Barbara. I had toyed with the idea of asking Anthea to help me, but I thought that considering the strain we had been under lately it might be a good idea if I went alone. All the fights we had been having disturbed me. Was this the beginning of the end with us? Was I doomed to always have the women in my life fall away from me?

This question haunted me. I began thinking of the ephemeral figure in Preston's painting as he hurtled himself alone and into the darkness. Being totally alone was a frightening thing. I had grown to be alone with Barbara, but there is something different in being alone with someone and being alone in open ground with no one there to help you.

How different I was from the youth who left high school into college. My father had just died and I was alone then. But somehow being in the environment of the campus and knowing that my time was scheduled for four years gave me a feeling of comfort.

And yet, I still jumped at the first opportunity to break my still solitude. There is a terror about being totally alone which was overcoming me. I wanted to have the courage to say to it, "Come and take me if you can. Explode me in your fireworks or let me fight it out." I could sense that something like this was needed. But how hard those words are to say and really mean. The condominium had not changed. Very few things were altered except that Barbara, anticipating my scheduled visit, had put all my clothes in a heap in the middle of the living room. Barbara always did have a winning way with her, I thought as I picked up clothes which were wrinkling in their random postures. I wondered if she was trying to create a situation in which I would have all wrinkled clothes that I would then have to iron or take to the cleaners. It would be the "Barbara touch."

I had borrowed Sam Massey's car and I was hauling the things to Preston's. The basement had been finished (as much as it was going to be) and I could put my hanging things on a clothes line that he had rigged up for me, and my books I could stack on the work bench and on the floor. I had never been one to buy a great many books as others in my profession were always doing. It seemed to me that since the library purchased all the books I wanted and since I could check out a book for twelve months at a time, it did not make sense to be spending large amounts of money on books which I could have for nothing.

As I hauled out the last of my first load and put it in the car, I got a sudden urge to resume my hobby of collecting leaves. It seemed to me that this might be a very relaxing hobby. There were plenty of trees in Jackson Park, especially on what they called the "wooded island". There was also Washington Park. I could take what I found back to the lab and put it all under the dissecting scope. There I could, in that timeless realm, classify my specimens into naturally abstract and artificial classes which we have devised for that purpose. It was an exercise in organizing the continuous homogeneity of nature which was arbitrary and relatively ad hoc. It was this aspect about taxonomy which thrilled me.

Preston was at his house when I got there. He helped me unload and went back to the condominium with me to pack up another load.

"Well, how is your budding artist coming?" he asked suddenly. Preston and I were un-boxing books at the time. I didn't reply but made a little face.

"Having a row?"

"How's that?"

"The woman you live with—you know, the artist?"

"Oh she's doing fine."

"What does she think about commercial art?"

"I'm not sure whether she is very interested, to tell you the truth."

Preston stopped and laughed. He found all of this very amusing. Helping himself to a drink of water he came back and sat down reverse ways in a chair so that his legs were straddling the back. "I know what her problem is. She thinks that commercial art is a sellout. She thinks that only hacks go into commercial art. It is the same with everyone. It's not an uncommon feeling."

"I don't know. She has not been very specific about her reasons. All she said was that she was not interested."

"Not to worry, my good man. I took the liberty of writing to Bellomy's in New York and asking them for their current catalogue and course schedule. I just got it yesterday. Registration for the fall term begins August 1 and any new applicants must have their materials in by July 29. She needs a letter of recommendation which I, of course, will be willing to provide. Show her the catalogue (it's back at the house) and let her make her own decision. You owe her that much."

Preston's speech impressed me. He was a genuine friend. How kind it was for him to put forth all the effort that he did. As he sat back in his chair with his hair ruffled and the flightiness of his personality showing itself almost at every instant, I couldn't help but nod my head at such a man. He reminded me in certain ways of Ronnie (though their manners and personalities were so different) in his attitude toward others. That evening when I got home I found another picture with a note attached. It told me that Anthea would not be home for dinner. I decided to warm up a can of chili and had just seated myself with a bottle of beer when Anthea came in the door.

"I thought that you weren't coming home for dinner."

She looked terrible. Her eyes were showing signs of fatigue and her face was drawn. "I was just in Glenview."

"Glenview? Who do you know—" and then I stopped. She had gone to see Glen and Martha. Anthea detected my recognition and flopped down on the couch. "Yes that's right. I wanted to see how they were. You know it's almost been a month."

I cocked my head in a way which she knew meant, "Well, continue."

"They are not doing well at all. Glen is undergoing physical therapy to help him gain use of his limbs again and Martha is under heavy psychiatric care. Glen has moved in with Martha to help care for the children. The absence of Ed is immense. And they have some problem about their medical insurance. There is some limit that they've exceeded and the cost of it all is wiping out Martha and Ed's savings. It's really very sad."

I shook my head. This news affected me too.

Anthea sat up. "But you know what gets to me the most is that Martha is just a wreck. I cannot imagine what it would be like to lose your husband and recover from violent rape at the same time. She cannot speak for more than five minutes before she flies into hysterics. She has medication to calm her, but it doesn't really work. She can barely get through each hour. Without Glen there, she'd have to ship her children to her parents. I think she should do that, anyway. But it's not my call."

Anthea buried her face in her hands. "The crazy thing is that she feels guilt about it. Like she did something wrong—can you believe it?"

It was indeed sad. Anthea had looked up to Martha as someone who Anthea admired. She had admired her for her strength, and now to have her fly apart like this must have been doubly disconcerting for Anthea. I had liked Martha too, though I was not as enamored with what I took to be her "act" as Anthea was. It just seemed to me that it was much easier to talk a strong case living in the suburbs than it was for someone living in the city. This was because in the city one has crime all around him all the time. The daily reality of it is omnipresent. In the suburbs people move (they think) away from crime to safe little homogeneous hamlets. They isolate themselves from the mainstream of American life in sterile, uniform housing developments. That is why violence is doubly hard on them. They cannot believe that it is really happening to them. How could anything happen to them? They moved away from all of that! They tried to move away from the problems of the city and yet not to the country, for they desired the jobs of the city and the culture of the city—only the problems of the city were repugnant to them.

I had viewed Martha as one of these people. So it seemed easier for me to understand why she had become unglued than it was for Anthea. It all made perfect sense.

Anthea was distressed and needed time to work it all out. We spent a quiet evening together: I read and Anthea drew. Just before it was time to turn in Anthea said, "I'm going to get it all down."

"Get it all down?"

"The whole night. I'm going to make a picture."

I nodded my head and went to sleep.

* * *

The next day I finished taking my things to Preston's. He was not there to help me for he had some things to do. I was surprised at the progress that had been made on the house. Except for painting the walls, the upstairs was completely done. Preston had done a very tasteful job on the place. It would be a pleasant spot to live. It was not too far from campus and not too far from the lake front. I liked walking on the lake front along the long park which Chicago has reserved as public use. Sometimes the waves would hit the rocks which separate the park from the water and the resultant spray would sail high over and into the park. On the other side is Lake Shore Drive. At times, the waves are so big that the water carries all the way onto the Drive! I had always been so far away from the waterfront in my old place that I rarely got down to it. Now, perhaps, things would be different.

I thought about Anthea. She would like the park here along the water. Many people ran here because there was fifteen miles of uninterrupted park leading all the way into Evanston. It made me sad that she had had to go through the experience of seeing Martha so beaten down by that ugly tragedy. Anthea was such a sensitive person. That is why, I believe, she has built up so many personal defense mechanisms.

I had so many different roles with Anthea. I was her lover, friend, and mentor. Each role called on different parts of me. I had never experienced such a relationship before. With Barbara it had always been the monotony of the master/slave: she commanded and I either obeyed or we fought about it. The process was a continual battle of wills. Each side was trying to get the political edge on the other.

All these thoughts were unsystematically moving in and out of my mind as I went back to the house to get my final load. In a few minutes I would be completely moved out. The divorce was moving very quickly and soon might be finalized. Then it would be over. Then I would have officially entered a new phase of life. I lifted the last of the books down the stairs and into the car. Then I climbed the stairs for the last time. I looked about the place which had been home for so many years and I sighed. What a different Andrew Viam had lived there than the one who now lives in Rogers Park!

And yet we were not totally removed from each other. There were similarities. How queer it seemed that a person could be so altered by a few events that he is no longer essentially the same. I wondered about Barbara. What would happen to her? Would she remain with Giles? I doubted that. He would never allow himself to get tied down, and he would soon move to someone else. But then what would she do? Perhaps because she felt relatively financially secure she wouldn't worry, but what would she do with no one to dominate? I wondered whether dominating a person was as bad for her as it was for the person being dominated? If this was true, would she ever realize it?

When one divorces someone there is such conglomeration of feelings that it is hard to know exactly *what* one feels about the other person. There is resentment and hate for all the felt injustice meted by the other person, and at the same time there is a weird sensation which is occasioned by that which made you fall in love in the first place. Though that might not be acknowledged by some, it is always there. And that prompts the thought: why did it turn out wrong? I know that if I married Barbara fifty times, that all fifty times we would be miserable. Her infidelity was not the cause of our divorce. If we had been happy, I would have tried to work it out between us. But we weren't happy. Our lives were full of pain caused by two natures which had grown apart (if they had ever really been together). For after sex and its appealing glitter wears away from a relationship there has to be something else there. For us, I believe, there was nothing. This was a very sad thought. Why couldn't we have made it? There was no answer. All that stared me in the face was the stark data of what we both were. We were two people ill-suited for each other. And even though things had been better at the beginning, all things considered our marriage had been a mistake. This was a very disquieting thought which caused my eyes to well with sorrow. In my heart I was saying goodbye to one phase of my life. And saying good-bye is always difficult. It was an admission that I was growing older and closer to the end of my existence.

I looked at the apartment and sighed. It was really all over now. There was no going back. In a rush of emotion I kissed the wall and then, as if repelled by this gesture, I turned and walked out. I put the keys under the mat as I left.

* * *

The next couple of days Anthea was completely absorbed in drawing. She did this alone so I rarely saw her. I had gone back to my work at the University on the paper I was planning to write. I also thought that I'd like to keep a diary of some of the things that had happened to me.

When I got home one day Anthea was waiting on the sofa. Next to her was the drawing pad. I had not noticed, but she had begun to use it. I felt touched that she had accepted my gift after all that time.

"Come in. I have something to show you," she said. She seemed happier than I had seen her in quite some time. In all honesty, she had been very moody since her visit to Millers. Now she seemed her old self: confident and full of vitality.

She seated me and I noticed that she also had a new hairdo. She had been growing out her hair, which had gotten almost to medium length already. It was pulled back and she had made two little braids which went across the side of her head. I rather liked it. The style gave a new image of her which I found very attractive.

"I want to show you the work I've been doing this past week."

"You've been working all week on drawings?"

I knew this to be true, but I asked the question all the same.

She smiled and flipped back the cover of the book. "Here are some preliminary sketches of the woods where we camped."

I was amazed. They were very good. Suddenly all the images of the trip we had taken and the emotional metamorphosis it represented came back to me with immediacy. Sketch after sketch seemed well balanced and full of remarkable detail. With the larger sized paper she was able to do better justice, I thought, to her powers.

There were twelve sketches in all and I wanted to look at each over and over again. We talked about them, and I shared with her my thoughts both about the pictures and the events which had occasioned them. It was perhaps the first time that we had actually opened up on the subject at any length. It was a good feeling to talk to her and hear what she also had to say. Of course, I could see what she thought as well. It is remarkable how much of a person's point of view and editorial comment can come across in a drawing. We sat there for several hours until the sun had gone down. I felt so close to Anthea that suddenly I was next to her and kissing her tenderly. We rolled over on the sofa and lost ourselves in each other for the first time in over a week.

Afterwards I suggested we go out to eat. Anthea liked this idea and began getting dressed. I looked again at the drawings. They really impressed me. Then I remembered the material Preston had gotten for me. I had not shown it to Anthea, but with talent like hers I knew that it could not be wasted. I went over to the pile of things which were mine (we had no desks to put things in) and finally found it. I opened the envelope and took out the catalogue and course schedule and the cover letter. There was something missing.

"If you are looking for the application form you won't find it there," said a voice from the other side of the room.

I turned my head. Anthea was standing there, smiling. She must have discovered the material by going through my pile of things. This made me feel a little funny since I wanted to be the one to show it to her (even though I feared that there would be another uproar about it—I thought that it would be best for her and ergo I would risk it for her). On the other hand, I felt relieved that this somewhat irksome task was taken away from me.

"I found the material last week." I smiled. "I was a little upset at first that you went ahead with it after I had told you what I thought of the whole thing. But then I read the note Preston wrote you and I understood it all."

Of course the burning question that I had on my mind was whether she was going to turn in the application form. As much as I was convinced that she ought to do it, something in me kind of wished that she would tell me that she would never consider such a thing because it meant leaving me. There would be a slow lapse dissolve and we would walk into the sunset.

It was not until we descended the stairs that I had the nerve to ask her what she did with the application form. She smiled and did not answer.

We went to the restaurant. Why didn't she want me to know? What was the mystery? I don't mind admitting that I was getting a little perturbed over all the fun and games. However, as the evening wore on I very soon forgot all about the art school and everything except Anthea and myself. Things were almost as they were when we emerged from our little Wisconsin journey. I was never so happy as I was that night. We had taken a bus to eat (the car was in the shop) and decided to walk home. We went along the lake shore and it took us two hours (for we went at a leisurely pace). How strange it seemed to me that I had missed all of this with Barbara.

Anthea and I walked hand-in-hand at times and at others simply next to each other as we made our way north. We didn't say much. It didn't seem necessary. We were comfortable.

It was not until the middle of the night that I awoke and thought again about the application, but I was not to find out the answer until a week later when Anthea greeted me with a bottle of cold duck.

"I was accepted," she said.

"What? To Bellomy's?"

"Well, not exactly accepted. But they told me that I was tentatively accepted subject to an interview which I'm to have in ten days."

"Ten days," I echoed. It all seemed so near. "What do they mean 'tentatively accepted?' That sounds kind of peculiar to me. Let me see your letter."

"All right, but first you have to have some cold duck." She poured me a glass and then brought me the letter. Apparently they had accepted her and the interview was more for her sake than it was for theirs. They wanted her to know more fully what she was getting into so that she might make the most informed decision. This was very decent of them. I thought that they must have quite a few applicants in order to risk losing one with such a process. I was favorably impressed by the gesture. We decided that we would go together and look for a place for Anthea. It was all so startling. Everything was happening so fast—all of a sudden. I had been toying about with this idea for some time, and now it was happening. I felt very sad all of a sudden. I didn't want to lose my Anthea. I knew that she talked of coming back to me after she had finished her eighteen months of training (and periodically in their breaks), but I knew too well what distance and separation might bring. I knew that there was a very good possibility that she was leaving me forever. And I was the very cause for my own misfortune. Why?

I asked myself why had I pressed so much for her to attend this school? Why?

But I knew the answer. I just didn't want to let it enter my mind when I was feeling so sorry for myself. I felt in my heart (or maybe it was 'feared') that I was spending my last days with Anthea. We took the trip to New York. Anthea saw the school and was able to get an apartment with two other girls in the outer village. She seemed pleased and excited at the prospect of really getting into something which was exciting to her. I knew that there would be much drudgery and routine in the months ahead (a fact, which I believe, she did not foresee), but on balance I thought that she was making a wise choice for herself.

I had never seen Anthea so happy. She had a new pride in herself and carried herself differently. I was envious in a way of someone entering a new field of work which offered so much promise to her. I suppose that it was partially from the perspective of a man who knew about how he would stand and always stand in his own field. My professional future seemed rather certain and mediocre. Hers, on the other hand, was full of promise. Such a future holds so many possibilities that it breeds excitement.

Anthea would never let me talk of our separation. It was mid-August and she was still talking as if we would be together forever. Anthea wouldn't let me go anywhere by myself. She clung to me as a child clings to her parent. This made things doubly difficult. For anticipating the parting, I had tried to build up a few defense mechanisms, but Anthea would not let me. She stayed near me and tried to please me as best she could.

On August 22 my divorce was finalized. Anthea and I went out to lunch to celebrate. "I've already looked into several firms in Chicago who might be interested in hiring someone from Bellomy's. I did not realize what a prestigious place it was until I heard some of their responses. I'll be able to come back and then we can buy a house or something."

"Yes," I replied trying to be as enthusiastic as I could. But I knew that I didn't believe any of it. I wanted to believe, but the cynic in me said that she would find someone else in eighteen months more to her liking than myself. I felt myself trying to be aloof while every corresponding effort for the same on my part was met with an equally sincere effort on her part to bring me closer to her. We went down to see how Preston's house was progressing. Preston was there to greet us. "Well, and how is the prospective art student?"

Anthea looked pleased. I felt sick.

We went inside and found that everything was virtually completed. "Your story is all done except for the staining of the book shelves I had built in for you. You could move in tomorrow if you wanted to."

I thanked him, but I wanted to stay where I was up to the very last minute. I wanted to hang on to Anthea and the life we had established together for as long as I could. It was strange, but I wanted our habits of familiarity to continue and yet at the same time I tried to separate myself from her. They were impulses working against each other.

I had moved in everything except the few clothes and personal items that I had left in the apartment. When we went into what was to be my bedroom, I saw a sight that took my breath away. On the wall was Preston's picture.

"I decided to sell you my picture at a very reasonable rate: nothing!"

"You can't *give* that to me."

"I can't? Oh, then I'll have to take it back," he said laughing.

I was very moved at all he had done for me. He had picked up a bed and used furniture at very reasonable rates for me and had generally gotten everything in very good order. I knew that he was a man I could trust and it would be bearable to live with him. But I could not get excited about it in any real way, for the day that I moved in with him would be the day Anthea would leave me.

We went directly home by way of the garage where the car was and picked up the old heap. It ran fairly well, though I had the feeling that it was only a matter of time before that clanking collection of squeaks and rattles started up again. When we were driving, I felt as if there was something that I wanted to say to her. The gift of the painting touched me in an unusual way. It seemed extraordinary to me that someone would simply *give* an artifact which took so long to produce. He could have gotten a thousand dollars or more for that, I told myself. But I knew that from the very first time that I saw it, I was attached to it.

Not since my childhood had I been so taken by a piece of art that it affected me in a highly personal way. The painting lived with me even when I was away from it. Its imprint was on my soul.

When we returned I could not hold back my urge to talk to Anthea. I felt so alone and at the same time I felt a bond of attachment to her. This feeling longed for some kind of expression. "I want to give *you* the painting," I said.

"That painting that Preston gave you?"

"Yes," I said.

She stopped a moment and looked at me very carefully. I knew that she was trying to gauge the kind of response that she would make to this. Why had I made the offer? I loved the painting, so it seemed odd that I would instantly give it away almost as soon as it was in my possession. But I felt that there was something in that painting that represented my change and I wanted Anthea to have that with her so that she could see it too and be reminded of it.

"I'll take it on one condition," she said. "If you promise to keep it as custodian until we are back together. That way it will be a token that I will return."

It was a pretty sentiment, and the open manner in which it was delivered almost made me believe that that day would happen. I know that at that moment I dearly wanted it to happen. Anthea, you see, saw things differently than I did. She was so intensely attached to me that she never doubted that she would return, but then I knew that people who are so extremely attached to something can often become disenchanted almost as quickly. My intensity was less than hers, but I thought that it would probably last longer. But then, all of this was simply guessing. She might return. We might buy a house together. We might.

*   *   *

The last week went all too quickly. Anthea clung to me every minute. She constantly declared her affection, and made me the focus of all that was Anthea. She wanted me to know that I had helped her in ways that I would never know and that she was living for me. "I will make you proud of me, Andrew," she would often say. I would respond, "I am proud of you already." But Anthea had something that she had to prove to herself and she knew it. This was somehow related to the new found respect and pride she had in herself. I'm not sure exactly how it all fit together (for psychology has never interested me), but it all made sense from my perspective. Going to New York was the only thing that she could authentically do.

How the days had sped by picking up pace until it was the morning of her departure. I was becoming numb from it all. I could not think about what I was about to do or I would not be able to do it. I dressed in a tie and then took it off and donned the outfit that I had worn the day that I met her on the bus. She was attired in new clothes that I had purchased for her only two days before.

"You look smashing," I said. But she only smiled and told me by the look in her eye that she recognized my outfit too. Neither one of us liked, by nature, saying goodbye to someone. It was an action that did not come easily. As a result, we were silent much of the way to O'Hare Airport. There was so much that I wanted to tell her. In most ways I felt that this was the last time that I would see Anthea. I wanted to tell her about how I was before I met her and all the positive alterations I had gone through—due largely to her presence in my life. I wanted to tell her how proud I was of her and how I wished her success in her new venture. But most of all I wanted to tell her that I wanted her to stay with me. There was a part of me that did not (could not) let her go. And yet I was driving the car to those cement runways which would carry her away from me.

I could not speak, and yet I wanted to tell her. As we approached nearer, I felt as if I were in some kind of dream and I was lying there, watching as an observer. This could not be happening to me. How could I let Anthea leave?

We arrived at the parking garage and got our little ticket. The airport did not seem too busy as we passed through security and onto her departure gate. I looked at her as we walked and I could almost image looking at her for the very first time. Her new hair length made her appear softer and not as cold. As we walked I noticed other men looking at her and I understood their gazes. They did not bother me, but in some measure I felt a pride over Anthea. But at the same time I saw a woman whose face also carried the memories and emotions of a summer which I knew I could never forget. So much was infused in her face for me which was entirely personal. None of the passersby could see these things when they looked at Anthea. For these things did not reveal themselves to casual observation. They were mine, and I cherished them.

We got to the gate twenty minutes early and made small talk about her plans when she got to New York and how she would take a taxi to her place, etc. Things we had gone over twenty times before were once more reviewed so that we might fill the time. And then it was time to board. We waited for the line to pass away and then I arose, and kissed her lightly upon the lips. Then I hugged her with all my might. We both shed tears, though I tried to hold mine back. I don't know why.

"See you at Christmas?" she said in a faint voice.

"Sure," I replied. I put her face in my hands and tilted up her head. "You know Anthea—" I could not say anymore. I kissed her forehead and then I handed her the carry-on bag. "Now go and get 'em. I know you'll do well."

And then she was gone.

*　*　*

I had already gotten back the deposit etc. on our little apartment in Rodgers Park and had packed up the car with my things. I did not want to return to that place. I drove directly to Preston's (and now my place, too) and proceeded to take the things up to my room. Preston was home, but knew enough to leave me alone. When I had put all the things away I lay down on my bed and stared at the painting. Then I discovered a little slip of paper in my pocket. It was a note from Anthea.

> *This is to let you know that I have reserved a table for two at*
> *Sol and Eddie's for December 22.*
>
> *Love,*
> *Anthea.*

I smiled. Could it ever be? The odds were certainly against it. My pessimistic nature told me not to get my hopes up. But that resolution was impossible. Just then I needed something. The painting inspired me to take a walk, so I went to the lake front. It was a very windy day and the waves were high. I walked near the rocks even though I was being sprayed by the water. I walked near the rocks because I wanted to feel all of it. I wanted to let all of the wind and water pass through me. The wind and spray were in front of me. The painting 'Naked Reverse' drove me through the tumult alone against all of it. I looked up and saw the skyline of downtown Chicago. It stood in stark relief against the sky. The summer was now over. September was about to begin.

Other Novels by Michael Boylan

Rainbow Curve, (2014) Fans of baseball's history will appreciate this compelling tale about race, politics, and corrupting power and one man's courage to stand up against it. *De Anima* #1.

The Extinction of Desire (2007) What would you do if you suddenly became rich?. *De Anima* #2.

To the Promised Land (2015) Are there limits to forgiveness: personal, corporate, political? *De Anima* #3.

Maya (Forthcoming) Follow the fate of an Irish-American family through three generations. It's the story of immigrants. *De Anima* #4.

Georgia (Forthcoming) A novel told in three parts. Explore racial identity through a murder mystery set in the early 20th century. *Arche* #2-4.

61912427R00137

Made in the USA
Middletown, DE
21 August 2019